Shelby
&
Shawn

A Novel By:

Mary Ann Parfitt

Mary Ann Parfitt

ISBN: 979-8-9867319-2-6

 Shelby & Shawn   ©   2023

Being single is not a weakness of being unable to find a partner. It is the strength of having the patience to wait for the one who is right for you.

 Shelby & Shawn © 2023

Dedication

To Drew, Leland & Lizzie,
for all the joy you've brought to my life.
May you grow to be strong, healthy, and
confident people.

Table of Contents

Chapter 1

Back To Reality

January 1, 2000, otherwise known as Y2K, went off without a hitch. No power outages, no computer crashes, no end-of-the-world stuff. Everyone who hoarded food, water, flashlights, and batteries in preparation for the crash was extremely embarrassed.

The manager of my office, who BTW didn't believe any of it, was supposed to go into the office on Sunday, which was New Year's Day, and check all the computers to make sure they had changed over to 2000 and were working properly. He didn't want to go in so he assigned a couple of our young girls to go in for him. They of course did not show up.

When I got home from my trip to Meadville on Sunday, I had a message on my voicemail from Jennifer O'Riely, one of the girls who was supposed to go in to check the computers. She said she was sick and did not make it in. She also stated that she would not be in on Monday either.

Her partner in crime, Kelly Stone, also called to say she did not make it in on Sunday and would not be in on Monday as well.

My manager, Lewis Shelly, had previously scheduled Monday off, so I knew he wasn't coming in. There was going to be trouble with all of this but I had no idea how much till it all hit the fan.

So I had a real mess when I came back on Monday. Not only did I have to boot all the computers to see if the time change had taken effect and no computer was affected by Y2K, I also had to do the morning deposits. Since half my staff had called off, I

          Shelby & Shawn   ©   2023

was very short of help.

In an office as busy as mine we couldn't afford to waste a minute doodling because when the doors opened the crowds would be pouring in. Being an auto club, we handled registration renewals and that was the one thing that brought everyone in at the beginning and the end of each month.

I worked as swiftly and efficiently as I could, keeping my mind on my task of turning on all the computers, logging in and checking for updates, then turning them all off again. Finally, a couple of the young girls arrived. Joy Marshall and Beth Kelly came in chatty and giggling, a sound most days I enjoyed. When they saw me they went on telling me about the exciting weekend they had.

Joy was young and dating someone she seemed very serious about. They had gone out on New Year's Eve to a club in Pittsburgh, drinking and dancing to the wee hours of the morning.

Beth was my age and not the big party type, so she spent New Year's Eve with family, playing games and eating at midnight like I used to do with my family pre-divorce.

"I am so glad to see you both," I said. "It sounds like you had a great time."

"So how was *your* weekend?" they both asked at the same time, giggling, suspecting I went away with someone but not knowing the details.

"I had a great time!" I answered. Then I put them to work straight away, dodging the question completely.

"Joy, could you please double-check the work that was

          Shelby & Shawn   ©   2023

done before you all left on Saturday? And can you tell me if the inventories got completed?"

Visibly disappointed at the lack of details about my trip, Joy responded, "we got them all done."

"Thank you so much! Jenn and Kelly both called off, so we're on our own." Loud moans escaped them both after hearing that. "But I'm truly grateful we don't have those tasks to do before opening."

"Beth, can you set up the office? I haven't even brought the cash drawer out yet."

"Sure!" she said and we went about setting up the office for the day, completing the deposits for pick up by the bank and getting the work checked before it went upstairs.

This was no sooner finished than it was time to open the doors. As I suspected we were crushed by people right off the bat. I ordered pizzas and let the girls eat at their desks since it was obvious they were not going to get a lunch break. After a fifteen-minute bathroom/drink break, we were right back at it.

Finally, I heard the doors to the building automatically lock. *Thank God it's 5:00.* We had to finish servicing those people who were sitting in the lobby before we could start the closeouts for the day, but at least we knew the end was in sight.

Once the last person was taken care of and out the door, everything was put away, and I let the girls go. "We'll have a full staff tomorrow and can catch up," I told them.

This has been a long, exhausting day, and I still have a long drive ahead of me to get home.

I wanted to spend time with my kids since I hadn't seen them in a few days. They stayed at their dads for the weekend while I was out of town. I got home last night at about 6:00 and Gene, my ex-husband, dropped them off at about the same time. They had to finish up homework and get ready for school today so we hardly got to chat at all.

I hate this drive; I thought as I got in my car. The traffic is heavy. It's dark and rainy which makes it more difficult to see, which slows me down.

I spent about three hours a day in my car. I swore as soon as something opened up closer to home, I would grab it. In the meantime, this promotion allowed me more money and a better life for my kids, although I was never home to share it with them and that took a toll on our relationship.

Raising teenagers as a single parent wasn't easy under any circumstances but being away from home a lot made it all the harder. Fortunately, we lived in a nice townhouse in a decent neighborhood now and the kids had friends whose parents helped look after them. I tried to share the responsibilities of rides to functions they wanted to attend, taking them one way or picking them up at the end. And I allowed them to have their best friends over when I wasn't home as long as they followed the rules I set for them.

Joel was back, living with me full-time again, after spending a few months with his dad. At 16, I pretty much gave him a lot of freedom. His best friend Tom Petric spent a lot of time at our house sleeping on the couch. He was a good kid and I trusted both he and Joel not to get into too much trouble anymore. They had gotten it all out of their system by then and settled down a lot.

Robin was the real worry now. At 14, She was always testing her limits and rebelling big time. This took me by surprise because as a child, she was so shy and quiet. Almost every day was a battle now to get her to go to school. When she didn't get her way, she threw screaming tantrums. And it didn't help that Gene spoiled her and gave in to her all the time.

Her best friend was Nickie Lyons. Nickie's grandmother lived in the complex and she spent a lot of time at our house as well. I liked that her grandmother, Grace Lyons, was just a couple of doors down and was always home to keep an eye on them.

On that exhausting day of work because of traffic and rain, I got home at 7:45 pm and the kids were not in a very good mood. They had eaten scraps for dinner and had been fighting over the television all evening.

When I walked in the door, I got bombarded with endless yelling and screaming. Fortunately, I had anticipated this and on my way into town, I drove through the dairy queen to get them their favorite flurries. I handed them the ice cream and they calmed down. We all sat down in the living room to catch up on what was going on in their lives.

Robin talked mostly about Nickie's cat having kittens and how much she wanted one. I reminded her in our townhouse complex we were not allowed pets.

"But why do other people have them?" she whined, and I explained for the millionth time,

"They had them before the rule was made to not have pets." I tried to explain to her again. She just didn't want to hear.

"But it's not fair," she continued. "If they can have them, why can't we."

"Because we moved in after the rule was made," I said.

"But they'll never know. I'll hide it and keep it in my room." She continued.

"I'll think about it," was the only thing I could say to make her let it go for all the good it did. I ended up giving in later and letting her have one.

Stop feeling guilty for not being able to give them everything!

Joel was bored with school and wanted to quit. "Mom, it's so overcrowded when the bell rings it's like a herd of cattle in the hallways."

"But you need an education if you're going to have a career. You can't get into a good college if you quit." I tried to encourage him to keep going. "It will pay off down the road."

"I'm not going to college. I can get a job," he argued.

This was an argument we'd had a lot. I knew he wasn't happy and since his room was in the basement and I didn't always check up on him, I suspected he skipped a lot anyway.

One time the school called me at work to ask if he was homesick. I had no idea he did not go to school, so I called him at about 4:15, the time he would have been getting home if he had gone.

I asked him "how was school today?"

"Good," he replied.

"The school called me. You didn't go to school today."

 Shelby & Shawn   ©   2023

"You tricked me," he yelled into the phone.

"You skipped school Joel," I stated. "Do you think that's okay? Stay in till I get home so we can talk about this."

He hung up angry at me for tricking him and I was sure he called his father. I didn't get any support from Gene with discipline. The kids always ran to him crying that I wouldn't give them their way. He always took their side and babied them while treating me with complete disrespect.

I snapped out of my thoughts, as Joel had been going on and wasn't backing down about quitting school. At this point, I was too tired to argue.

"It's late and we're tired. Let's talk about it some more tomorrow." I said.

We finished our ice cream and called it a night. Robin went to her room. I cleaned up some dishes and Joel put something on TV to watch.

At about 10:00, I was dozing off on the couch. I said, "I'm headed for bed, sweetie. Good night. I love you." I kissed him on the forehead and went to bed as well.

"Night mama. Love you."

 Shelby & Shawn   ©   2023

Chapter 2

The Weekend Away

Once the lights were off and the quiet of the night settled in, my mind went back to my weekend away with Shawn Cavalier. We had so much fun dancing on New Year's Eve with his sister, Kelly, and her boyfriend, Brad Stevenson. When we woke up in our hotel on New Year's Day, we both seemed different … closer. There was a comfort between us I couldn't explain; smiles, loving looks, joking back and forth, pillow fight kind of playfulness.

But he was always respectful of my decision to practice abstinence until marriage. In fact, he seemed to support it, almost appreciating it. I could sense him thinking *I'm not ready*.

I was disappointed when it was time to think about checking out. *I don't want this to end.* We showered, packed, and headed to Perkins to meet Kelly and Brad for breakfast. They continued to be very affectionate, and it seemed to bother Shawn some. He and I were quiet and ate, looking at each other occasionally with a light smile, and that loving look in his eyes.

When we finished eating, we said our goodbyes.

"It was so nice to meet you!" I said to Kelly and gave her a hug. Shawn and Brad shook hands, and he gave Kelly a big brother hug, picking her up off the ground and shaking her, laughing.

On the way home we were quiet for a long while. I was looking out the window enjoying the view of the country, farmland, cows, and horses. I loved the outdoors and back-to-nature adventures, hiking, and kayaking. It brought me a lot of joy. I felt closer to God and at peace with my life.

I always wanted to live in the country and raise my kids on

a farm. Gene grew up on a farm and I thought that to be his dream too when I married him, but it didn't work out that way. I wonder if things might have been different if we had followed that dream.

Suddenly Shawn snatched me out of my thoughts saying he wanted to talk with me about his situation. I knew his wife, Sarah, was really giving him a hard time seeing Kenny, his four-year-old son. There was a lot of anger and hostility between them. If they didn't resolve that it would affect Kenny in a very negative way.

"I am struggling with my divorce and fighting for custody of Kenny. I can't focus on anything else right now. I really have strong feelings for you Shelby, but I'm not ready yet to make a commitment. And I don't know how long that's going to take." He explained.

"I understand," I said, and I truly did. "I have that experience with Gene, and it doesn't get better unless both parties are willing to work on it together. I appreciated you being honest and upfront about it. I have feelings for you too but I value our friendship and would never want to do anything to interfere with your relationship with your son. You take all the time you need to get your life together. I'm here if you need me."

"I can't tell you how much that means to me. I don't want to lose your friendship either. I can't afford to lose any of my friends right now. I need the support of my friends to get through this custody battle and divorce."

I knew he was speaking of Roy Booth now and I didn't want to go into that with him. After all the trouble Roy had caused in our singles' groups, it would be hard to be friends with him again. He destroyed Randy's group by spreading vicious rumors about him taking advantage of the women in his group, so no one trusted him again. Then he came after me, acting like we were a couple and telling people things about me that were not true.

But I knew if my relationship with Shawn was to grow, I would have to work things out with Roy. I would have to find a way to make Roy understand that we are all friends and just spending time together. It would be hard, but Shawn was worth fighting for. And it wasn't fair that Roy's interference could affect my relationship with him.

As I lay in bed thinking about all this, I became very weary and eventually fell asleep. I have no idea what time it was.

Chapter 3

It's Al's Birthday

I woke up late the next morning and had to rush to get to work. The traffic was always backed up on the parkway west and the time between the Churchill and the Wilkinsburg exits took longer than the whole trip it seemed.

I really need to get a transfer to the Greensburg office or find another job. It would be much closer to home, which would be a huge change in my whole life. I would be able to focus more energy on my home and spend more time with my kids. I feel like I don't even have a day off because that day is spent catching up on cleaning my house.

At least I would have a full staff today and Lew would be back from his vacation. Beth and Jenn were opening, and they had already started the bank deposit and were preparing the work upstairs when I got there.

I stuck my head in the door to Lew's office. "Got a minute?"

"Come in." He said in a grumpy voice. He was staring at his computer looking miserable.

"So, you heard about the girls not showing up?" I asked.

"Yeah. Guess I'm in trouble for that."

"I haven't heard anything."

"I have a meeting upstairs on Friday." He sighed.

     Shelby & Shawn   ©   2023

"I hope it goes well." I walked out of his office feeling his dread.

I went out on the floor to help the staff. There was the license deposit left to do and checking that amount of work for errors took forever. We always had two people do it to make sure we found as many as we could before it went out. At 9 am the crowd poured in. The rest of my six-day workweek went just like that. We were busy and I was exhausted by Saturday.

Fortunately, Saturdays were only half a workday and I got home a little after 3:00. I was resting on the couch when Cindy Woodward called and asked if I wanted to go out that night. The kids were out with friends. I hadn't even seen them yet.

"Al Malone is a member of the VFW and they have some guitar players there tonight. It's his birthday and he wants some of us to go see this guy." Cindy said. "Al can get us in and the drinks are cheap."

"I don't know," I said exhausted. "It's been a long week and I don't know where my kids are." I laughed.

She laughed too. "Well let me know by 7:30. That's when we'll be heading over. Call me at Al's. We're doing dinner at his place first." I had a feeling they were doing more than dinner, but okay. I was pretty sure they were dating and keeping it hush-hush in case it didn't work out.

That seems to be a strong characteristic of the dating scene today. It's no wonder with all the gossip going around. Everyone just wants to be private. My only issue with this is 'how MANY people are you dating privately?'

I looked at the clock. It was 5:30 now and I hadn't even thought about dinner. I said I would let her know and hung up the

 Shelby & Shawn   ©   2023

phone. I immediately called Grace. I could always find Robin there or Nickie here on the weekends.

Grace answered the phone. "Hi Grace. It's Shelby. How are you?

"I'm doing well, dear," she replied. "How are you getting along these days?"

"I'm good. I'm looking for Robin. Is she there?" I asked.

"Oh yes." She said, "Here, It's your mom." I heard her say as she handed the phone to Robin.

When Robin got on, I asked, "Have you had dinner yet?"

"No." she said, and I heard Nickie say something in the background. "Can I spend the night here?" Robin asked, directing her attention back to me. "We're going to order pizza and rent a movie."

"Alright," I said. "As long as it's okay with Grace. Do you have your key in case you want to come home in the middle of the night?"

"No. I'll come over and get some clothes and my key in a few minutes." She hung up without saying goodbye. A few minutes later they came bursting in the door and ran up the steps to Robin's room.

It didn't take her long to grab what she needed and back down they came.

"Goodbye," they called as they ran out the door. They were both so full of energy.

Oh, to be young again.

"Hey," I called loudly to get Robin's attention. "I may go out for something to eat in a bit."

"Okay," they acknowledged they heard me as they slammed the door shut.

I decided to take a long hot bath. I ran the water and added some bath salt to soak in. The fragrance was lavender and vanilla, a scent that calms me enough to make me sleepy. I must have dozed off. When I woke up, I heard a noise downstairs and wondered if Robin and Nickie had changed their minds and decided to stay here tonight.

Then I realized it was Joel's voice I heard. I got out, dried off, and put my robe on to exit the bathroom. In my room, I called Cindy at Al's to tell them I would meet them there in a bit. It was 7:00 now and I had to dress and do my hair.

Still, in my robe, I went downstairs. He and Tom had come in and were raiding the fridge, making sandwiches and such. When they saw me, they both said, "hi mom."

"What are you two up to tonight," I asked.

"We're just going to hang out here if that's okay," Joel said.

"Sure is," I said. "I'm gonna go grab a bite with Cindy as soon as I'm dressed. Help yourselves and be good."

"Okay," they said as I went upstairs and dressed to leave.

I decided to keep it casual since it was cold, and I was too tired to dress up. I threw on a pair of straight-leg jeans, a blue sweater with a cowl neck, and my black shoe boots with low heels.

     Shelby & Shawn   ©   2023

I was comfortable and warm.

I arrived at the VFW at 7:50. I had to knock at the door and wait for someone to answer. A man came to the door and I asked if Al Malone was there. The man called out for Al and I heard Al call back "let her in." As I entered, I had to laugh, realizing that we were the only people there besides the bartender and the guitar player.

Al and Cindy were on the dance floor for a slow tune. Another friend of Cindy's had joined them and was sitting at a table. I didn't know her and when I sat down, she introduced herself as Gail Thomas. She had short grayish-blond hair and looked much older than I thought she was. Her skin was wrinkled and dry, giving her the appearance of having health issues. She also coughed a lot and admitted to being a heavy smoker.

"I'm from Murrysville," she said. "I attended a couple of Cindy's Starting Over Single's meetings but I'm not sure about all this single stuff. My husband left for another woman after 22 years of marriage. And now I have all these health problems and he leaves for some young bimbo. How am I going to get on with my life?" She was on the verge of tears and getting hysterical.

"I'm so sorry." That was all I had a chance to say before Al and Cindy joined us and Al asked me to dance. Another slow song was playing so I got up and danced with him though hesitant to walk away from this poor woman pouring her heart out to me. Besides that, I was starving and just wanted to eat.

Now Al was a cute little munchkin, with black hair and big brown eyes. He was about two inches shorter than me so when he pulled me in he put his face in my chest.

I smacked him on the head. "Cut it out!"

     Shelby & Shawn   ©   2023

"But it's my birthday!" He looked up at me with a pouty, whiny face.

I pushed him away, rolling my eyes. *So immature.*

"What's on the menu?" I asked, walking away from him.

"They had stopped serving food at 7:00." He called after me.

"Dang," I said rather annoyedly as I walked back to the table. "I'm famished. I haven't eaten all day and I don't want to be drinking on an empty stomach."

"Well," he said. "I know a place they'll be serving food."

At the table, we told the others "We're headed for Yesterday's."

Cindy laughed. "How'd we make that decision?" she asked.

"I haven't eaten today and thought I would be able to eat here. Al says they aren't serving food anymore. I need food!"

"Well, I guess we better go get food," Al said, and everyone agreed except Gail. She did not come, and I never saw her again.

Cindy said she was newly separated and was not accepting it well.

"I saw that!" I said. "She was on the verge of a breakdown before you guys came over and interrupted her."
That happens a lot with people coming into single groups. Sometimes they just aren't ready yet to move on and that is pretty

          Shelby & Shawn   ©   2023

much what we're about, learning how to move on.

We arrived at Yesterday's, our favorite hangout because the owners were strict about not letting in the riff-raff. They had a dress code policy and didn't allow drugs around the place. It was a nice family atmosphere.

DJ Larry played oldies every Friday and Saturday night. He packed the place with a good crowd of people every weekend. We had to scramble and squeeze into a table in the back against the dance floor railing.

It wasn't long before Sonny Jones, another regular in Cindy's group, showed up. I ordered a burger and had to wait almost an hour for it. When it came, I gobbled it down like a horse.

"You weren't too hungry," Al said, laughing as he watched me. I mumbled a few words of "I was starving" that could not be understood with my mouth full of food. It was too loud to carry on a conversation so after a few dances, I called it a night.

"I'm taking off," I said and stood up, putting on my coat.

"But it's still early," Cindy said.

"I'm sorry," I said. "I'm so tired and I have to be up early for church tomorrow." I gave Al a peck on the lips and wished him a happy birthday as I got up to leave.

"Bye!" I waved as I walked out.

It was snowing as I walked to my car, that wet snow that doesn't make good snowballs but makes everything icy. The seats were freezing, and I shivered as I sat there waiting impatiently for the engine to warm up. *I just want to get home to bed.*

The drive home was slow because the roads were covered and slick. I walked in the door at 11:30 to find Joel and Tom sleeping on the couch and floor of the living room. After changing into jamas and brushing my teeth, I crawled right into bed and fell asleep immediately.

Chapter 4

We Need Support

What felt like a minute later the alarm went off. I crawled out of bed and into the shower. As I stood under the water trying to wake up a thought came to me. Cindy had not asked me what I did on New Year's Eve. Shawn and I had been very discreet as far as I knew. No one should have known we went away for the weekend together.

Knowing these groups, there was nothing anyone could keep secret, as hard as we tried, thinking of Cindy and Al trying to build a relationship without interference.

This is why I stepped down as leader of my Starting Over Single group last fall. The difficulty with Roy Booth had caused us so much trouble, and Sharon Geesey had made it impossible for me to continue to lead in a responsible way.

I couldn't think about it now, but I knew I had to come up with a way to work things out with Roy if I wanted to continue to build my relationship with Shawn.

I was serving as Eucharistic Minister number one at 8:30 mass the next morning. There were six of us but the minister in the first slot had to be there early to set up for the priest and put out the wine and host to be consecrated. The candles had to be lit and the goblets put out for each minister. It would also be my responsibility to stay after and help clean up.

I loved the volunteer work I did for the church and the people I interacted with. But on the other hand, it was so hard to see all the happily married couples and families around me, wishing I had that, missing that life.

We don't choose divorce. It's not what we want when we get married.

It was a life-saving grace to have that emotional support when you're a single parent. It was vitally important to let the church community know how much this support is needed since the Catholic Church is very marriage-oriented and frowns on divorce. Not everyone was welcoming to me or my kids. It was a stigma we carried.

Everyone says kids coming from divorced homes have emotional issues. Well, yes. Sometimes they do. And that is why we needed emotional support from our Christian community. It takes a village.

I continued to send out that message every chance I got.

I arrived at the church at about 8:10 and started my tasks right away, setting out the chalice and ciborium, pouring the wine into the pitcher, having the host for the priest in place, making sure the candles were lit, and finally carrying everything down the front.

When I reviewed the checklist, there were a couple of things I missed. Fortunately, Father Jon was serving that morning. He was always ready to pitch in and help set up. Together we got it all done in a jiff. I took my seat in front of the church for Mass.

When it was time for the ministers to go up, I joined the others on the altar behind Father Jon. From that viewpoint, I could see the entire congregation. Standing in the back left side of the room was Shawn.

When our eyes met, he smiled, and I thought I saw a twinkle in those beautiful blues. I smiled back but kept my senses about me to the task at hand. I took my responsibility as a minister seriously and did not want to make a mistake. As Father stepped up to me saying "the body of Christ" I said "Amen" and received my host. I went to the right to administer to that side of the church.

Once everyone had come forward for communion and the church was clearing out, I took my remaining host back to the altar for Father to put in the tabernacle. As I walked back to my seat I glanced at the back of the room. Shawn was not there.

When mass was over, I went to the front to pick up the trays carrying the empty chalice, pitcher, vases, and other items to take back and clean.

"Here, I'll help you with that," Sam, another minister who was serving said as he helped to carry the two trays, so I didn't have to make two trips.

"Thanks so much for your help, Sam!" I said after we washed, dried and put everything away. I picked up my coat and purse, bidding Sam goodbye. I went out through the gathering area and did not see any sign of Shawn.

I ran into a few other people I knew who were lingering there, talking to Father. After chatting with them for a few minutes, I begged off, saying that my kids were at home and I had to get to them.

My kids had stopped going to Church with me a year ago. Joel was the first to rebel. He said he just didn't believe it anymore. I tried punishing him for a while by grounding him on Sundays, but that only made it worse. When I talked to Father Jon about it, he said the same thing.

"Let him go. They'll come back when they're ready," was his advice at the time, so I had to let it go. Robin stopped coming shortly after that. It broke my heart because I knew they wouldn't

          Shelby & Shawn   ©   2023

come back. Gene was an atheist, and he was a big influence on the kids that way.

Now as I walked out to my car still looking for signs of Shawn, I wondered if this was going to be our relationship now, catching glimpses of him here and there. But when I got into my car I noticed on the window, lying under the windshield wiper, a note. I got out and grabbed it. It said, 'Hi Trouble, Shawn' and had a smiley face.

Calling me 'trouble' was a standing joke between us now. I laughed. That's cute. I'll take it, I thought, and let my heart feel the joy of building a relationship in a healthy way. *Taking it slow.*

I spent the rest of the day doing nothing but hanging out with the kids, playing games, and watching movies. I made pasta for Sunday dinner, a tradition for me growing up, with meatballs and homemade bread, except my bread wasn't homemade. *Like I have time for homemade bread.*

The next morning, I got to work a little early. I didn't have to get started on anything right away because the other girls had come in early and handled everything. I went to the lounge to have a cup of coffee. We had vending machines with half-decent coffee and a snack machine you didn't dare purchase out of unless you saw them refilling it that day.

As I was sitting at the table sipping my hot coffee, Lew came walking in looking like he just saw a ghost.

Oh, that's right. His meeting with the bigwig's upstairs was Friday.

He plopped down in the chair in front of me and put his face in his hands, rubbing his eyes.

"I have been asked to resign," he said.

"Oh no," I said, trying to sound surprised though I wasn't. Did he think he could shirk his responsibilities like that and not have a consequence?

"I have two weeks and they gave me a nice separation pay." He sounded like he was trying to convince himself this was a good thing.

Lew was 34 and had no wife or kids so I imagined getting another job would be easy for him, especially with the experience he had now. And they were giving him an out that would not ruin his reputation. I had to commend the company for that. Pittsburgh had been his only office, but it was a big one, with three receptionists, four license clerks, two travel agents, and four insurance agents.

"Oh. Well, that's good." I said, feeling totally stressed out now.

There were two of us as supervisors under him when I got transferred there, but Taylor Martin left shortly after I started, leaving me to learn the job on my own. I came to Pittsburgh from a small office of three people. Talk about sink or swim.

And in two weeks, I won't have a manager!

 Shelby & Shawn   ©   2023

Chapter 5

The Best Invites

The next few weeks went by quickly. The weather was snowy and cold. I didn't have much time off being the only supervisor for the office and having no manager since Lew left. It was hard to get anyone to cover that big an office.

But I decided to take a long weekend from February 11th through the 14th. The girls said they'd muddle through without me, and I knew they could handle it. I had no real plans for Valentine's Day because I wanted to keep my options open just in case. My hunch was correct. On Thursday night at 10:00 Shawn called me.

"Hi Shelby. How are you?" he asked when I answered the phone.

"I'm good. A little tired from work but I've taken some time off to get a break this weekend." I said. "How are things going with you?"

"Things have been busy for me at work too." He told me about some of his stressful situations at work and I talked about my manager leaving and how hard it was on me. We talked for an hour about work, kids, and life stuff. It dawned on me for a moment that Gene and I never talked like that. *Gene was the talker. I was the listener.* Suddenly we realized what time it was.

"So hey. The reason I called is I have Kenny this weekend and I'd like to invite you over on Saturday night to spend some time with us. I thought we'd order a pizza or something. Are you free?"

"I am free Saturday night," I said, trying not to sound as excited as I really was. "Would it be okay if I brought some stuff to do for us, like maybe crafts or something?"

"That'd be great! So how bout 6:00?"

"I'll be there!"

I couldn't wait. Robin was taking Nickie with her to Genes for the weekend. She was excited about that. Joel was hanging out with Tom at his house. I didn't have to worry about them being home alone. I would do something special with them on Monday for Valentine's Day, maybe take them out for dinner.

It always helped me to plan on spending time with my kids when I could so I wouldn't feel so guilty spending time with other people's kids.

And going out for dinner was enjoyable now that they were older. When they were young, Ground Round had a kid's night, pay what you weigh, but they had to order from the kid's menu. Joel always got furious about it. I would let him order something for me off the kid's menu and I would order what he wanted off the adult menu and we'd swap. That pacified him for a while but not long.

Friday night Gene pulled up at 6:00 to pick up Robin and Nickie. Nickie loved Gene as much as Robin did. He did have his way with young girls, making jokes and teasing them. He made them feel cute and special. Robin had him wrapped around her little finger.

That was one of the qualities that made him appear attractive to the ladies. One of my favorite memories of him as a husband was sitting in the rocking chair rocking our babies. He said he used it in his favor.

Unfortunately, he used it in his favor while we were still married.

I stood at the door and watched them pile in and drive off, waving, and saying a prayer for God to keep them safe. The phone rang so I closed the door and went to answer it. It was Cindy.

"Hey, some of us are going down to Yesterday's tonight," she said. "Are you coming down? Al and Sonny will be there and a couple of women from my group."

"Gene just picked up the kids and I have some errands to run. Maybe I'll stop in for a drink after," I told her.

I was really excited about spending Saturday evening with Shawn and Kenny, so I wanted to find some fun things for us to do. I headed to Fun Party Store first.

Hmm. What would a four-year-old boy like to do?

It'd been so long since Joel was four, I'd forgotten. But now thinking of Joel at four made my heart go soft. He had a face full of freckles, big brown ornery eyes, and the cutest giggly laugh that the ladies just loved. Robin at four was the prettiest blue-eyed blond. *I miss those days. It is true they go by too fast.*

I found some construction paper to cut out hearts. I bought glue, stickers, and little kid's scissors; I assumed Shawn didn't have any of this stuff. Maybe we could make a Valentine to take to his mother, I thought.

From there I went to the supermarket to get some stuff to make cookies. I figured the premade sugar cookie dough would be best, so I didn't make such a mess in Shawn's kitchen. I knew he wouldn't have roller pins or cookie cutters and I didn't want to get into that much expense. I got white icing and food coloring and of course, sprinkles.

     Shelby & Shawn   ©   2023

What kid doesn't like sprinkles?

When I came out of Fun Party Store, snow was covering everything and coming down heavily. I figured it was cold enough to keep the few refrigerated items I'd bought in the car, so I headed down to Yesterdays. Cindy was there with Al and Sonny and a few others I didn't know. They waved me over and I made my way through the crowd. It was packed again.

As Sonny found a chair for me, Cindy introduced her new members as Greg, Joyce, and Mary. They were from out around the Delmont area and found out about our groups through the church bulletins I advertised every week to help her out.

I sat down and ordered a drink, peach, and ginger, my favorite alcoholic beverage. I looked over at DJ Larry and waved. He knew I'd be requesting a song as I always did. A couple of times he'd let me get behind his podium and look through his collection to find new songs to play. He had a good selection of music. All oldies.

I chatted with Joyce and Mary while Cindy was out dancing. Most nights you couldn't get us off the dance floor but tonight I wanted to spend some time meeting these new people, though it was hard to hear with the loud music and crowd.

Greg Altman was very tall and very thin with blond hair and green eyes. A slow song came on and he asked me to dance.

"Sure," I said and got up to meet him at the end of the table. We walked out on the dance floor stepping right into rhythm with the song. When I put my hand on his shoulder, I could literally feel his bones. "Don't you eat?" I asked, squeezing his shoulder and making a joke about how skinny he was.

          Shelby & Shawn   ©   2023

Fortunately, he was a good sport and laughed. "No, I don't actually." He said. "My wife and I are getting divorced, and we are still living in the same house so it's kind of awkward right now."

"Wow!" I said. "That would be."

"Well, it's my house and I'm not giving it up. And she thinks it's her house and she's not giving it up … so I guess we're stuck until the lawyers decide whose house it is."

"Have you ever seen 'War of the Rose's'?" I asked.

"No." He answered. "What's that about?"

"Well, you better not watch it. It's about a couple getting divorced and neither one will leave the house. It doesn't end well." I laughed. "Although it might be a warning for you."

He laughed and said, "I won't watch it."

Another slow song came on and we danced right through it.

We finally made our way back to the table only for Cindy to drag me back out for her favorite song by Shania Twain 'Man I Feel Like a Woman'. A few more dances and I had to have something to drink. Greg moved on to dance with Mary while Cindy and Al went out on the dance floor as another slow tune came on.

I drank my peach and ginger down pretty fast and went up to the bar to order a sprite, abiding by my two-drink limit. Of course, that took forever so I said hi to Larry while I was up there.

"How's everything going?" He asked me.

     Shelby & Shawn   ©   2023

"Busy at work and the kids keep me on my toes," I replied. He had met my kids when we were here for a spaghetti dinner one night with the group. It was a BOGO night one Wednesday and everyone brought their kids to eat.

"My daughter just turned 16!" he said. "You think you got troubles!" He laughed in a sad pathetic way.

I had to laugh too. I would be experiencing that sooner than I wanted to think about. I moaned and said "I feel your pain. Hang in there."

My sprite came and I downed it fast causing my throat to hurt from the fizz. I gave Larry a wave and went back to my table to say good night.

"It was nice meeting you all. I will be sure to get newsletters out to you when I get your addresses." I was the only leader who wrote newsletters before all the groups went under and I kept that going after I stepped down. I made it part of Cindy's group since hers and the volleyball group were the only ones still going.

"Hope to see you at some of our events again soon."

They all bid me goodbye and yes, we'll see you soon and away I went thinking *we'll see*. Most of these people came once or twice and if they didn't find what they were looking for at that time, they didn't come back.

And what were they looking for? Instant love!

Cindy's group was still getting some crowds though. And then the volleyball group was still active. I thought about Randy Brown's call last week to let me know that they needed players so I could put an ad in my newsletter for them.

"You should come back Shelby," he had said. "We could use you. You're a good player."

"I don't know," I wasn't sure what my reception would be like if I went back because of the way I had left. After I had been directed by Catholic Charities, who oversaw the groups, that I was not to call the men in my group anymore, I resigned as leader. "Do you think I'll be welcome?" I asked. "After all the trouble Roy had caused us?"

"Absolutely! Everyone's been asking where you are." He said. "Everyone knows how much trouble Roy caused you and nobody holds that against you."

"Really?" It was good to know I hadn't isolated my friends. I still hadn't talked to Roy about anything or had a chance to patch things up with him. "Well let me think about it. Maybe I will."

I planned to ask Shawn when I saw him Saturday night to ask what he thought also.

Leaving Yesterday's, the snow was really coming down and the roads were getting bad. I got home at about 11:00 and put my groceries away. My townhouse was empty and quiet. I turned the TV on to watch the news and opened my drapes so I could watch the snow come down out the sliding glass doors leading to the deck.

The wooden deck was completely covered with almost a foot of snow already. The trees were heavy with the glistening white laying in the crevasse and the branches looked as though they would break right off the trees. It was a memorizing winter wonderland, crisp and beautiful.

My thoughts went back to the farm where Gene's parents lived when we dated. The lane going down to the house was a windy, long dirt road with potholes you had to swerve hard to avoid. In the winter the road was nearly impassable without a four-wheel drive truck.

But the beauty was spectacular. Acres of farmland covered in a blanket of white. I loved it there and we would have stayed after his parents divorced and moved away. But Gene had not been any kind of farmer who could manage that much work. Nor could I keep up with that big farmhouse after having a baby. We were both too young. We were not ready for all this. It was best that we moved to the city. *Or was it?*

Just then the door flew open with a blast of cold air as Joel and Tom came in. My spell was interrupted, and I realized I missed the news entirely.

"Where have you guys been in this weather," I asked.

"At Brian's. We didn't realize it was getting so bad," Joel answered. "Tom's sacking out here tonight."

"I should think so," I said. "He's not driving in this weather. I'm heading to bed." I started up the stairs as they raided the kitchen helping themselves to snacks and drinks.

"Night Mom!" they both called out. "Love ya!"

"Good night, guys! Love you too!" As I said my nighttime prayers, I thanked God for my terrific kids.

Chapter 6

The Separation

They had turned out to be terrific kids despite what we'd been through. I handled it the best I could considering I was not at all prepared for what was coming. We were living in Pittsburgh, so I was alone, with no one around to help me. I remember the day Gene moved out.

Six months prior, Gene was believed to have lung cancer, but further tests proved negative. Those couple weeks waiting for test results were stressful and caused Gene to lose his temper a lot. One day he blew up and began hitting our oldest son aggressively and uncontrollably. I stepped in to stop him and he grabbed me up by the front of my shirt and hit me in the face. We began counseling immediately after that.

But it changed him. He bought a sports car, started wearing gold chains and bought himself a diamond ring. In counseling, we explored all the difficulties in our marriage. After six months, we decided we needed to separate for a while. We talked about living apart but continuing to see each other and our counselor, Phil Malony. Our goal was to work our way back together.

My hope was that Gene would learn to be more responsible. He had never lived alone and didn't know how to take care of himself at all. He handled money terribly, always borrowing from family and friends. We were always in debt because he spent money before he had it. I also believed he was taking drugs, mixed with alcohol, making him very unpredictable. I found out later I was right.

There was a woman he worked with named Sherry, who I met at his Christmas party. He told me her husband was abusive and she was leaning on him for moral support. So I befriended her at the party, *the trusting soul I was*. She had come to the house once or twice when I was at my part-time job to get away from her husband when he became aggressive, *so she said.*

The afternoon Gene moved out her husband came to my door looking for his wife. It turned out Gene had rented a U-haul, gone to her house, and completely wiped him out. I told this man I didn't know where she was or anything about his wife. When he left, I called Gene at work to confront him.

"Where's Sherry, Gene? Her husband was here looking for her." I asked him when he answered the phone.

"Where do you think she is?" he replied and laughed.

"What happened to you living on your own so you could grow?" I said completely shocked.

"I don't want to live on my own. Sherry and I are together now." I didn't even know who this man was I was talking to on the phone.

"Does this mean you are not coming back ever? How am I supposed to proceed from here and plan my life? How am I supposed to take care of my kids?" I was so very angry and upset. I began to cry.

"I'm confused right now." He seemed to soften. "I don't know what I want. I'll come back when I'm ready." He said, sounding sympathetic then becoming more aggressive again. "I'm in control now and you'll have to wait and see when I'm ready." It was like two different personalities.

I hung up the phone completely lost. Four days later the bank notified me that my husband had removed his name from the bank account. They said they would issue me new checks and

 Shelby & Shawn   ©   2023

adjust my statements. If I had any questions I should call. I was terrified now.

I called Gene. "What am I to do without any money to feed my kids? You know I only work part-time hours on the weekends. And now I'll have to pay for a babysitter." I was trying to stay calm, but I was nearly hysterical.

"I'll deposit $150 dollars a pay into your account. And I'll come to watch the kids on the weekends while you work." he told me. I have it all planned out.

"I can't live on that. What are you doing? None of this makes any sense. Are you still coming to the next counseling appointment? We need to talk this out."

"Yeah, I'll come."

"I'll see you there," I said and hung up. I wasn't eating or sleeping, and I felt like I got kicked in the stomach most of the time. The kids became very needy and clingy sensing my stress.

I was calling my mother and sister a lot for emotional support. At that time, with landlines and no cell phones, they were considered long-distance calls. The next thing I knew my phone was shut off. I had to go to a neighbor and call the phone company to get the phone back on in my name.

The gas and electric companies came next. They at least called me to let me know he was shutting me off so that I could put the accounts in my name with no interruption.

Once the neighbor found out what was going on she came over to check on me often. Her teenage daughter offered to babysit so I started picking up more hours at Ames where I had been working part-time for two years. It was still minimum wage pay

     Shelby & Shawn   ©   2023

and paying a babysitter. I wasn't going to make ends meet like this.

At the next counseling session, Gene came in with an arrogant attitude and demeanor.

"I'm going to live with Sherry for now. If I change my mind, I'll come back." He told Phil.

"What is it you want from this?" Phil asked.

"I'm confused. I don't know what I want," he said. "I'll come back when I'm ready." He was smirky, almost laughing.

"And what am I supposed to do in the meantime?" I asked. "Look, you need to figure this out. I'm not going to sit around and wait for you to decide you're coming back. You have a month to make up your mind."

He just laughed. "You're not in control anymore. I'll come back when I'm ready."

I left that day feeling broken and beaten. I had three kids, nowhere to go and no one to help me. My mom told me to come home.

"Mom, you don't have room for me. You and daddy on social security can't support us." I told her. "Plus, we have all this stuff. What are we going to do?" I was trying to be strong for my kids, but I was crying a lot and I had not even a minute to myself. The kids were so emotional they just clung to me all the time.

On the weekends when Gene came to watch the kids, I came home from work and asked him what he was going to do.

"I told you I'm in control of this and I'll come back when I'm ready. Don't pressure me." He kept saying that.

So, one weekend, I took the day off on Sunday and when Gene came to watch the kids, thinking I'd be going to work, I had a picnic lunch packed for us to take the kids to the park. He was agreeable to go but was very angry about it.

We spent the day playing with the kids. I made sure not to bring up any problems or put any pressure on him to reconcile. I bent over backward to be kind and loving toward him. I even jumped on a swing with the kids and asked him to push me too, laughing as he did.

When we got back to our place, I put the kids to bed and came out to find him sitting in the living room. "This was a nice day. I appreciated your effort to be together." He said and he started crying. "I don't know what is wrong with me. I'm so confused."

I held him and we ended up making love on the couch. I fell asleep after but woke up an hour later to find him gone. I went to bed and cried myself to sleep. I didn't call him at all after that.

But I decided to try the last tactic. I knew how jealous he was. I got a babysitter one evening during the week and told the kids I had a date for dinner. I went out and had dinner alone and did some shopping, coming back late. The following weekend, when I was at work and Gene was at the house, the kids told him I went out to dinner on a date.

When I got home from work, he was indeed very hostile and angry. He wanted to know who I went out with and how I knew him.

"It's none of your business. You don't live here anymore." I didn't tell him anything. He became very aggressive with me physically and I had to ask him to leave.

     Shelby & Shawn   ©   2023

At our counseling session that following week, I confronted him.

"What are you going to do?" I insisted. "Your time is up. You can't keep stringing us along. What are you telling Sherry? That you're confused. I doubt she'd be going along with this if she knew you were telling me you'll come back to us when you're ready."

"I told you I haven't decided yet! Don't worry about her." He was loud and aggressive, almost spitting his words at me.

"Why couldn't you just be honest about this in the first place?" I said. "This whole thing could have been handled differently."

"Shut up!" He interrupted me. This time he did spit the words at me, and I snapped. All those years of suppression, all those times he told me to shut up, built up to this.

I looked at him calmly and said, "Don't tell me to shut up! Don't ever tell me to shut up again. Get out."

He just sat there with a sick grin on his face. "She's crazy. She needs to be 302'd"

"She said get out," Phil told him. Reluctantly, he got up and left.

I felt numb but I didn't cry anymore. Then Phil began to tell me a story:

'Once there was a kingdom where there lived a great king. Someone put something in the water that made the people of the kingdom insane. Everyone drank the water except the king. The

 Shelby & Shawn   ©   2023

people began to fret over the king. They wondered what was wrong with him and thought he was insane. Finally, the king drank the water, and everyone rejoiced because their king was sane again.'

Then Phil said to me "Don't drink the water, Shelby."

I truly understood exactly what he meant. I saw Phil a couple more times before I moved back home. Through our sessions, we concluded that Gene, thinking he had cancer, had experienced an early mid-life crisis. I believed it was the drugs he was taking. He had always been an addict, living a lie our entire marriage. It was only a matter of time before it surfaced.

My mother and father hired a moving company, moving us and all my belongings into her basement. They set up my queen-sized bed in the game room with my TV where the kids and I slept. They hired a lawyer for me to file for child support. It took a month to get a date set for a court hearing that I had to go to Pittsburgh for.

Gene was so angry; he and his girlfriend came in the middle of the night and took my car. It was in his name, so I had no recourse against him. Dad and my brother-in-law took me out to buy a car dad cosigned for. It was a cute little chevy cavalier sport and I liked it better than the one Gene took from me.

Once I had my hearing and the support started coming in, my dad had to cosign for my townhouse until I was able to establish my credit and get on my feet. It took years and Gene fought me every step of the way. He made my life as hard as he possibly could.

But I overcame it. So did my kids.

One year later, Gene left Sherry after dumping her with all

          Shelby & Shawn   ©   2023

his bills. She wrote me a letter telling me she would testify in court for me and asked if she could see the kids. I never replied.

Chapter 7

Valentine's With Kenny

Saturday night, I knocked at Shawn's door promptly at 6:00. I was a little nervous. I had met Kenny before but in a group setting. We'd never had alone time. Shawn opened the door and as I stepped in little four-year-old Kenny came running over to me and hugged my legs. He was adorable.

"Hi Kenny," I said.

"Hi Cellby. Are we going to make cookies." he couldn't pronounce my name and it was the cutest thing ever.

"Yes, we are if you'd like to," I said.

"Yeah!" He jumped up and down as I stepped inside, and Shawn spotted his neighbor friend coming down the hall with his girlfriend.

"Hey, John. What're you guys up to tonight?" Shawn asked them.

"Hi John," Kenny said when he saw them.

"Hi Shelby," John said to me when he got to the door.

"Remember John?" Shawn asked. "He was here one night when we were watching football."

"Oh yes. I remember you." I was surprised he remembered my name.

"And this is my girlfriend, Beverly," John said.

"Hi Beverly," I said.

"Oh, you can call me Bev. I like it better. Beverly sounds so formal." She said,

"OK, Bev it is," I said smiling.

"Well see you later," they said.

We all said our goodbyes and Shawn closed the door.

"The pizzas should be here soon. I ordered cheese and pepperoni. Didn't know which you'd like better." said Shawn.

"Thanks! I like em both." I said. "And what kind of pizza is your favorite?" I asked Kenny.

"Cheeeese" he said like he was getting his picture taken. We all laughed.

"Well let's get these cookies made. Do you have a cookie sheet?" I asked Shawn as Kenny was jumping up and down calling "YEAH" again.

He said, "I think I do." and we laughed at that. "Let's try under this cabinet." His apartment was a small one-bedroom efficiency with very little cupboard space.

Sure enough, there was a cookie sheet under the cabinet thank goodness. I took it out and found a knife to cut open the cookie dough package and then set up the table with the sprinkles. I cut the pieces of cookie dough and put them on the sheet.

"Put sprinkles on them like this," I showed Kenny, before putting them in the oven. "Now let's find cups for the icing."

     Shelby & Shawn   ©   2023

"In the top cupboard," Shawn reached and got them for us.

I gave Kenny a spoon, "Put a spoonful of icing in each cup, then add drops of food coloring to each and stir." Shawn was helping him so he didn't squirt food coloring everywhere. He got a big kick out of watching the icing turn colors. I wondered if his mom had ever done anything like this with him.

What was even funnier was Shawn seemed to be enjoying this whole thing as much if not more than Kenny. As we waited for the cookies to cook and cool I spread the craft stuff on the living room floor.

"Would you like to make Valentine's cards? We can cut hearts and flowers and all sorts of shapes."

We made cards and pictures, cutting and gluing each piece the way a four-year-old would, making a huge mess, but laughing the whole time.

Just when the cookies were cool enough, we could ice them the pizza came. We ate pizza and cookies while doing crafts.

"This is the most fun I've had since my own kids were little. We had craft night once a week. I really missed it." I said to Shawn.

Shawn kinda casually asked out of the blue "So when are you coming back to volleyball? You should come back. We really need you."

"Did you and Randy talk about this?" I smiled thinking this sounded awfully familiar.

"No, why? Did he tell you to come back too?"

     Shelby & Shawn   ©   2023

"Yes. He mentioned it," is all I said.

"Well, everyone's been asking where you are and why you quit coming. You really didn't need to quit. We need you. Our teams are dwindling down in numbers."

"Well, I've been thinking about coming back," I said.

"I hope you do," he said and started wrestling with Kenny.

As they played around in the living room, I cleaned up the kitchen and did the dishes. By then it was time for Kenny to get bathed and ready for bed. I gathered my things and gave Kenny a hug.

"Thank you for a wonderful time this evening Kenny," I said to him.

"Tell Shelby thank you for everything," Shawn said to Kenny.

"Thank you, Cellby," he said.

I then gave Shawn a big hug before I left and thanked him too for a wonderful evening. As I drove home, I made a mental note to call Roy and see if we could patch things up. I wanted to make sure he would be comfortable with me coming back to volleyball before I just showed up there. After the way the situation was handled with Roy when he caused trouble with our groups, and him being asked to leave, I would not blame him at all for not wanting to talk to me again.

Sharon Geesie at Catholic Charities did not handle the situation very well for us. Being a counselor, she should have had the skills to help people manage conflict. Using Randy to take Roy out of the group is not the way I wanted it to go.

I wanted to bring Roy into Sharon's office to have a one-on-one meeting with him using her as a mediator, to supervise what was being said. I just wanted Roy to understand that we were all just friends, spending time together, supporting each other, and helping each other heal from the effects of broken relationships. But he was lying to her too so her hands were tied, I guess, as far as what she could do.

He was taking everything out of proportion by saying we were taking advantage of people. And the fact that he was telling people he was dating me in order to keep the other guys away from me was very manipulative and controlling. His behavior was destructive to my group and Randy's.

He tried to cause a lot of trouble between Shawn and me because he was so jealous. I had considered these guys my best friends. I loved them like brothers. Including Randy.

It was because of all this that I left my Starting Over Single group and stepped down as leader of this church group through Catholic Charities. We were a bunch of adults acting like high school kids. I didn't want to be a part of it anymore.

It was going to be difficult to talk to him after all this time but I had to try.

Chapter 8

Making Up

I was very nervous the next morning when I picked up the phone to call Roy.

"Hi Roy. It's Shelby," I said when he answered the phone. It was 8:30 but it sounded like he had been up already. I remembered one time when we were hanging out together, he told me he was up every day very early, like 5 am. He would send me lots of emails in the wee hours.

"Shelby!" he seemed very surprised. "Hi. How are you?"

"I'm fine. I hope I didn't wake you."

"No, I was up. What can I do for you?" His tone was cold.

"I'd like to get together and talk to you if I could?" I asked him.

"Oh. What about?"

"Well. I prefer to discuss it in person. Can I buy you an ice cream?" I said. I really didn't want to get into it on the phone.

"Really," he sounded very apprehensive. I didn't blame him after the way he had been treated by the group leaders and Catholic Charities. "Sure. Where and when?" he said finally.

"How about The Meadows on the Mt. Pleasant Rd?" I asked. "Say today at about 12:00?" I'd be just getting out of the church and could go straight there. That would give me a chance to pray about what I wanted to say and ask God to guide my words for a faithful outcome. *I would be much calmer.*

"Okay. I can make that," he said. "I'll see you then."

"See you then," I said and hung up.

The conversation felt strained, and I began to regret the decision to call him. I hoped the actual meeting would go better. I really wanted to resolve this conflict with him in a way that would allow us to become friends again. Or at least be able to be together in the same place without being too uncomfortable.

I wasn't serving at church so when I got there, I was able to go straight to a seat and kneel for prayer. I spent a lot of prayer time asking the Holy Spirit how I should handle this and to please guide my words to heal this relationship. Then I said the rosary while I waited for Mass to begin.

People were pouring in since Lent had started. It looked like we were going to have a full congregation today. That meant Mass was going to run a little longer. I didn't want Roy to get there first and think I wasn't coming.

After Mass was over at 11:40 I stayed about 10 minutes longer just to get my thoughts together about how to begin the conversation I was about to have with Roy. Because he had lied so much before, I wished I could have done this with someone who could have been a buffer between us. But that didn't work out the last time and there was no one I could trust now, so I was on my own.

I got in my car and drove to The Meadow's, which was a custard shop right down the road from the church. It only took me 5 minutes to get there so I arrived early, but Roy was already there as I thought he would be. He must have been as anxious as I was. When I walked in, he stood up and came over to me.

        Shelby & Shawn   ©   2023

I kept a little distance between us but smiled and said, "thank you for meeting me."

"Sure," he said with a shrug.

"What kind of ice cream do you want?" I asked, leading us to the counter. "I'm buying so have anything you like."

We both ordered chocolate ice cream. His was in a cone and mine in a cup. I paid and handed him the cone.

"Thank you," he said.

"You're welcome," I said. "A peace offering."

We found a table and sat down just enjoying our ice cream at first. Then I began:

"Roy, I want to apologize for what happened to you with the singles group. I think there were a lot of misunderstandings and miscommunications that led to all of that. We really felt like you were turning on all of us and when Cindy went to Sharon at Catholic Charities that was what we all thought. I wanted Sharon to just sit down with you and me to talk about it but that was not the way she chose to handle it. I'm sure she thought she was doing the best thing."

I paused for a moment to eat some of my ice cream, and he replied:

"Shelby, I never meant to cause all that. It wasn't my intention to get anyone into trouble or kicked out of the groups. I was concerned about people being taken advantage of. I felt you were being taken advantage of too. That's what I told Sharon. I was just concerned about some things that I thought were wrong with some of the leaders."

          Shelby & Shawn   ©   2023

"Okay, I get that. But do you understand that we were all just good friends and spending time together? We're adults Roy. We can make decisions for ourselves about our relationships. Just like you and I have a right to be friends and do things together. Do I have that right with Shawn or Randy or anyone other men? No one had a right to interfere with our relationships."

"I understand that now. Thank you for meeting with me and talking to me about this."

"I'm glad we can talk and be friendly again. I plan on coming back to volleyball and I didn't want to make you uncomfortable."

"You should come back," he said. "We all miss you and we need more players."

I laughed, "you just need more players … right?"

He laughed as well. "We really do need more players."

We finished our ice cream and went our separate ways, still maintaining some distance between us as we walked out. That trust was going to take a long time to rebuild if it ever did. I tried to remember him as the friend I loved spending time with so much. I knew we would never be that close again.

At least he took some responsibility for his part in everything. I was very surprised about that. I expected him to lie again. Maybe he was really trying to change. I hoped so, cause the alternative is he just told me what he thought I wanted to hear.

I went back to volleyball that following Friday night. When I walked into the gym, I was welcomed by everyone. I soon discovered that Kari Young had been slowly backing out of the lead because of some health problems. She didn't tell anyone, but she ended up having cancer. We didn't find out until after she passed away.

Bobbie Gaines was taking over for her. I was glad to see her becoming more involved and I spent some time explaining to her about the other groups and how we coordinated our activities together. She didn't seem to understand it and I wondered how committed she was going to be leading this group. There were still quite a few of the old players and we were able to have a balanced team of people.

That night was my weekend to have the kids home, so I took Robin and Nickie with me to volleyball. The girls didn't like playing so they sat on the sidelines to cheer us on. At one point they got a little too rowdy and I yelled for them to calm down. They had so much energy.

It was so good to be back with my friends. Roy and Shawn were there of course, and we hung out talking for a while in between games. It felt comfortable but not quite the same. Randy Brown was still coming but he hadn't brought his kids with him this time. He and Bobbie spent time together.

Bobbie had brought her daughter, Rae, who was crazy about Randy. She always hung all over him. I'd hoped they'd get together. They seemed right for each other. Bobbie's dream was to live on a farm and Randy wanted more kids. I was curious to see how all that would play out.

At one point Shawn pulled me aside and said, "Roy told me that you guys talked things out and are okay now. I'm so happy to hear that. It was really nice of you to make the effort to do that."

"Thank you for saying so. I really wanted to clear the air and come to an understanding of what happened. I didn't want

 Shelby & Shawn   ©   2023

there to be any bad feelings left between us ... especially if I was coming back to volleyball. I wanted to make sure he was comfortable with me here."

He smiled and said, "Kenny wants to know when you're making cookies again."

"Tell Kenny any time," I winked and smiled as others joined us and we changed the subject.

After Volleyball we headed to Eat N Park for some nourishment. The guys were always hungry after playing. Randy came but Bobbi did not.

The girls ordered burgers and shakes. I just had some decaf coffee and pie. No spit wad battles anymore. The staff had been getting annoyed with us for making a mess of the dining room so that they had to stay late and clean up.

It was hard to explain why 40-year olds sometimes had to act like 10 year old's. When you've been through a divorce, you understand that sometimes you just gotta cut loose and have fun sometimes. I guess they call that getting in touch with your inner child. It was an important part of our healing process.

The girls started singing "you've lost that lovin feelin, ohhhh that lovin feelin …. "The guys joined in "you've lost that lovin feelin … now it's gone … gone … gone … woah oh oh oh oh" thumping hands on the table ….

The food came and we ate, talking about everything and nothing. Randy was asking the girls how school was going. Shawn and Roy were talking about the upcoming basketball season. Tara and Kari were talking about buying air bikes. I sat back and took it all in. Just being together was enough. That feeling of having an understanding from others who have been through it too.

We got home around midnight. Robin and Nickie went to Robin's room to watch a movie. It was awesome having them with me tonight. I went straight to bed myself. Thank goodness I was off the next day and could sleep in. I needed it.

 Shelby & Shawn   ©   2023

Chapter 9

Moving Up

When I got up around 8:30 the next morning, I had a burst of energy. I put some cinnamon muffins in the oven and got started on cleaning the living room. I took everything down off the walls to wipe off, vacuumed behind all the furniture, and washed the cobwebs from every corner. From there, I moved on to the dining room and kitchen walls and on up the hallway steps, washing the walls and railings.

At about 11:00, the girls came running down the steps crying "we smell something good."

"There's cinnamon muffins and chocolate milk," I said.

They grabbed a muffin and a pint of milk each and ran into the living room to get on the computer. They were pretty smart, and I had to be double checking them all the time on there, so they weren't getting into anything harmful or hurtful. I had set up parental controls, but they quickly found a way around them. So, I made sure I got on there every day to see what kind of stuff they were looking at.

At 11:30, I got a call from work. It was Dawn Brady, the President of Operations for The Auto Club in our region.

"Hi Shelby. Sorry to bother you on your day off. I hope I'm not interrupting anything." She said.

"Oh no! I'm just cleaning, and I don't mind an interruption from that," I laughed.

"Well, I won't keep you." She said, laughing. "I would like to know if you can come in a half hour early Monday and come straight to my office."

Hmmm. I knew this was going to be about Lew leaving but what direction would this go in? "Sure, I'd be happy to," I said.

"Okay. We'll see you Monday morning at about 8:00 then."

"See you then." I hung up and sat there for a minute thinking.

What opportunities would this open up for me? I had been looking for another job closer to home but now I was wondering if I should just sit tight for a while and see where this leads. There was no way I was going to keep driving to Pittsburgh for much longer but there were offices closer to me that would work out. And I do want to buy a house so I can look for that anywhere. I was starting to feel excited about my future again.

I got married a week after graduating from high school and had a baby in the first year. I was a stay-at-home mom so when Gene moved out, I literally had to start my life over with two kids to raise. I put myself through school, got this job, and began to work my way up. After eight years, I was a supervisor hoping to be a manager someday. That day may have come.

I got up and started cleaning again but this time I was whistling while I worked. It felt good to get things done. But I started to think about that drive and how unhappy I was with it. And being a manager would mean longer hours in this office.

I really have to give this some thought.

I got up at 5:30 a.m. to get ready. I decided to dress professionally in case this turned into an interview for the management position. I wore a deep purple suit with a pink blouse beneath and black flats. I did have to work all day and I didn't want

     Shelby & Shawn   ©   2023

to be uncomfortable in heels.

The traffic was light but still took me an hour and fifteen minutes instead of an hour and a half. I went straight to Dawn's office on the third floor. There was no one downstairs yet but several of the executives were there on the administration floor. Her secretary asked me to have a seat.

I waited about ten minutes before Dawn came out and called me in.

"Good morning," she said. "Have a seat." She directed me to a big table at the other end of her office. I sat in the chair at the corner while she sat in the other corner chair.

"I'm not sure if you've heard about Lew Shelly, but he is going to be leaving," she began.

"Yes, I did hear from him that he would only be here another couple of weeks," I said, carefully watching my words for confidentiality's sake.

"Though I have not put the bid out yet, I am looking ahead and trying to place someone so that we won't have to go without a manager in this big office for too long. I've been watching you Shelby and I see how committed you are to your work. You have a very good work ethic, and you seem to be a very good leader. The staff here seems to like you. How would you feel about the position of manager here when Lew leaves?"

As I thought, the position is here in Pittsburgh. I thought about it all day yesterday and it just isn't what I want.

"I'm sorry, Dawn, but I'm having a hard time with this drive and the number of hours I'm spending away from my kids. I have two teenagers at home, and they need my supervision more right now."

"How old are they?" she asked kindly.

"They are 14 and 16. Too old for babysitters but still not quite old enough to be on their own so much. I have been looking for another job closer to home with another company because of this."

"Well, you are very valuable to us and we don't want to lose you. Let me see what I can move around. Can we talk about this more in a couple of weeks?"

"Yes, Thank you very much. That means a lot to me." I was truly touched that she said that.

"I'll be in touch." She stood and walked me to the door.

I went down to my office, greeting the staff as I walked through the lobby, letting them know I was available if they needed me. When I checked my phone calls, I had a message from Randy on my voicemail, something about a title, so I called him back.

I got his secretary, Shannon, who knew me well from our dating days. "Hi. This is Shelby. Is Randy around?"

"Oh, hey, Shelby. He's expecting your call. Let me find him."

"Hi. Thanks for calling me back." He said when he picked up the transfer.

"Sure. What's up?" I asked.

"I bought Liam a used car. I wanted to know what to do.

I've only ever bought vehicles from dealers, and they always did everything."

I chucked. "We hear that a lot," I said. I went through the checklist of everything he needed to bring in.

"I think I have all that," he said. "I'll be coming after work at about 4:00. Do you wanna go for a bite to eat after you get off?"

"Yeah. That'd be great. I can tell you my news."

"I'll look forward to hearing it. See ya later."

"Bye." I hung up and called the kids to let them know I'd be late getting home. Then I got to work on some reports that needed to be finished.

Randy arrived at about 4:30. I had one of my girls do the transfer for him while I helped get the office ready to close. When they finished with him, I let them know I'd be leaving. Beth and Kelly were going to finish closing out.

We walked out together but got in our own cars and drove to Church Brew Works on Liberty Ave. in Pittsburgh. This is a brewery occupying a renovated Catholic church. A gigantic copper kettle sits where the altar once was. The stained-glass windows are still in place, shining light into the restaurant.

The house brews are named after their place on the altar: pipe organ ale, bell tower brown ale, and pious monk dunkel. The food is amazing as well, offering contemporary versions of steak, pizza, burgers, or unique pierogi combinations. *It is one of Pittsburgh's finest!*

The place was not yet crowded so we had our pick of seats. We found a bench in the back against the wall. Randy ordered a couple of samples of the different beers they had. I tasted a couple of his but ended up with a sprite.

"What's this news you have?" he asked.

"I may be promoted to manager. My current manager is resigning. They need someone to fill the position but I'm struggling now to work these hours, drive that distance, and raise teenagers. I told them I would need to consider all that. The operations manager, Dawn, asked me to wait and see what she could come up with. She said she'd let me know. I'm not sure what's brewing, but I'm a little excited."

"That sounds exciting." He didn't sound particularly excited. Randy was an extreme Old Testament type who believes the man controls the woman and the woman is obedient and submissive. When we were dating, I wasn't allowed to make a decision without his permission, and he got very angry when I did.

Our food came. We ate and talked about what the kids were up to, he told me about the car he bought, and I told him about my conversation with Roy.

It was late when we finished eating. He walked me to my car and I drove home.

He's a good friend...

But we understood why it would never be more. I worried about him driving after all that beer.

 Shelby & Shawn © 2023

Chapter 10

Kari and Tara

Kari Myers approached me at volleyball Friday night.

"Hey, Shelby. I decided I can't continue to play volleyball. A few weeks ago I broke my finger and it's not healing right. I'll continue to come to collect the money and pay for the gym for us."

"I'm sorry to hear that, Kari. What's this now? A broken figure?" I took her hand to check out her finger. It was a little crooked but otherwise looked fine. "It looks okay to me. Well, maybe you'll be able to play again in a couple of months after it heals."

"Yeah. But it isn't healing right, and I don't want to take the chance of it getting all busted up. I'll still come to see everyone and say hi."

I thought something was off but there was no arguing with her. She was trying to back out of this responsibility.

"Bobbi's taking over for me as far as collecting the money and bringing the ball and key on Friday nights."

"Well okay. We'll miss you. Keep in touch."

She came for a couple more weeks and watched us play. She even went out afterward with us to eat but she never ate, and she looked thinner and more peaked each time. We always jagged around with her about how skinny she was. *If only we'd known.*

"You better start eating," Randy said to her one night. "You're gonna disappear into nothing. Can I buy you a burger?"

"No. I'm just not hungry." She'd say laughing.

Finally, she stopped coming. She called Tara, her best friend who also came to volleyball, and had her collect the money to pay for the gym when Bobbi wasn't able to.

"What's going on?" I asked Tara when she called to talk to me about it.

"I don't know. She's not even telling me and I'm her best friend."

"Well, we can't force her to stay with us. I'll go visit her when I get a chance and see if I can get to the bottom of things. If not, we have to respect her privacy." I felt as helpless as she did.

"Yes, you're right. In the meantime, I'll take up the slack for carrying the ball and collecting the money. Bobbi doesn't always come. Maybe down the road, we can all take turns or something."

"Okay. If you can't make it, let me know and I'll get it from you."

"Thanks." She hung up and I knew she was crying.

A few days later, I went to Kari's house to visit. She came to the door and opened it but stood blocking me and did not invite me in. She looked terrible so I thought I woke her from a nap or something.

"Hi. How are you doing? Did I wake you?" I asked, feeling awkward about standing outside her door like that.

"I'm fine. Yeah, I was just napping." She said but not budging. She seemed to be blocking me from seeing in as well.

 Shelby & Shawn   ©   2023

"Tara told me she was taking over for you and I just wanted to let you know how much we appreciate everything you did for us. Any chance you'll be coming around to see us, just to say hi."

"Well, I'll try but I don't know if I'll make it any time soon. Ya know, I have some other stuff going on," she said.

"Okay. Well, I won't keep you."

"Yes, I'm very tired. I just need to get some rest," she said leaning on the door.

"Well … take care of yourself." I hesitated to leave her just feeling something wasn't right.

A few weeks later, Tara called me crying hysterically. "I just heard from Kari's brother. She passed away. Apparently, she had cancer for a while now. She never told anyone. Not even me. Why would she do that?"

"I'm so sorry Tara. She probably didn't want us to pity her or something. Maybe she was just uncomfortable with all that emotion … She didn't want people crying over her. Is there a funeral service we can go to?"

"No. Her brother said she didn't want anything. They are just going to cremate her. Just like that, she's gone." She was crying so hard now I didn't know how to console her.

All the signs were there too, and we didn't see them. There was nothing we could do. Ya can't make someone tell you they're dying.

"Maybe we could do something for her as a group?" she said. This seemed to perk her up a bit. "Like a dinner or

          Shelby & Shawn   ©   2023

something."

"How about if we plan some sort of mass for her? I can arrange it with Father Jon and Our Lady's Church. We'll have a mass and go out to eat after." I suggested.

"Oh, I would love that. Can you do that?" She seemed to be genuinely comforted by this. I was glad I was able to calm her.

"Yes. Pick a date and let me know. It can be a Saturday night or Sunday morning. I'll set it up and then we'll invite everyone."

"I'd love that. Let me look at my calendar." She picked a Saturday night two weeks away. "I think we should go to Perschetti's for dinner. That was her favorite restaurant."

Fortunately, when I called Father Jon and explained the situation to him, he was able to accommodate us. The next Friday at volleyball we gave everyone the details.

"The Mass for Kari starts at 6:00. The first five rows to the left of the church are reserved for us," I told them.

"And the side room at Perschetti's is reserved for us for 7:30," Tara added.

Thirty-six people showed up. The mass was dedicated to Kari and Father managed to say a few words about us.

"Today's Mass is being dedicated to Kari Myers, a member of our Christian Singles group, who passed away a few weeks ago. She was a well-loved member as you can see by the large turnout of people who came to celebrate her life and say goodbye to her."

After mass, we all drove out to Jeannette for dinner at

 Shelby & Shawn   ©   2023

Perschetti's. The evening went smoothly, and we were all glad to be together to celebrate Kari and the time she spent with us.

Tara came up to me after we ate. Everyone was mingling around.

"This was very nice. Thank you for helping me put it together. I miss her so much and just needed this closure."

"I was happy to help you with it. I miss her too. I'll never forget running into her at Starlake one night at the Santana concert. Macy Gray opened for him, and she was loving her, singing along and such. She was quite a character."

"Yes, she was. I don't understand how I missed this." She started to beat herself up again. "All the signs were there."

"All the signs were there but we all missed them. We couldn't have known if she hadn't told us. We kept asking her if she was all right and she'd say fine. She didn't want us to know. We didn't have any control over it."

"I know. That's the hard part. Not having any control. It's just going to take time."

We hugged and let it go, moving on to talk to others there about other things. Life goes on.

Chapter 11

Who's Dating Who

It was well into March when one Saturday afternoon my friend, Norma Pierce, called me and asked if I'd want to go get a drink somewhere. I knew Norma from church. She was a widow, very high class, wealthy and proper. She had stylish gray hair, thin, and always wore long skirts and high heels to be taller.

She and Anne Sard had attended my Single's group regularly when I was leading. We had gotten very close, often going to dinner, movies, or attending concerts.

She said, "I'm feeling so lonely and could use someone to talk to."

I suggested Yesterday's since that was my favorite place. "It's a family-type lounge/restaurant with a dress code, a great DJ, and a good reputation for not being a dive," I told her since she had not heard of it.

We agreed to meet at 7:00. The kids were with Gene, so I took my time bathing and dressing to go out. I had been working so much and was too tired to go out on the weekends, so this was a treat. I thought of inviting Andrea, but she did not like this type of place, and she did not dance so I quickly dismissed the idea.

When I arrived, I got a table against the wall at the far end of the lounge to the right of the door. Norma came in shortly after 7:00 and spotted me right away. We ordered some food, and she began telling me about this trip she went on.

"I went with the church group from St. Catherine's," she said. "It was a cruise to the Bahamas. I was very excited to go. The ship was beautiful, and I met the captain. He and I were flirting and sort of star-struck with each other."

Now mind you Norma is 62 years old. To hear her talking this way, so excited to meet a "distinguished-looking man" in her words, was rather humorous to me.

"If I hadn't been with a church group, we may have had a shipboard romance," she said, her eyes rather ornery looking.

"Really?" I asked. "Just like the love boat?"

"Yes. He was very good-looking," she said again.

It was all I could do to keep myself from chuckling out loud. Suddenly the door from outside swung open and a crowd of people came in with a burst of cold air, first two women and a man, and it took me a minute to realize these were Shawn's friends, John and Bev.

Walking in behind John was Shawn. They went to the corner booth along the same wall as us but on the other side of the door. As Shawn turned to slide into the booth beside the woman I didn't recognize, he saw me. I tilted my head sideways and smiled. He smiled back, waved, and sat down beside the woman I was beginning to understand was his date.

I focused on Norma, and we continued to talk and eat our dinners. Finally, DJ Larry came in and set up and began playing at 8:30 which was early for him. There was already a big crowd and immediately the dance floor was packed.

After several songs were played, my favorite swing song came on, Brown Eyed Girl. I glanced over to see Shawn stand, hold his hands together in a prayer position and bow to me asking for a dance. I excused myself to Norma and got up walking to him. He took my hand and led me to the dance floor where we stepped right into sync in a perfect swing dance.

After that was a slow dance and he pulled me close to him. We didn't even talk … just let the music move us calmly and sensitively. When the song was over, we both bowed to each other and went back to our tables.

Norma said, "Wow you guys look good together."

"Thanks!" I said. "He's a good friend and we've been dancing together for a while."

"It looked like more than friends from my view," she said.

"Well maybe down the road," I said. "But not now. He's in the middle of a divorce and he's pretty sensitive right now. He has a long road to go. But I'm hopeful."

We both finished our drinks, and the music was getting loud as was the crowd. It was time to leave. I didn't even look for Shawn as I walked out. I hoped he was having fun.

On Wednesday Greg Altman from Cindy's group called and asked me if I'd like to go out and have dinner on Saturday night. Now normally I'd want to leave my schedule open in case Shawn called to ask me out but after seeing him on a date last Saturday I decided I had better keep my options open and go out and have fun too.

There's no reason for me to sit around waiting for someone who could take a long time getting his life together and then maybe not even pick me.

So, I said yes to Greg Altman for dinner Saturday night. The kids were home with me this weekend, so I skipped volleyball Friday night to spend some time with them. I ordered pizza and rented a comedy called The WaterBoy with Adam Sandler.

After the movie, we played Monopoly, the board game. Robin had to be the horse, Joel always got the car, and I always took the hat. Since the game takes forever to play out, we played for an hour or so and got bored.

Robin headed to her room. "I'm going to bed. Come on Shadow." She scooped up her new kitten she named Shadow. I had finally caved and let her have it since I didn't plan on staying in this townhouse another lease cycle.

Since Joel didn't have a phone downstairs in his room, he had to get on the phone in the living room with a girl he'd met and wanted to learn more about.

"Can I have some privacy?" he asked.

Since he and Tiffany had broken up, he wouldn't tell us anything about who he was meeting. And of course, until he was ready, we didn't pry. I gave him his privacy and went to my room to get ready for bed.

I wasn't sleepy yet, so I sat up and read some of my meditations from a book called My Utmost for His Highest by Oswald Chambers. This was a meditation book that Randy had given me when we were dating. It was a good read and I enjoyed it very much. I was able to fall asleep quickly after just a few short pages and reflections.

On Saturday night Joel went out with his new girlfriend. She picked him up since he didn't drive yet. Robin was staying at Nickie's grandmothers. I decided to dress up for my date with Greg.

I wore a knee length deep red skirt and a cream-colored V

     Shelby & Shawn   ©   2023

neck knit sweater with a pearl sequence on the front. I wore cream-colored heels that matched the sweater. I hardly ever wore heels any more, but Greg was so tall I could pull it off.

Greg picked me up promptly at 7:00. *Hummm A man who is punctual. I liked that.* We exchanged some casual conversation in the car on the way to the Four Points Sheraton for dinner.

Now at the Sheraton, there was a room for the bar area and dance floor and a room for the dining area with a folding wall between. At 9:00 when the band started, they opened the wall for both rooms to dance. Our reservation was in the back of the dining room at a corner table. It was quaint and quiet.

I ordered a peach and ginger to start, and he ordered a beer. We looked at our menus and decided what to eat. I didn't want to order anything too expensive though he looked like he had money. I remembered his situation with his divorce and kept it simple.

Most of the guys in these groups were in the process of getting divorced so dating was just friendly and casual. I knew they were all just getting back on their dating feet so to speak. Men who were looking for more than that didn't stick around long.

As soon as you say, "I practice abstinence till marriage", they turn tail and run. Who does that anymore? Not many.

Once we ordered, we relaxed and were able to talk better. "So how are things going for you," I asked without being specific.

"Well," he kind of chuckled. "My ex busted a hole in my bedroom door last night."

"Oh no!" was all I could think of to say.

"Yes. We were having this huge fight over our stuff, and

     Shelby & Shawn   ©   2023

she accused me of taking some of her stuff out of the house which I didn't but she's just extremely unreasonable right now."

First, I wondered if he was telling the truth about not taking her stuff. All men accuse their ex-wives of being crazy. Then I wondered if I should be seen with this guy for fear this woman really is crazy.

"Are you sure you want to continue living there with all this going on?" I asked.

"Oh yes. If I leave, I lose the house and it's my house. I owned it when we got married and she moved into it. Besides, she makes more money than me." He chuckled again. He seemed to be able to find the humor in all of it.

"Well, be careful, please. I'd hate to read about you in the papers." We both laughed. "So, what kind of work do you do?" I asked.

"I work for a company that orders parts and supplies for overseas companies. It's a lot of computer work and it's starting to take a toll on my eyes. I had some surgeries a while back and things improved a lot, but I still struggle to see, especially at night. That's why I'm usually looking for rides when I go out at night. So, what about you … what do you do?"

"Well, I work for The Auto Club in Pittsburgh right now. I'm hoping for a transfer back to this area to be closer to home."

"That is a long drive for you. How long does that take?

"I spend about three hours a day in my car, out and back."

So, I talked about my job, my kids, my divorce and he was a very good listener. Soon our food came. I switched to sprite,

         Shelby & Shawn   ©   2023

and he continued drinking beer. At 9:00 they opened the door to the bar and dance floor. The band was starting to play oldies, mostly 80's stuff and it was very loud. We had a slow dance before we left, and he drove me home. At my place, he walked me to my door, said good night, and left. As I walked in, I thought playfully, *it's barely 10:00. Not even a kiss good night.*

I went upstairs to change into my comfy clothes and back downstairs to get a glass of wine. I opened the drapes to the patio and settled on the couch to watch some TV. As I watched the snow come down on the deck I thought about the evening with Greg. It was nice and comfortable, and he was easy to be with.

But that situation was a bad one. It reminded me of another man I dated whose wife really was crazy. She followed us around and tried to break into his house when I was sitting in his kitchen. I wasn't getting into that mess again.

Look how far I've come in wanting a healthy relationship. And a big part of wanting healthy is recognizing unhealthy.

I guess I'd have to keep him at arm's length until he gets all that resolved. I felt bad for him but who knows what her side of the story is. The wine made me tired, so I went to bed. Church was early the next morning. As I drifted off to sleep, I thought of Shawn and wondered what he was doing tonight.

Chapter 12

Decisions Made

Monday morning when I arrived at work, there was a message on my voicemail for me to go upstairs and see Dawn Brady at 1:30 this afternoon. I took my half hour lunch at 1:00 and grabbed a bite to eat fast while preparing for my conversation with Dawn. When I got upstairs, I was directed to go in, she was waiting for me sitting at her desk.

"Hi. How are you, Dawn?" I said, taking a seat on the other side of her desk.

"I'm good. How are you?" she said pleasantly.

"I'm doing well."

"I've been thinking about our conversation the last time you were here, and it turns out there's going to be a position open in Somerset for a manager. Betsy Stiles is the manager there and she has a lot of experience, so we're bringing her here. The Somerset office is small. I'd like you to consider this position. That is closer to where you live, right?"

"Yes, it is," I said excitedly. "Somerset is about 20 minutes down the turnpike from me. And I'm looking for a house so I can probably look in areas that would be closer to the turnpike. Thank you so much for this opportunity. Yes, I would like to be considered for this position."

"Okay," she smiled. "I have some paperwork for you to fill out and there's a process you have to go through, but I don't think you'll have any problems. I'll email you all the forms and applications and let you know when we'll need to do an official interview. It's all just a formality. You'll be considered a manager trainee first and then just move into the manager position after six months." She stood and extended her hand; I stood and shook it and thanked her again as I left.

I spent the rest of my day in a daze, unbelieving that all this was happening. I didn't have any management education or experience. All I had was business school and a few classes in Psychology. I started doubting myself and wondering if I could do this job.

When I came to Pittsburgh as a supervisor, I didn't even blink. It just seemed right. Now, as I drove home that evening, I felt unsure, and unprepared. This was going to be a challenge for sure. I prayed for direction, confidence, and peace.

It's funny that when you've had a hard life and things have always been difficult, it's hard to accept when good things are happening. It doesn't feel comfortable because it's not what you're used to. You feel like something has to go wrong, like waiting for the ball to drop.

When Gene and I separated, I really struggled to get on my feet. I had to work part time jobs while going to school and shuffling my kids from daycare to babysitters. When you live in that survival mode for so long, getting it out of your head is the biggest challenge. That feeling of being a failure lingers for a long time.

And if the ex continues to be a source of battering for you it's even harder to recover.

Not too long ago, in a drunken stupor, Gene called my house and left a message on my machine calling me every foul name in the book for no apparent reason except he felt like it. I called the police and asked if I could press charges or get a restraining order or something. They sent a very kind officer named Jones over to talk with me and as soon as he walked in I played him the message.

"Who is that" Officer Jones asked in a very offended tone.

"It's my ex-husband," I said.

"How long have you been divorced?" He asked.

"Almost 10 years. There's no reason for these messages. He just gets drunk and calls randomly for no reason. I have two teenagers. What if one of them had gotten this message before me."

I can't believe you've been divorced for 10 years, and he is still harassing you like this." He said. "There isn't anything legal we can do because it isn't ongoing daily harassment but I'm going to give Gene a call and talk with him about it."

Officer Jones called me back a couple of days later and said that he'd had a heart-to-heart talk with Gene and if it happened again, I was to call him immediately. It didn't happen again. In fact, things with Gene did get a little better after that.

But often you may feel like you don't deserve to succeed or be happy and that's a dangerous place to be mentally because it makes you self-destructive. You may be unknowingly sabotaging yourself in ways you can't possibly recognize.

Thankfully they do have these programs and support groups to help people through this. There are many good counselors around; you just need to find one who is right for you. I went through years of counseling with my kids and individually to help us understand behaviors and be able to communicate better with each other.

 Shelby & Shawn   ©   2023

We didn't always do it right, but we never stopped trying.

When my husband was attempting to take custody of the kids, we each had to go through psychological testing for the courts. My counselors got me through all that and I was very thankful to them for helping me keep my kids. Losing them would have been the end of my life.

Having experienced all of this helped me to understand others going through this and what this felt like. That's why the support groups were so comfortable for me. I could say 'I know how you feel' and mean it.

It was easy to understand what Shawn was going through and why he needed to go through it without interference. It's so much to handle emotionally and it's all you can handle at the time. As much as I wished I could do more for him, I couldn't. All I could do was be his friend.

And protect my own heart.

Chapter 13

I Sowed My Oats

Looking back on the first year after Gene and I separated, I experienced a roller coaster of emotions, anger, depression, and pain. Once I settled into my new townhouse and my money started coming in, I was able to think about some goals. I got the kids to register for school to start in the fall. Joel was six and Robin four so she would go to head start preschool.

I then registered for school myself. I had wanted to be a teacher coming out of high school but my mom, being the strict Italian Catholic she was, said "get married … let your husband take care of you." The week after I graduated high school, I married Gene. *See how that worked out.*

I signed up for Psychology with a special education minor at the community college. I decided my goals were to finish school, build a career, establish my credit and eventually buy a house. I began my journey at 30 years old with two kids to raise, after our oldest son decided to stay with Gene and wanted nothing to do with me. *So much pain for all of us.*

Gene took me to court every six months for two years having the support reduced. I had to move us into a lower income house when my support got so low, I couldn't manage the rent at the townhouse.

I picked up jobs here and there to make ends meet, cleaning offices, serving beer at a bowling alley snack bar, cooking in a small diner, and waitressing when I could find something to fit my schedule. I transferred to a business school, with a placement program, to take computer science so I could find employment faster.

Gene also canceled his weekend visits often in the first few months, especially if he thought I had plans or a date, leaving me without help with sitters. When I was home with the kids, I was exhausted and yelling all the time. I still had to study to keep up with my grades, plus helping the kids with their schoolwork while cooking, cleaning and shopping.

During all this, I made some friends. Liz was a waitress at one of the places I worked until I couldn't manage the hours and was let go. Her sister, Nancy, worked as a bartender at a club called Billy's. She asked me to go down and have a drink with them on a Friday night when Gene actually picked up the kids.

It was a nice club with a big area for dancing. The owner, Billy, was a nice guy and always let us have a drink on the house to start. Nancy's friend, Joyce, worked as a server and her sister Kathy came in often. We all became good friends and got together almost every weekend. When Gene didn't take the kids, my sister Deb would take them overnights or my neighbor's teenage daughter would babysit so I could get out for a while.

I know my mom's underlying hope for me was that I would find another husband but that was the furthest thing from my mind. Since I never experienced this scene, I was ready to go wild. This was the only outlet I had for my pain, depression, and anger. Gene got to walk away from all the responsibilities to go have fun with his new girlfriend. I was gonna have some fun too.

So, I dated a lot of guys, had a few short-lived affairs, a couple of one-night stands, and mostly hung out with my girlfriends, dancing and laughing up a party almost every weekend. These women were the only reason I survived during that dark time.

This party phase only lasted a year. Gene became so enraged that he could not stop me or have control over me, he

 Shelby & Shawn   ©   2023

accused me of being unfit and tried to take the kids off me. I went through psychological testing at mental health, and he hired a private detective to follow me around.

So, I had to settle down and become a responsible mom again. I never forgot those days and those friends who helped me survive.

When I graduated from business school, I got a job and began to work our way up out of poverty. My friends fell away when I stopped partying with them, and we went our separate ways.

I moved us back into a nice townhouse in a good neighborhood and our lives became a little easier.

I thank God every day for his gift of Grace and forgiveness, knowing my ways were sinful during that dark time. I found my way back to the light with many good Christian people to show me the way once I asked for it.

Chapter 14

The Big Dance

John and Bev started coming to volleyball with Shawn and Roy. When I arrived on Friday night, they were all sitting on the bleachers on one side of the gym. Randy, his kids, and some others were using the volleyball to shoot some baskets while waiting for others to arrive. I walked over to Bobbie who was also standing with Shawn and Roy to give her my money for the rent on the gym.

"Hi everyone," I said, and they all responded with hello in unison. Bev got up and came down to stand next to me. I was passing out some fliers for Cindy's events and I handed one to her.

"Oh, what's this about," she asked.

"It's for single people," John answered her before I could.

"I'm single," she said.

I smiled and explained what the group was about. I told her about Cindy's group and some of the others that have kind of dwindled down, and how we all plan events together. As it turned out Cindy was going to have a dance at her church in a couple of weeks. One of her group members was going to be DJing for the event. We were all to bring some food to share. It sounded like fun.

"I want to go to this," Bev said to John.

Shawn looked at it and said to John, "that does look like fun. Let's go."

"Okay," John said, stepping off the bleachers to put his arm around Bev's neck. "And what's this 'I'm single' stuff your talkin about." She just laughed.

When Shawn stepped off the bleachers, he bumped me with his shoulder and said "Are you going to be there?"

"Yes," I said and smiled.

"Good," he said. "I'll need a dance partner."

I gave a flier to Bobbi and Randy but neither of them showed an interest in coming to the dance.

Everyone had arrived and we began to play. I enjoyed being back with my team and I loved playing volleyball. I was very bad at it when I first started but I had gotten good since then. I never really considered myself athletic. I tried playing basketball in middle school and they told me I had weak ankles and couldn't run well. I could ice skate though, but my feet leaned in, so I guess I did have weak ankles. That didn't seem to be a problem with volleyball though. I was as good as the guys.

Three weeks went by quickly and it was the night of the dance. I hadn't heard from Shawn except to see him at volleyball and we were always friendly yet distant there. I didn't know what to expect tonight. Since it was still wintry cold, I wore a black below the knee skirt with a burgundy sweater and black flat boots. Shawn was not much taller than me and I liked looking up at my guy while dancing with my head on his chest.

I arrived shortly after 7ish, and it was crowded already. Cindy had the place decorated with streamers, tablecloths and candle centerpieces. Colored paper mâché balls were hanging from the lights like chandeliers. It looked very nice.

     Shelby & Shawn   ©   2023

Shawn, John, and Bev were at a table nearest to the door. They waved me over. As I approached, I saw Shawn's arm resting on the back of the chair next to him.

"Been saving this one for you," he said.

"Oh, thank you. I must take this cake over. I'll be right back."

"Here, let me take your coat and we'll go up together." He got up as I put the cake down and took my coat off, walking over to the rack by the door to hang it for me. Then he walked over to the food tables with me, and we both got a drink and some food.

"What kind of cake did you make?" Shawn asked.

"It's dark chocolate with Hershey chocolate icing."

"I think we need to cut that right away," he said and went to find a knife.

Cindy spotted us and came over. "Hi. Glad you could make it." She said to me,

"Wouldn't miss it," I said. "Everything looks awesome. You did a great job!"

"Thanks. It was a lot of work, but we had fun putting it together."

"Nice to see you, Shawn. How are you?" she asked as he came walking back with a knife to cut the cake.

"I'm gonna be great in about a minute." He said cutting the cake and slapping a big piece on his plate. We all laughed.

"I'll have a piece of that as well but not so big," I laughed.

"You got a nice turnout here," he said to Cindy.

"Yes, we counted about 46 who came through the door so far. (*With single groups, it's always about the turnout*) There's plenty of food for sure and a nice variety. I think everyone's having a good time."

"Looks like it," I said. "Well, we're gonna go sit down and eat. Talk to you later." We headed in the direction of the table when Shawn reached up and grabbed a hanging ball to hit me in the head with. I laughed as it stuck to my hair and made some static, so my hair was flying everywhere. He thought that was hilarious.

On our way back to the table I noticed Greg had come and was sitting with some women on the far side of the room. I gave a little nod as I went by, and he waved. We sat down at our table with John and Bev who had also gotten some food and drink. The music was loud so talking was difficult. When we finished eating, we got up to dance. John didn't like to fast dance, so Bev and I went up with some of the other ladies from Cindy's group. John and Shawn came up for the slow dances.

There was a big difference in Shawn lately I had noticed. He seemed calmer, more confident, and sure of himself. And he was much more playful. I was happy to see him that way. And I was very much attracted to him as we danced. Again, I knew I had to keep those feelings under wrap remembering our conversation on the way home on New Year's Day and knowing what he was going through.

He said he wasn't ready, and I had to respect that he had to go through this process his way. There was a closeness between us, but he was always respectful of me, minding his boundaries and not crossing any lines of intimacy that would confuse the relationship. I appreciated that.

Later in the evening Greg came over and asked for a dance. "Are you having fun?" I asked when we got to the dance floor.

"Yes. There are many nice people here and Joyce gave me a ride tonight, so I didn't have to drive. Although I don't like to stay away from the house too long cause I'm not sure what the wife's doing when I'm away," he said.

"What do you think she'd do?" I asked, thinking he was being really paranoid.

"She gets her boyfriend to come over and take things out of the house when I'm not there," he said. "Some of the stuff is hers but most of it is mine."

What a strange situation he was in. I wanted to offer him support and encouragement but didn't want to get too involved with that.

"Wow! That must be so hard to live like that. I hope that all gets resolved for you soon," was all I could think of saying.

The dance was over, and I noticed Shawn dancing with a woman I didn't know. We both arrived back at the table at the same time as John and Bev. He pulled my chair out for me and we sat down.

John said "Shelby, we've been talking about going on a hike one of these weekends just the four of us if you'd like to come along. We thought the mountain trails in Ligonier would be nice when the weather gets warmer."

"I'd love to," I said. "I've been to Linn Run a lot with my

          Shelby & Shawn   ©   2023

kids. Adams Falls and Flat Rock were our favorite places to go hiking when they were younger. I haven't been there in a long time. That would be a lot of fun."

"We thought we could either pack a picnic to take along or go to a restaurant in Ligonier," said Shawn.

"Okay," I said. "I'm game for either one. Just let me know when." I looked in Shawn's eyes and felt what I saw there. Love. Things were winding down and people started leaving. We all walked out together and said our good nights till next time.

I didn't say anything about my possible promotion to anyone, but it was on my mind. I wondered how it would change my life.

        Shelby & Shawn   ©   2023

Chapter 15

Memorial Day Weekend

Spring was in the air and as the weather got warmer, we started looking for outdoor things to do. One event was our single's picnic sponsored by Catholic Charities. It would involve all the groups and the leaders planned it. This was one way the Catholic Church showed support for their single community. It was a big event that included separation, divorce, widows, widowers, and foster parents.

"We're holding this year's picnic at Mt. Oden Park on Sunday of Memorial Day weekend," Cindy said when she called me to talk about it. "Sharon's already reserved the pavilion. It's big and there is a field to put up a volleyball net or play baseball if we want."

This was a popular event with the groups because we invited the families, brought all the food, and planned activities.

"I'll make a pinata for the kids, if that's okay, and a double chocolate cake. I'll decorate it myself for spring."

"That'd be great. I'll put you down for the cake."

The other leaders shared the responsibilities of food and drinks. Some of the elderly women from my old group liked the bingo games.

"I'm bringing bingo for your older women," she said tactfully and laughed. "And some neat prizes."

"I'll make up treat bags to fill up with the candy when they bust the pinata."

We had a beautiful day that Sunday. The kids all had a blast busting the pinata and filled their bags to the top with candy. The old ladies loved the bingo prizes Cindy picked out.

Later in the afternoon, the crowd thinned out except for the teens and the 'middle-aged' kids who were hanging around to start a baseball game. Some of the adults set up the bases and got all the equipment ready to play.

Some friends of Shawn's were there, and I heard them talking about Shawn taking Kenny on a camping trip this weekend with Bobbi and Rae. I had not seen him since the dance except at volleyball where I saw he was friendly with Bobbi. Rae was still drawn to Randy, but I did notice that Bobbi was trying to push her toward Shawn.

After hearing that, I felt sad but kept things in perspective. We had no commitment or even an intimate relationship for me to have any negative reaction to this. I was glad he was enjoying himself and figuring out his life. I know how important this process is when going through a divorce to rebuild your life and find yourself again. He needed that and I wanted to see him grow confident and be happy.

I helped clean up some of the tables and put away stuff before joining the baseball game. "Hey, can I try pitching?" I asked. So, I took that position for a while. I wasn't very good at it so I switched to third base.

My batting wasn't great either, but we had some good laughs about it. At one point I ran into someone when we were both going for the ball. I almost knocked her down and gave her a bloody lip. Oh, did I feel bad! The teens really showed us old fogies though and they let us know it too.

I missed my kids not being there. I wanted to keep them at

home, but Gene had plans for them at his place this weekend. At least they would be home tonight, and I was off Monday so we can do something together then. I would leave it up to them to pick what they wanted to do.

After the game we finished packing up, taking a lot of food home with us. When I got home, I really needed to shower and change from running in the heat all day. Feeling refreshed again, I laid on the couch to read for a while then must have dozed off.

The next thing I heard was the door flying open and the kids running in like they each wanted to be the first one in the door, so they were knocking each other over for it. Fortunately, no one got hurt in the crash and they were laughing so that was a good sign they'd had a good weekend.

"Hi, you two," I called out and they came into the living room, plopping down on the couch with me almost crushing me. I gave them big hugs and asked, "How was your weekend?"

"Fine," they both said at the same time.

"What did you do?" I pushed the subject, or I would have to settle for one-word answers.

"We went to see Uncle Mark and Aunt Anna in Ohio. And our cousins and everyone … It was like a family reunion." Joel said.

"It was a long drive," Robin said. "And we couldn't stay overnight cause there was no place around to sleep, so we had to drive home late last night. Then Dad woke us up early this morning to help him with some stuff at his store."

Gene owned a store in Millvale, his new live-in girlfriend owned it so I could not claim it for child support, where he sold

        Shelby & Shawn   ©   2023

guns and outdoor stuff like hunting, fishing, and stuff. It was my understanding that it did well, but I knew Gene and he was bad at managing money, so I wondered how much of what he said was true.

"So, what do you guys want to do tomorrow?" I asked. "I have tickets for Idlewild and the soak zone if you want to go there.

"I just want to go hang out with my friends," said Joel.

"Can I ask Nickie to go with us then?" Robin asked.

"Okay," I said. "Go call her and let me know if she's allowed to go." Of course, I knew she would be. She was always with us, just another one of my kids and I loved her like one.

Robin used the phone upstairs and came back down a few minutes later. "Yeah, she's allowed. What time are we leaving?"

"Whenever you guys wake up and get going," I said. "No hurry to get there. They'll be open till 10pm."

Soon Nickie came in the door with her overnight bag, called "hi!" and went straight up to Robin's room. I had all that leftover food, but no one wanted any of it. So I ordered a pizza and waited an hour for it to come. When it arrived, I yelled up the steps to come and get it.

Joel had come up from his room downstairs already and we all crashed in the living room with pizza and drinks. We agreed on a movie and enjoyed an evening of relaxing together. After the movie, we were pretty tired, so we were in bed by 11.

          Shelby & Shawn   ©   2023

Chapter 16

Idlewild's Soak Zone

The girls were up the next morning at 10:30 excited to go to Idlewild. I made them pancakes for breakfast and we packed up a picnic lunch of sandwiches, chips, and drinks in the cooler. That leftover food came in handy now.

"We'll get ice cream there like we always do. And Fudge!"

We left the house at quarter of 12 and arrived at 12:30. There was a pretty long line waiting to get in but we had our tickets, so we were able to go straight through. I drove all the way to the back near the soak zone to park and we headed straight there. We walked through the shower rooms, changed into our bathing suites, then out the other side where the wave pool was.

It was a hot day in the 90s and not a cloud in the sky. We managed to find a couple of lounge chairs and set up there with our towels and cooler. Once we settled in the girls were off to do their own thing.

"Be careful and check in once in a while," I called after them.

After covering myself with sunblock, I splashed around in the water a bit then lay on the lounge to just enjoy the warmth of the sun. As I closed my eyes to let the sun beat down on my face my mind wandered to Shawn and his camping trip with Bobbi this weekend.

I had to admit I was jealous. It brought back memories of her going after Randy when I was dating him. I began to wonder if it had nothing to do with the man and more to do with beating me out. I decided it wasn't worth wasting my energy on. She had a right to be dating and exploring relationships just as we all did. I couldn't fault her for that, especially if Shawn was asking her out.

But my memories came flooding over me, the times we spent dancing, the night we went to Meadville, all the fun times we had, and my heart ached.

What's going to be will be. I have a full life with my kids, career, and volunteer work. I have a very active social life and keep it all balanced very well. In fact, do I really need a man? It would be nice to have one, but I really don't need one.

That's a bad mentality to have. Men don't want to hear that. Sadly, it is hard to find a strong man who can let a woman be strong without feeling intimidated by her.

But it was true. I had so much in my life. I felt very fulfilled being independent. Joel would soon be a senior in high school and Robin was begging to be homeschooled. Shawn was just beginning to raise a child.

I was looking for a house to buy. I realized after the kids moved out, I would live alone for the first time in my life, since I went from my parents to my husband and then the kids.

Suddenly water splashing on me disrupted my thoughts. I looked up to see the girls standing over me ringing their long-wet hair on my stomach. They burst out laughing as I screamed and jumped up to chase them into the water and splash them back.

After playing around with them in the water for a while we decided we were hungry so back to the lounge chairs for some sandwiches, snacks and drinks. I had packed lunch meat on hoagie buns and chips. The drink choices were water, Pepsi or iced tea.

We divided up the food and each grabbed the drink of their

choice. As we sat on the lounge chairs eating, the girls told me of their water slide fiasco.

"I hate when my bathing suit rides up just when you hit the water." they were both saying. As much as they hated this it was obviously hilarious as well because they were choking on their food laughing.

A fresh coat of sunscreen and the girls were off to ride the water slides, bunched-up bottoms and all, leaving me alone with my thoughts again. I cleaned up the garbage they left around me and packed up the remaining food items we didn't finish back into the cooler. There was still a small amount of ice in it to keep everything cold for a while longer.

The sun was going down on the other side of the park now that it was approaching 5:00 and the breeze was cooling off a little. I had already turned over a couple of times to roast evenly on both sides, but I could start to feel the burn.

I decided to find some shade, pull out a book and wait for the girls to be tired enough to go home. It was about another hour when they came walking over, looking exhausted.

"We are tired. Can we go now?" Robin said.

"Sure," I replied. "You both look burnt to a crisp."

"I can feel it," said Nickie. "Especially on my face."

"We have to get some ice cream," said Robin.

"I want to get fudge too," I said.

As we walked to the showers to change our clothes, I watched them ahead of me. They were two beautiful teenage girls,

          Shelby & Shawn   ©   2023

shapely with long flowing hair. I made a mental note to start
having talks with Robin about boys. Not necessarily sex because
we'd had that talk long ago but what teenage boys were like and
how to protect herself. I'm sure Gene had probably made
comments about staying away from boys as jokes, but I doubt if
she took him seriously.

We walked through the park, stopping to play a few games
along the way, and arriving at the ice cream stand to find a long
line. The girls grabbed an umbrella table that someone had just got
up from while I moved ahead in the line finally arriving to order.
Nickie then came over to help me carry everything back to the
table. While enjoying our ice cream I subtly brought up the subject
of boys.

Trying to sound casual I said, "So did you girls see any
cute boys today."

They both giggled and talked at the same time, "there was
this one kid, oh the one with the goggles, what about the one with
the hat on, oh and the kid that had blond hair and a silly mustache
that looked fake, yeah he was weird."

"What about guys in school? What are they like?" I asked,
nonchalantly pushing the subject a little further.

"Oh they're all childish or geekish," Nickie answered.

"There's a kid in my math class whose kind of cute but he
doesn't even notice me," Robin said.

"Have you tried to talk to him?" I asked.

"No," she said. "I'm not ready yet. Maybe I will some
time."

"Oh okay. Well, you should wait for the right time." I said. It seemed like I didn't have too much to worry about. They were still not thinking about boys too seriously yet. We finished up our ice cream and I bought my fudge before we headed home. We were all exhausted from the sun and were in bed early that night.

 Shelby & Shawn   ©   2023

Chapter 17

Wow! A Promotion?

On Tuesday afternoon, I got a call from Dawn upstairs. "Shelby, I have all your paperwork here processed and everything looks good for your transfer to Somerset."

"What about the interview I was supposed to have," I asked.

"Well, as I said, that was just going to be a formality so we're going to forgo it and just move forward. So tomorrow I'd like you to go to the Somerset office with Betsy. She is going to show you the ropes around the office. They open at 9am. Plan on spending the day till they close at 5."

"Okay, Dawn. Thank you. I'll look forward to it." I was so excited I decided to get out of work early and was home by 5:30. The kids were surprised to see me walk in the door. I went into the living room where they were sitting and watching TV.

"I have some good news," I said, turning off the TV and sitting in the chair facing them. "I got a promotion at work. I'm going to be trained to be a manager and I'm transferring to the Somerset office. It's about 20 minutes down the turnpike and the hours are 9 to 5 which means I'll be home more."

"Wow mom, that's great!" said Joel.

"Awesome!" said Robin, not really sounding excited.

"Well, thank you both," I said happily. "I'm gonna get started on dinner."

I was cooking dinner when the phone rang. Joel answered it and called for me, "It's for you mom."

"Hello," I expected it to be Cindy since I hadn't heard from her in a while.

"Hi. It's Shawn," he sounded upset. "Are you doing anything tonight?"

"Hi Shawn. I was just making dinner for my kids. Is everything okay?" I asked.

"I'm sorry to interrupt your dinner time," he said.

"Well, have you eaten? Would you like to come over for dinner? I have made spaghetti and there's plenty enough for you."

"I don't want to impose," he replied.

"It's no imposition. We'd love to have some company."

"Okay. Thanks. I'll head over there now." he said, sounding a little more cheerful.

Twenty minutes later Robin and I had finished setting the table when he knocked on the door. I opened it and said, "hello. Good to see you."

He gave me a big hug which he seemed to need but felt as good to me as I'm sure it did to him.

"Hey, Robin. How are you?" he asked, and Joel came up the steps from his room. "Joel. How ya doin?"

They both replied good, and we all sat down to eat. He asked the kids about their classes, and they talked about activities they were interested in. The conversation seemed to flow smoothly with everyone getting a share at talking. Shawn told stories about the funny things Kenny did over the weekend camping and fishing. He didn't mention Bobbi in his stories. I wondered for a moment if that wasn't the source of his upset.

We all finished dinner and Robin said, "I'll clean up the dishes mom."

Joel jumped in and said, "I'll help her if you guys wanna go relax."

"Wow," I said looking at Shawn in surprise. "Would you like to go for a walk? There's a cemetery behind the townhouses we can walk in or the college across the street has some nice walking trails."

"That sounds great," he said. "Dinner was delicious, and I'm stuffed full. I could stand to walk some of this off."

We grabbed our jackets because it was still cooling off a little in the evenings and started walking in the direction of the cemetery. The road through it wound back and forth up and down. We took our time strolling casually, neither of us saying anything at first. Then Shawn began to talk.

"Sarah is dating someone, and it looks serious," he blurted out. "I'm scared they are going to take Kenny off me or turn him against me."

"Oh Shawn, I've seen Kenny with you. He adores you. No one could ever turn him against you, and he'll never stop loving you. If you continue to see him and spend time with him, showing him how much you love him you'll never lose him."

I tried to comfort him and what I said was true. He was

amazing with Kenny, the way they laughed and played together just made my heart warm. You could just see the love in him for Kenny.

"Do you think so? But what if they start making up reasons to stop giving me visits? I'll just be devastated."

I knew he would be too. "You're letting your fears get the best of you. I don't believe that will ever happen. You're a good father and they'd have no reason to do that to you. Besides, you're dating and trying to move on with your life too. That's all she's trying to do. We don't know how any of this is going to work out but trust that it'll work out for the best."

"You think?'

"I'm sure of it."

"Thanks! I guess I just needed a sounding board. Someone with some calm and sense to bring me down from this. Sometimes my mind just spins and spins over this stuff. It keeps me up at night and my job suffers then."

"I know how that feels. I've been through it too. It will get better." I said, giving him a little shoulder bump and nudging him sideways. His shoulder bumped me back a little harder nudging me almost over a tombstone. Then he had to reach out and grab me back up, so I didn't fall. We both laughed.

"What're you tryin to do, knock over a headstone," he joked.

"Oh me! Who shoved who." I laughed and pushed him.

"You started it. Watch you don't get pulled into one of these graves," he said, making an eerie ghost sound. "oooooooo" grabbing and shaking me.

"I should be in one of these graves," I said, getting serious.

"What are you talking about?" he asked but he knew about my teenage years. I had told him the stories about running away from home and taking an overdose of pills.

"I've done some pretty stupid stuff. I should be dead. I don't know why I'm here!"

"You're here for me," he said. He had stopped walking, turning to me to take me by the shoulders he kissed me. It was soft and easy and just as quickly he let me go. We turned to walk again more briskly now as it was starting to get dark and there were no lights up there.

"Well, I got some good news at work today. I'm getting a promotion, training to become a manager, and I'll be transferring to the Somerset office." I told him how this all came about.

"Well, congratulations! That'll be a much easier driver for you," he said then went back to talking about himself. "My divorce is almost final. We're just working out the last details of the house and some other financial issues. I'll be glad to have it done."

"I'm sure it will be a huge load off when everything gets worked out on paper and you can relax about all of it," I said, my heart full of love for him.

We had gotten to his car by now and he said, "Thanks for the spaghetti and for being my best friend through all this."

"I'm more than happy to have provided both," I smiled, and he laughed.

"I'll see you soon," he said, getting into his car and driving off. Something felt different but I couldn't put a finger on it.

I went into my house and the kids were watching television. We all sat in the living room and talked for a while until it was time for bed. They both said they really liked Shawn and wanted to know if we were dating. I explained he was getting divorced, and we were just the best of friends.

While I was lying in bed reading, the phone rang. It was Cindy.

"Hey, long time no see. What have you been up to," she asked.

"Working and working and more working!" I laughed. "That's all I ever do. And what about you? Where've you been?"

"I met a guy." She said,

"Really? Tell me all about him." I said.

"Well, he's very tall so it's really funny," Cindy is very short so yes that is indeed funny. "But he's soo good-looking," she said in this dreamy voice.

"And does this good-looking man have a name?" I asked, laughing.

"Chad. His name's Chad Blake. So, I'm having this little dinner party on Saturday night for all my friends to meet him. Can you come? Please say you'll come."

"Sure, I'll come. What time shall I be there, and can I bring anything?" I asked.

     Shelby & Shawn   ©   2023

"Well come around 7ish and just bring yourself."

"Okay. See you then." I hung up thinking of Shawn and wishing I could invite him along. But I still wasn't sure if Shawn was going to end up with me. Things seemed to be pointing in that direction, but I didn't want to take it for granted. Anything could happen. I needed to guard my heart and wait patiently for God to work on this.

So, the next morning, I reported to Betsy at the Somerset office. She showed me around the office, introduced me to the staff and talked to me a little bit about the job, what would be expected of me and how everything works. She gave me a key and set up my code for the security system.

I kind of had a feel for it already being a supervisor and not having a manager around all the time, I really did the job myself anyway. We spent the day working on the paperwork to get me transferred into all of the systems and showed me how they all work, running reports and getting the information I needed for that.

So, I was to report back to Pittsburgh for the rest of the week to close things out and pack up any stuff I wanted to take with me. I would permanently be in Somerset starting Monday.

Chapter 18

A New Group

When I arrived at Cindy's on Saturday night, Greg, Sonny, Mary, and Chad were there. Al showed up shortly after me with his new girlfriend, Sandy, who uncannily looked just like Cindy. We will have a long serious discussion about that later. The table was set and dinner was served. I couldn't help noticing I was seated beside Greg who I was very surprised to see here.

"How are things going with you?" I asked as we sat down passing a bottle of wine around to fill our glasses. Cindy had made a juicy roast with mashed sweet potatoes and string beans cooked perfectly, buttery, and still a little crisp.

"I'm much better that my divorce is over, and my wife is out of the house, thank you!" he said with a sigh of relief. "That was the roughest thing I ever had to go through, and I'll never do it again."

"Well good for you. That it's over, that is. Don't sell yourself short though about getting married again. Just pick the right one next time."

"And how do you know that it's the right one?" asked Sonny. I've been married twice, and I thought both of them were the right ones." Everyone laughed.

"Well, I guess that's true," I said. "You can never be sure. But I think if you know who you are and know what you really want, then take the time to know someone to make sure they are who you want, then you have a better chance of working things out in the long run."

     Shelby & Shawn   ©   2023

Mary said rather nervously "I think you just must believe in love and go for it. You can't ever be sure it's going to last. We don't go into marriage thinking we'll end up divorced, especially in the Catholic Church. They make you go through those classes, and you have to have all your sacraments, or you have to agree to raise your kids Catholic and they don't believe in divorce."

"The Catholic Church is too old-fashioned. They need to get on the ball with things … like letting priests get married," said Chad. "Then they wouldn't have had that scandal."

It always comes to that. The Catholic Church is always under fire. I wanted to dodge that subject, so I went in a different direction.

In a very calm voice I exclaimed, "well I think all churches want you to stay married. I don't think any church wants to see its people get divorced. But Catholics are rather strict about divorce and annulments and all that. They do stand by their rules, but they need to be more lenient about welcoming single people into the church, whether separated, divorced, widowed or widower, there needs to be a welcome place for us.

We're single Christians but we're human. We can have morals and values we live by, but we're out there in the world meeting people, dating, and living. We're going to have situations to deal with. We're going to need to set boundaries. We're going to face conflict just like everyone else. We may not always make the best decisions. Sometimes we may fall flat on our faces. That is why we need our Christian community, not to be judged by them but to be there for us when we fall, to help us back up."

Cindy said, "that's what we've tried to do with these groups that we've started. But people come and don't find what they're looking for, so they don't come back. The groups dwindle down and soon no one's coming to the activities or the meetings."

"That's true. Because most of the time what they're looking for is a mate, an immediate connection." I said. "The ones who come back are the people who are just looking for friendship and fellowship … other single people to do some fun activities with. They're not looking for hookups, romance, or love. No one is going to find true love at a glance. That's a fairy tale and it doesn't exist."

"But if you find those things, hey all the better, right?" chimed in Sonny jokingly and everyone laughed.

"But that is very true, Sonny." Cindy said.

"So not to change the subject but on a different note," said Greg, "I have a suggestion for an activity I'd like to take the lead on." I got the feeling he was uncomfortable with this conversation.

"What's that?" I asked, glad he had changed the subject.

"It's the peddle/paddle at Ohiopyle. Bicycling 6 miles up and canoeing 6 miles down. It's an all-day event. They set everything up for you. I can get the costs and schedules to you in a week or so. We just need a date."

"That sounds like a lot of fun," Al said to his girlfriend.

"Oh, I'm afraid of water." She replied. "But maybe I could try it." She said seeing the disappointment on his face.

"I'm all for it!" I said excitedly. "I love doing that kind of stuff. Call me with the details and I'll make sure it gets put into the next newsletter. And a date should not be a problem for me because I have some news about work. I am being promoted to manager in the Somerset office. I have some training to do but I start down there on Monday and I will be off every weekend now.

          Shelby & Shawn   ©   2023

It's not as far to drive so I'll be home earlier in the evenings also."

Everyone was very excited and happy for me. At that point, the men got up to go outside and smoke or just shot the breeze with guy talk while the women cleaned off the table and did the dishes.

"Chad seems very nice," I said, and everyone agreed. "And he is good-looking. Where'd you find him?"

"I was doing a bus tour of Pittsburgh and he was on the tour also. He was with some women, but they didn't seem to be getting along very well. They fought the whole time. I caught him when she wasn't around and gave him my phone number. We've been dating ever since."

"You got rid of her just like that huh?" I said laughing.

"He told me they'd only been dating a short while and he was going to dump her anyway," she said. "At first she drove by the house once in a while but that seems to have stopped."

"You better watch you don't have a stocker on your hands," Mary said. She seemed genuinely concerned and I agreed, remembering a situation I was in like that once.

"Oh, she doesn't bother me," Cindy said laughing. And that ended that conversation.

The men came back in, and the talk turned more casual through the evening till I finally decided it was late and I had an hour's drive home. I bid my goodbyes and made sure Greg had my phone number to call me about the peddle/paddle he was planning.

I had switched to soda an hour ago to clear my head for the drive. It had begun to rain which created a bit of fog on the river traveling down route 28. When I got off the exit I stopped at a

 Shelby & Shawn   ©   2023

Sheetz for a coffee before getting on the turnpike toward home

As I drove, I thought about Cindy. Mary was right to be concerned. She was putting herself in a situation we try very hard to avoid in the single world. I have even had speakers come in to talk to my group about dating practices, dos and don'ts, internet dating, and the bar scene.

It can be scary out there which is another reason why we need so much support from the church and our Christian community. We need a safe place to go to meet other singles for those who are looking for a healthy relationship. But unhealthy people are everywhere. All we can do is educate them to help others understand what is healthy and what isn't. The choice is up to them.

The next morning in church, Father Jon was presiding. He saw me come in and asked if he could talk to me after Mass. I told him I would wait in the Sacristy for him to finish greeting in the gathering area.

I was helping Joan and Tom Mitchell clean up while waiting for him when Sam Demetri came in to turn off the camera which was recording the Mass. Patty Message, the religious director, came in to check on the pamphlets for the ministers distributing to the homebound. We were all standing around talking when Father came in to change out of his garments.

"Shelby," he began as everyone dispersed to other areas of the church to finish closing everything down. "I have a woman in the church who is separated from her husband and is struggling. Would you be willing to call her to offer some support?"

"Oh yes. I'd be happy too."

"In fact, what does your schedule look like these days? I

mean, do you find yourself having any free time in the evenings?"
He asked.

"Well funny you should ask that right now. I am getting a promotion at work and I'm transferring to the Somerset office, which is much closer a drive than Pittsburgh, so that's going to free up a lot of my time. Why do you ask?"

"We know you're not leading the Single's group through Catholic Charities anymore and we know there is such a great need for it, as you've reminded us so much." We both laughed at this. "We'd like to ask if you could get something started again here, directly through the church."

"Oh, I would love that!" I was truly excited. "How do you want me to get started? Who do I answer to?" I had so many ideas and questions.

"Shelby, I trust you to put everything together yourself. Just let Patty know what you need, and she will make sure you have it. Thank you. We appreciate you doing this."

"Thank you for the opportunity. I can't wait to get started. I'll put some ideas together and call Patty as soon as I get it all figured out."

"Great! Enjoy the rest of your Sunday."

"I will. You too." I left feeling so excited. I couldn't wait to get started making plans for this. When I got home, I got out a notebook and started jotting down ideas. Later I called Cindy.

"Hey," I said when she answered the phone. "Guess what?"

"What?" she laughed.

"I was just asked by Father Jon to start another single's group through the church."

"Get out! That's so great!" she exclaimed, just as excited as me. "You'll be able to do so much more now, since you're not under Sharon's rule."

"That's right! And Father Jon has given me the okay to do whatever I want. I just have to okay the schedule through the office, and I can use the old hall to hold the meetings again? I've been writing down some ideas for how to proceed since I won't be asking counselors to come and speak any more."

"I'll coordinate some of my activities with you. And I know you'll come up with some great ideas. You always do."

"Thanks for your support!" I said. I really did appreciate her friendship. "Hey, your dinner last night was nice. I enjoyed meeting your new boyfriend. Is this going to be a serious relationship?"

"Who knows!" She said, "You know how this goes. We never know how long it's going to last."

"I know. The older we get the less likely we are to find a life partner." I agreed.

"The older we get the less we want one," she said and we both laughed but knew how true it was. I was starting to get set in my ways and focused on my career.

I thought about it more after we hung up. When I told Shawn the other night about getting a promotion, his attitude changed slightly. Men don't want women who are strong and independent. They want women who need them, who are vulnerable, especially men who are insecure to begin with.

     Shelby & Shawn   ©   2023

I was slowly changing more and more over the years from a woman who was weak and dependent, unsure of myself, and scared of everything to a strong, confident, independent woman. It was getting harder to be vulnerable, to let others take care of me, and that may stop me from finding true love.

Later that evening, I was able to find time to call the woman Father had asked me to talk to. Her name was Melissa.

"Hi Melissa. This is Shelby Good from Our Lady's Church. Father Jon gave me your number and asked me to call you."

"Hi." She seemed hesitant to talk.

"Is this a good time to talk?" I moved slowly not knowing exactly what her state of mind was like.

"Yes. It's okay." She said, still hesitating.

"I lead a support group at the church for those going through a separation or divorce. Father tells me you and your husband are separated."

"Are you separated?" She asked me.

"I am divorced, and it has been the most difficult experience of my life," I said.

"What happened?" I told her a little bit about my separation and divorce which seemed to encourage her to talk.

Then the floodgates opened. She talked for over an hour about her situation. I encouraged her to come to a meeting, but she was not ready yet. I did convince her to come to dinner with some of the women in the group and she was open to that. I sent her the

        Shelby & Shawn   ©   2023

information and she came to one dinner but never came back.

I ran into her years later to find she went back to her husband. "That was very courageous of you," I told her. I could only imagine the strength it took her to overcome the pain she endured during her period of separation, knowing he was with someone else. We hugged and shared a moment of prayer. Sometimes it goes the other way.

 Shelby & Shawn © 2023

Chapter 19

A Different Life

Monday morning, I reported to Somerset to begin my management training. Betsy was there to greet me. "Hi. I can't stay long. I had cleaned out my desk and office so you can move your things right in." She said.

"Thank you!"

"I'll just carry my stuff out to the car and take off. I'll be back later in the week to check on you. Call if you need anything."

"Okay. Well, see ya." I was surprised she was leaving me alone so soon.

I had the computers configured to my settings already and the first thing I did was check my emails. It was a good thing I did because Dawn had sent me a message from maintenance that they would be there that day to paint and bring in new furniture for me. I was blown away!

They showed up around 10:30 am and began taking everything out. The room was not huge, about nine by eleven; big enough for me to have a desk with chairs, a filing cabinet, and one on one conversations with my employees when necessary.

While they were painting, I spent some time with my staff, getting to know everyone and learning about what they did. I wanted them to know I was there for them at any time they needed anything; my door is always open.

It wasn't a big office, but we had room for a receptionist, Wendy Smart, a middle-aged woman with short black hair, and a short, stocky build. a two license clerks, two travel agents Melissa

Cary, a young, thin blond, and Amy Scott, a middle-aged redhead. My insurance agent was Brian Ranger, an older gentleman, tall, thin and gray. The license clerks were Tara Perry and Annette Winger, both in their 40's, with brown hair and average build. They were all very friendly and welcoming.

When the painting was done and dry, at about 3pm, they started moving my new furniture in. They brought in a nice new desk, new chairs, and 2 five drawer file cabinets with locks and keys for security items. I hadn't expected them to get all this done in one day. I was able to unpack a lot of my boxes, not that I had much to bring with me from Pittsburgh and get some of my files in order.

I stayed after 5:00 to watch the girls close the office to make sure my keys and codes would work. I wrote down the safe combination and made sure we had duplicate keys for everything that was locked in the office. Soon we were ready to go home for the day.

The drive was less than twenty minutes to get to my house. I was home before 6:00; I was used to getting home between 7:00 and 8:00. I walked in the door smiling for the first time in a long time.

"Mom, you're home already," said Joel and Robin, sounding very surprised and happy.

"I am! And I'll have dinner ready in no time so we can eat early for a change."

We sat down together, and I was able to ask them about their day. I even helped them with their homework. It was a most pleasant evening.

I was able to learn my new role as office manager quickly,

so the rest of the week went better. I had lots of CBTs to take and some conference call meetings. I answered directly to Dawn, and she was very easy to work with. So, I got things done in that 9 to 5-time frame.

I saw the kids off to school in the morning and came home earlier, which gave me so much time in the evenings to enjoy dinner, the kids, and a personal life. Joel and Robin seemed so much calmer having me home more. It was a life changer.

In another week the school year would be over, and the kids would be home all day on their own. I was trying to think of things to keep them busy and ideas for some vacation time this year. I didn't want them to have to sit around all summer doing nothing. They deserved to have some fun.

In the meantime, I had my new singles group to put together. I determined that Thursday nights would be a good night for me to have my meetings at the church.

I called Patty. "Is the church hall available on the second Thursday night once a month?"

"Yes, it is." We coordinated our schedule and booked that night for the singles group through December. My first meeting would be in June.

Now to get the word out. I called Donna, the office secretary, to put an ad in the bulletin. "I was just calling the group Christian Singles. Put the date and time in. Also, say to bring a covered dish to share."

Then I called Cindy to put the word out to her group. "I'll update the newsletter and email it to you if you'd hand it out to your group. I'll also hand it out at volleyball." I told her.

"Are you excited?"

"I really am," I said. "It'll be so good to get that kind of support back in my life. I only have a couple of weeks to decide how I am going to conduct the meeting itself."

"I'm sure you'll figure something out. You're always very good at that." She was always so encouraging, I thought as we hung up.

I knew the covered dish dinners were always a favorite. Everyone brought something to share. Single women, especially widows, loved making food for others. But what kind of topics to discuss? I would have to see what kind of crowd came, the age range, and the interests, that all played a factor.

I thought I'd keep the first night just casual since I didn't really have time to book a speaker or plan an event anyway. I will just explain what the group was about, and how we would function, and go over the newsletter with upcoming activities. I had sign-up sheets for email and phone numbers to be notified of any changes or cancellations that may occur.

I was going to be very careful with this group this time around. I needed to set clear boundaries and make sure there were no misunderstandings with the members. I decided there needed to be at least three people signed up for an event or it would cancel. I didn't want anyone to be uncomfortable with a one-on-one event.

Wednesday night I was going up to the church to see if any of the old items were left from the last meetings, I'd had last year. As I was leaving, Robin asked, "where ya goin?"

"To the church to check on supplies for my meeting. Do you want to come?"

          Shelby & Shawn   ©   2023

"Yeah."

When we got there, the closest still had boxes containing paper products for the dinners, cups for the coffee and a coffee maker, name tags, and some other stuff we had left in there. Robin helped me repack it all, making a list of things we still needed. We stopped at the store on the way home and got everything on the list.

I paid upfront and would pass a basket around to collect a dollar from everyone to offset the costs. I also picked up some cupcakes as my contribution to the dinner.

"Hey, what about me?"

Of course, Robin had to have cupcakes at home too, so I got those for her. We went home and ate them while I talked to the kids about my Second Thursday of the month meetings and what I'd be doing there. They were very supportive.

"So, while I have your attention here, you guys are done with school in a few days. What are you going to do with your summer?" I asked them.

"I don't know," they both said at the same time.

"Well, I'd like you to find a project to work on and maybe read a book or two. I'd also like to plan a vacation or maybe someday trips with you, so perhaps you can think about what you'd like to do."

"Okay! We'll think about it." they said and off they went to do their own thing.

Thursday after work I went home to feed the kids before I went to the church to set up for my first meeting of the Christian

Singles Group. I arrived at about 6:30 and my good friend, Anne Sard, came early to help me.

The meetings would run from 7 to 9 so we had plenty of time to get everything ready. At 7:00 people started pouring in with food. Anne was stationed at the food tables and made sure everything got organized while people found seats.

I was overwhelmed at the turnout. There were 38 people I counted after I got the signup sheet. I was even surprised to see an old boyfriend of mine, Shane Patrick, come in. He sat at a table on the side with two other guys I had never seen before. They didn't look like the kind of guys who would come to a church singles group, and they never came back after that first night.

Greg Altman had come and a few others from Cindy's group were all sitting together at a table in the back. Once I felt no more were coming in I went to the podium and introduced myself:

"Hi. Welcome! I'm Shelby Good. I'll be the organizer for this group. Thank you all so much for coming. I'm thrilled to see such an amazing turnout. First, I'd like to tell you a little bit about myself:

I'm from Greensburg. I'm a divorced, single mom of two teens, ages 15 and 17. I've attended this church most of my life, so it feels like my spiritual home. Being single can be a lonely place so it's very important to have support from your Christian community. That's why we've started this group.

The meetings will be held every second Thursday of the month here at the church. We'll always have a covered dish dinner to share with each other. We'll have a newsletter that will announce any events going on throughout the month. I will have those available at every meeting on the table with the signup sheets.

Please make sure we have your name and phone number in the event of changes or cancellations. Some of the events will include movies, concerts, dinners, and more. If you have any suggestions let us know what you'd like to do, and we'll try to get it on the schedule. So now before the food gets cold let's go by tables starting to the right here and help yourself to some food."

As people got up to get food, I went around to the tables to meet people one on one to see if anyone had questions. Mostly people asked if we would schedule this movie or that concert or if we could go eat at certain restaurants? At one point Shane came over to me and asked how I was doing.

"I'm fine. It's good to see you here. Did you get some food?"

"No. I'm not going to stay. This isn't really my thing. Do you have any other things going on I might be interested in?" he asked.

"Well, there's a volleyball group that plays on Friday nights at the Center on Route 30 at 7pm."

"That sounds interesting. Maybe I'll see you there."

"Okay. Well, thanks for coming. Have a good evening."

"You too. Good to see you," he said and as he turned to walk out the other two guys at his table walked out with him. I imagine they were going to the bar. *Good luck to them.*

I walked over to Greg's table to say hi to everyone there. "How's it going Greg? Did you ever get the information for the pedal/paddle you told me about?"

"I did," he said. "I was going to call you then Cindy told me about this and I thought I'd just give it to you here." And he handed me a sheet of paper with all the information on it.

"Oh, thank you! I'm really looking forward to this. Is there any day that's better for you, like a Saturday or Sunday?" I asked, since he was putting this all together, I wanted it to be convenient for him.

"Nope! Either one. How bout you?" he asked me.

"I'm good for either too. So, let's do it on Saturday. I'll put the information in the newsletter and is it okay if I put your name and number as the contact?"

"I don't mind at all. Once I get a number for how many people are going, I'll call and make the reservation."

I was thrilled to have his help on this. It's not something I would have thought of on my own, but I was really excited about going. I loved the water, and I knew I would be good at this. My dad always let me, and my girlfriend take the row boats out when I was a teen. I had a knack for it. I had a knack for just about anything outdoors. So this was going to be fun!

By then people were finishing up their meals and walking around mingling. I went to the table where the sign-up sheets were to make sure everyone signed in and got a newsletter. I also wanted to make sure I got everyone's phone number and email address. It was much easier to communicate that way with a large group of people at a time.

Soon they were saying good night and dwindling out. Anne stayed to help me clean up. We just stuck everything back in the boxes except the leftover food no one wanted. I took some home for the kids and she took a little home for herself. We counted the

     Shelby & Shawn   ©   2023

money together and kept a tally in a notebook of what we took in and what expenses I had covered that I had receipts for.

Anne said, "I'd like to put together a concert night if that's okay?"

"That'd be awesome!"

She liked the Westmoreland Symphony Orchestra, and they did concerts at the Palace Theater in Greensburg. I was happy to let her go ahead and take the lead on that. She would take the calls, collect the money and get the tickets.

I was ecstatic to have all this help. This was a wonderful group of people to work with. So committed and responsible. We turned out the lights, locked everything up and went home. I had a really good feeling about this.

Chapter 20

Hiking

On Saturday morning, Shawn called and wanted to know if I'd like to go hiking with him, John, and Beverly in the mountains. We hadn't talked at all last night at volleyball, so I was surprised to hear from him at this short notice.

Since the kids were with Gene and I had all weekend alone, I decided to go. They picked me up around 11:30. Shawn was driving, and John and Bev were in the back seat, so I jumped in the front.

"Hi!" They all called out at once.

"Hey! How y'all doin?" I asked. "Where we headed?"

"Linn Run State Park," John said. "Have you ever been there?"

"Sure! I've been there a lot! I used to take the kids there when we didn't have much money to do anything. We'd spend a whole day up there sliding down the water slide. We'd take a picnic lunch. It's so nice up there."

"Bev and I have never been there," Shawn said. "We can't wait to see it."

"Oh, I think you'll love it! You should take Kenny up some time." I said. "There's a natural water slide. Well, you'll see it when we get there."

"So, I heard you got a transfer and promotion," said John.

"Yeah. How's the new job going?" asked Bev.

     Shelby & Shawn   ©   2023

"Yes, I did and it's going great. I started in Somerset a couple of weeks ago. I really like it and the hours and drive give me so much more time at home with the kids." I told them a little about the office and the drive, mostly John and Bev were interested and asked questions.

Soon we were at the Adams Falls parking area where the entrance to Flat Rock was. We parked and got our stuff together, water bottles, backpacks and so forth. The trail went along the stream flowing down from the mountain about a half mile before we reached the area called Flat Rock.

Flat Rock was a natural water slide about 100 yards down to a whirlpool at the bottom that was only about 2 or 3 feet deep and not very wide. The rest of the area was all rocks and water flowing through or laying in small puddles in the crevices of the rocks. Beyond the whirlpool the water narrowed and continued down the mountain.

It was a beautiful day but there had been some rain, so the stream was flowing briskly along the rocks to that point. There it deviated in different directions. There were places to sit along the stream, putting our feet in the water to soak.

The day was hot, but the water was ice cold coming down from the mountain and our feet froze in no time. Orneriness got the best of us as we began kicking and splashing one another, squealing and laughing from the cold water hitting us. When we'd had enough playing and were shivering wet, we put our shoes back on and continued our hike.

We climbed up the bank on stone steps to the top lot where there were picnic areas and another trail to Adams Falls. The trees were more open here and the sun dried us quickly. About a quarter mile in we came to a hill going down to a small wooden fairytale bridge above the falls.

We went across the bridge and around the right side to get a better view. The falls were also flowing swiftly from all the rain. There was a steep hill down the other side beneath the falls, but it was muddy and slippery, so not wanting to end up covered with mud, we didn't attempt to get down there.

The foliage was still coming alive from the spring thaw and the flowers were not yet blooming. The trail that went back deeper into the woods was not marked sufficiently from that point on, so we went back the way we came.

When we got back to the car Shawn asked if we all wanted to stop for a bite to eat in Ligonier, at a place called Carol & Dave's Restaurant. We all agreed we were hungry. When we got there the dinner rush had not arrived yet, so the place was empty.

It was a nice, quaint place, with a rustic atmosphere, cabin type decor, and old fashion browns and rust colors. The food was reasonably priced with decent portions and was delicious.

Shawn told us stories about Kenny that made us laugh. Bev told us a little bit about her kids, I never knew she had any, a 10-year-old boy and 8-year-old girl.

"John gets along with them really well," Bev said. "We're actually talking about moving in together."

"Oh, that's exciting!" I said. "How soon?"

"A month or two probably."

"Well, congratulations!" I said.

I then went on to tell them about Greg's idea to do the

peddle/paddle at Ohiopyle and how we would be scheduling that soon. Shawn said he didn't know how to ride a bike and John said he was afraid of water. Bev was a full-figured woman, so I didn't see her wanting to do this either and she said nothing.

We finished our meal and I excused myself to use the bathroom before we headed home. When I came out, Shawn had paid my check.

"Well thank you." I said. "You didn't have to do that."

"I wanted to. Thanks for coming today. I had a good time." he said.

"Me too." We smiled at each other, and our eyes locked with that loving look as we turned to go out the door.

It was about 5:30 when I got home. Cindy had called and left a message on my answering machine about going out, but I was way too tired. I called her back to let her know I would pass. I took a hot bath and just relaxed, feeling content, the rest of the evening with a good book.

I would be serving mass in the morning.

Chapter 21

Planning Events

One evening at the beginning of July I got a call from Greg right after dinner.

"Hi Shelby. I hope I'm not interrupting anything," he said.

"Not at all, Greg. We had just finished dinner and the kids ran out to meet their friends. How are you doing?" I said.

"I'm good. I have the information about the peddle/paddle. Can I give it to you now?"

"Sure! Let me get a pen and paper here," I hunted around to find these things because they were never where I left them. "Okay! Go ahead!"

"Well, the peddle part is $8.00 for the bike rental. The canoes are $20, so two people in a canoe would be $10 a person. If they just want to paddle, they can ride up with the Outfitters to the meeting place. When we arrive with the bikes, they will take them and have the canoes for us there."

"Wow! That's a great setup!" I said. "And that's not a bad price. I'll get this in the newsletter for the July 13th meeting and we'll announce it then. What date are you thinking of doing this?"

"How bout Sunday, the 30th?" he said. "That would give everyone a couple of weeks to decide and call me. Then I can call them for the reservations."

"That sounds like a great plan, Greg. Thank you so much for taking the lead on this. Is it okay if I put your phone number in the newsletter?"

"Yes, that would be fine. I would appreciate the calls. It gets kind of lonely here now that the house is empty." His voice saddened some and I could hear the depression in his tone.

This would be a good thing for him, to keep him busy and get him back to enjoying life again. I imagined he was experiencing something like PTSD if his situation was as bad as he told me it was. Now that his wife was finally out, he could start to heal and move on.

"Great! Thank you again! I'll see you at the meeting then." I said, wrapping up the call. I got right on the computer and updated the newsletter with the new information. I printed out a couple of dozen color copies to pass out at the meeting.

From the list of people who did not show up or could not make it to every meeting, I had an address list to mail to them. I also attached one to an email going to Cindy for her group to sign up if they wanted to participate.

My supply of envelopes and stamps was dwindling so I made a note to remember to pick up some of this stuff at the office supply store. Also make an announcement at the meeting for donations to offset some of the costs for this stuff.

Donna, in the church office, always told me she could make copies for me, but they were not in color, and I liked them in color to show off the picture I used for our mission statement. It was a young girl on her knees planting a small branch that said, "we grow what we plant."

I arrived at the meeting early on Thursday to set it up before everyone got there. Anne came early too with her covered dish and dove right into helping like she always does. We had rectangular tables along the wall for the food and drinks. We moved the round tables to accommodate eight people at a table and within proximity of each other so those at one table could meet and chat with people at other tables.

Soon people were arriving in pairs. I greeted them at the door and directed them to sit anywhere they liked. We had some new people who were always so uncomfortable at first. I try to chat with them to help ease their discomfort and break the ice before sending them to sit, especially if they are alone.

At 7:00, I made the announcements about the upcoming events from the newsletter and pointed out the signup sheets with contact information for those wanting to participate. Greg's pedal/paddle and Anne's Westmoreland symphony concert at Seton Hill College on July 22 were the highlights of the month.

I left it up to them to handle reservations and collect the payments in whatever way worked for them. I was glad I did not have to handle that part. I was going to attend both events, so I gave them my payments right away.

After the announcements, we all got plates of food and were free to mingle around the room. I sat with Anne and Greg at the same table to eat. When I finished eating, I walked around the room to talk with everyone individually, asking for suggestions for topics to be discussed and events they might want to attend.

It seemed codependency was high on the list. Everyone seemed to have some level of struggle with this issue, though they didn't know what it was called or that it even had a name. The complaint was "I tend to take on other people's problems all the time and then I get hurt."

That's typical codependency; when combined with enabling it could be a serious personality defect causing ongoing

     Shelby & Shawn   ©   2023

relationship issues. I can relate to this subject because I have codependency tendencies although I do not enable them, which is why my relationships always end, because I couldn't fix the problem and I refused to live with it.

It takes a great deal of soul-searching to become aware of this personality defect and a very long time to change the pattern. I recognize it in myself but have not yet gotten it under control. It's like having a sign on my back that says, "Men with problems set up camp here." Yes. Codependency is getting put on my list of topics to discuss at an upcoming meeting.

When I got home, Joel and Robin were watching a movie. I sat down on the couch with Robin and gave her a big hug, mostly because I needed it. She groaned and pulled away. Teen Robin was very different from child Robin who was attached to my hip 24/7. I didn't try to hug Joel, figuring I'd get the same response. Hugs were not abundant these days in this house. Mostly what I got was 'I hate you.' That was abundant.

Ah the life of raising teenagers. I still considered myself truly blessed to have them. They are unruly but they are rising to the challenges in life. It was different when I was a 'stay-at-home mom.' I was much better able to take care of my home and family. They were happier too. But this world today does not allow us that luxury. Single parents have to work to provide. Which leaves the kids to practically raise themselves. It's a double-edged sword.

I asked them if they wanted to do the peddle/paddle with us and they both said no. I checked the calendar to make sure that would be their weekend with their dad, and it was. When the movie was over, I chased them off to bed. I wanted to call Cindy before I went to bed myself.

"Hey," I said when she answered the phone.

 Shelby & Shawn   ©   2023

"What up?" she asked.

"I wanted to make sure you got the email with the updated newsletter. I think Greg has a few people signed up for the peddle/paddle already."

"Yeah, I got it and passed it out already. A few of my people are interested in that. Should I have them call you?"

"No. Greg is taking the lead on this, so they need to call him. His number is on there. He's making the reservations. I think we will just pay when we get there. There are releases to sign and stuff." I explained. "But he'll set up where to meet and what is required. I'm going. How bout you?"

"Oh no," she said adamantly. "I don't do bikes," she laughed.

"You can just come for the canoe part of the trip," I said.

"I don't do canoes," she said, and we both laughed.

"Okay! Well, if you change your mind …." I let the comment trail off.

I said my goodbyes and went to bed.

Friday night when I got home from work, I made dinner for the kids. They were just finishing when Gene pulled up. They jumped up, grabbed their bags and ran out the door. After cleaning up the kitchen I went to play volleyball. No one was there yet so I hung out waiting for whoever had the key.

I didn't know who was carrying the ball and key this week. It seemed to be changing all the time now. I wasn't sure how the money was being handled or the bill was being paid but it must be

     Shelby & Shawn   ©   2023

getting taken care of because they hadn't kicked us out yet.

Soon others started showing up, but no one knew who had the ball and key. One person thought Shawn had it, another person thought Randy had it but Randy was here and he didn't have it. Finally, Tara showed up with the ball and key. I was going to ask about getting better organized with this, but I didn't want to be responsible and have to be there every Friday, so I kept quiet and left it to them to figure it out.

While the guys were setting up the net, I passed out the newsletter and made a point to call attention to the peddle/paddle since these were all outdoors people and enjoyed doing sports and athletic activities. No one was interested.

The Saturday of the concert was my weekend to have the kids home. I made sure they were going to be taken care of. Robin was staying with Nickie of course. Joel and Tom were going to a party and would not be home until I got home.

As I took a long bubble bath, I thought about what to wear. It was a simple summer concert, and I didn't think it was going to be too dressy. It was a nice, pleasant evening, not too hot, so something cool with a sweater.

I got out of the tub and went straight to my closet. I found a cute peach colored dress with little white dots all over, buttoning down the front, slightly above the knee, with a white V- neck sailor's collar. I had a white sweater to go with it. My legs were tan, so I didn't need any stockings with my white sandals. I wore my hair down straight with a little makeup on.

I picked up Anne at 6:00. When she got in the car she said, "You look beautiful!"

"I'm not overdressed, am I? I asked.

      Shelby & Shawn   ©   2023

"No, you're perfect." She was wearing blue slacks with a light flowered summer top, and she also brought a sweater.

"And you are too," I said, and we giggled. "Who else is meeting us there?"

"Norma, my friend Mary is joining us, and Stephanie, I forgot her last name. She was one of the new girls at the meeting, the one who walked with a limp. She has diabetes, you know."

"I think I just chatted with her for a few minutes. Well, I'm glad she could come. Hopefully, I'll have a chance to talk with her more tonight."

When we arrived at the Seton Hill Concert Hall, we were to meet the other ladies, we never had men attend these events, at the front door. Anne had all our tickets. Norma and Mary were both there waiting for us. They seemed to already know each other. We waited about ten minutes for Stephanie to show up. I hoped and prayed that she would come; otherwise, Anne would have to eat the cost of her ticket. Unfortunately, that happened in these groups sometimes and it really made it hard to get people to help with events.

But soon Stephanie came walking up the sidewalk and we all introduced ourselves to her. Anne gave her the last ticket and we went inside. We were able to get good seats in the center about midway back, so the music wasn't too loud for us.

I made sure I got the seat beside Stephanie, so I was able to talk to her for a while before the musicians came out.

"So where are you from?" I asked.

"Greensburg." She said, "My husband recently died from

complications of diabetes. I have diabetes too." That was the reason for her limp. It was tragic because she was so young, in her early 40s, and so was her husband.

"I'm so sorry."

Then the concert started, and we were silent to enjoy the classical music. I truly loved these concerts. The music just seeped into my soul. It was very healing. The first year I was married, my favorite movie was 'Love Story.' I bought the soundtrack of classical music from the movie and played it all the time. My husband didn't share my love for it so that was the only exposure I got to it, until now.

On the way home we stopped for some dessert and coffee at Eat n Park. It was a very enjoyable evening. I just loved spending time with these women. They were so nurturing to me.

The following week went by quickly and it was time for our peddle/paddle. Greg had sent instructions to meet at a cafe near the Outfitter's where we would be getting our supplies. There was Joe from volleyball, and he brought his 19-year-old son, Joy Shannon from my group, Al and his girlfriend Sandy, Sonny, Greg, and I. Once we gathered as a group, we followed him over and into the office to pay and pick up our bikes and helmets.

Many of us had brought a small backpack to carry our snacks, lunch, and drinks in. The pedal part turned out to be a slight upgrade that took a great deal of leg power, so we had to stop often and rest. Joy was heavy-set with short blond hair and glasses. I wasn't sure how she would handle this peddle part, but she held her own.

They had benches available about every 500 yards to stop and sit for a while. The trail was right along the river, so the view was beautiful, but Sandy had never been in a canoe before. She

       Shelby & Shawn   ©   2023

was getting nervous every time we went by water that was flowing fast.

Once we made it up the river, the Outfitter's crew was waiting there with our canoes. They stayed to make sure we all got in and were headed downstream. Al and Sandy weren't 100 yards offshore when their canoe tipped over. Sandy got hysterical and would not get back in the canoe. They had to go back to shore and ride down with the crew to their car.

The rest of us were paired off with two in a canoe, Joe and his son, Sonny and Joy, and Greg and I. Sonny put Joy in the front, but it was not balanced very well so they were struggling not to tip. Since this was my first time on a river in a canoe, I was grateful to have Greg behind me steering. He was very strong and got us through the rapids easily.

About two miles into the trip, Greg called out "Is anyone hungry yet?"

"Yeah!" Everyone called out.

We found a place on an island to pull over. Everyone had brought lunches and drinks for a picnic. We ate as we talked and laughed, splashing in the water to cool off before getting back in our boats to finish the rest of the trip down river. It was the most fun I'd had in years.

When we reached the putout area, we had to get our canoes to the left so we could pull up at the exit, jump out and carry our boats up the ramp. It was tricky because if you didn't get over in time and went beyond the takeout point, you were fighting the current to get back to it. Greg and I got out easily, then helped the others by wading out into the water and pulling them over.

I considered myself strong and in very good shape, but this

     Shelby & Shawn   ©   2023

trip really took a toll on me. I was completely exhausted. The drive home alone was a real chore. At home, I soaked in a hot, hot tub for an hour. All the kids were there so we ordered pizzas because I definitely was not cooking.

It was fun to tell them about the day and share some time with them.

"Ah, now we wish we would have gone with you," said Joel.

"Well, think of things you'd like to do in August," I said.

In August, I was taking a week off work, so we were planning some day trips as our vacation this year. They had some suggestions and I liked them, so I said we'd look into it more when we were ready to go.

I was so sore the next day that I called off work to take another day to rest.

Chapter 22

One Vacation Day at a Time

I woke up on the first day of my week-long vacation excited about some of the plans we'd made. Today is Monday and we were going to Laurel Caverns, which is the largest cave in Pa. On the way home, we would stop for dinner.

I let Joel and Robin sleep in while I made some cinnamon rolls, bacon and chocolate chip pancakes for breakfast. I kept them warm on the stove while I went to take my shower, dry my hair and get dressed for the day. By that time, the kids were stirring.

"Rise you guys. It's vacation time," I was calling through the house. "Breakfast is ready." It was more like brunch at 11:30 but we would not have to worry about eating again till dinner.

They came into the kitchen and sat down at the table looking sleepy still. I put the plates out with all the food, brought out the syrup and the chocolate milk. Right away they perked up. They didn't get a big breakfast like this very often. I was determined this week was going to be the best of my time I could give them. We ate heartily.

"What are we doing today?" Joel asked.

"We're going to Laurel Caverns for a tour and then we'll stop for dinner on the way home." I said, talking about our plans for the day. I cleaned up the kitchen while they went to get showered and dressed.

We left the house at 12:30 with an hour and a half drive to get to the caverns. Joel sat in the back to sleep more on the way down. Robin held the map and was the navigator. She did a good job of it and we found our way there without a problem. We got there just in time to join the 2:00 group tour.

The tour was very fascinating and educational. The upper cavern entrance is a "network of interconnecting grid-like passages" and its lower cavern, which is unlit, consists of "watercourses into a dendritic system of passages." We were led through by a guide with a flashlight. Our group freaked out a little when we got to that part because they made a point to show us the bats sleeping right above our heads.

When we came out at the end, the kids were just looking at me and cracking up. Because of the humidity in the cave, my hair was sticking straight out like a bush. Oh, how was I going to stop at a restaurant looking like this? I hadn't even brought a hair- band to pull it back. This remained funny to them for the rest of the trip.

We went back up around to the souvenir shop but there wasn't much they liked there. I didn't want to spend a lot on junk so they each just picked a little trinket.

"We're hungry." They said together.

"Okay. How about this quaint little place called Caporella's Italian Ristorante in Uniontown." I said. "I found it in an ad for travel."

"That sounds good!" So, we decided to eat there. The food was excellent, and we took our time eating. The kids talked about what they liked in the cave most. "I liked the history of the caverns." Joel said. We all liked the light and sound show. I just enjoyed their company.

We stopped at a local video store to rent a movie for the evening. Robin wanted Matilda, so we all agreed on that one. When we got home, we changed into comfy clothes and relaxed for the evening. The next day we were going swimming at

Ligonier Valley Beach.

Now Ligonier Valley Beach is a swimming pool. It was very big with grass on one side of it and sand on the other. There were two slides, two diving boards and the water level went from two feet up to eight feet. We'd been coming here for years, and the kids loved it when they were young.

Now they were getting kind of bored with it unless they had their friends with them, so they had to entertain each other except when I came in the water. "Race ya across," I'd say, jumping in near them to splash them first. Then they'd both attack me. We packed a cooler full of stuff and stayed all afternoon and when the sun started to go over the other side, we came home.

"Ok. Up to bed." I made the kids get to bed early. "Tomorrow's the big day. I have tickets for SeaWorld in Aurora, Ohio."

This was going to be a three-hour drive; a distance I had never driven by myself before. It would be mostly turnpike which I knew I could handle. There would be rest stops along the way if I ran into any problems. I had an old Hyundai Sonata that was pretty beat up. I was a little nervous but very excited about taking another step on my journey to strength and independence.

We had such a great time. I dragged them out of bed at 7:00 a.m. to get right in the car and go. They could sleep on the way up. I had packed cereal bars, snack cakes, and juice drinks in the car for them to eat since we weren't stopping for breakfast. We arrived just when they were opening at 10 am.

We got a schedule and planned our day, making sure we saw every show. Shamoo, of course, was the highlight of the day. We sat halfway back but still got drenched. We fed the dolphins and held the birds. I let them buy whatever souvenirs they wanted since this was our first real family vacation.

Being thrown into poverty after the divorce, it took so long to get on my feet just to be able to feed and provide for them, there was no extra money. When they were young, a Friday night out for us was walking around the mall, letting them play with the sample toys that Circus Toy Store put out, then getting them a 99-cent ice cream at Murphy's. On Sundays, we would walk to the playground or drive to the mountains, if I had gas, to hike the trails. The kids look back on these times fondly, realizing that was all we could do without money.

It was very late when we were driving home so we stopped at a rest stop to use the bathrooms and I grabbed a coffee to stay awake. As we continued, the kids slept. I thought about how far we've come together. The time we spent living in the 'not so great' house, in the 'not so great' neighborhood, when they looked in the fridge and cupboard not knowing what they were going to eat that night for dinner, and I always managed to scrap something up to put on the table for them. They stuck with me through it all, through all the crying, all the sadness, all the mistakes, the deadbeats, the moving around, and they just kept going … as I did. *I love them so much.*

As we pulled up to our home, I also remembered the times I was able to pick them up and carry them into the house, into their beds, sound asleep. Those days were definitely over. We walked into the house like zombies and dropped right into bed. It was the best exhaustion I'd felt in a long time.

Thursday was a sleep in day. We didn't get up until 10:30. Today would be school clothes shopping day, so we got showered and dressed and headed to the mall. We had lunch in the food court, each of us picking a different restaurant to order from.

"I want Chinese," said Joel, and we went there first.

Robin picked pizza, "Two pieces of pepperoni please."

They got us a table while I got my cheese fries, and everyone was happy.

We spent all afternoon walking through the shops, looking at clothes, and shoes and they both needed new winter coats. Gene would be picking them up tomorrow and he offered to help with whatever they needed, so I decided he could do socks, gloves, and coats.

I knew Robin wouldn't let him get her underwear, so I took care of that for both of them. They each picked three outfits to start, a pair of shoes and a pair of boots. That would be good till Christmas when they got clothes from everyone including grandma. My mother always gave them a big box of clothes with one small toy or a gift card. She felt Santa brought them enough toys.

On the way out of the mall, we had to get cinnamon pretzels to take home. Ummm. At the house, they dumped all their bags in the middle of the living room floor and started trying everything on, showing me how it fit. That's when it hit me how grown they were and how soon they'd be leaving home for college or marriage. At that moment my heart sank. I just wanted them to be babies again.

They went and put all their stuff away to run off and do their own thing for the rest of the day. They'd had enough of mom this week and now needed some time with their friends. Tomorrow I will wash all the new stuff, go through their old stuff for donations to goodwill and look at my own wardrobe. Most of my clothes were my sister's hand-me-downs and they were very nice, but I wanted to treat myself to some new stuff.

 Shelby & Shawn   ©   2023

Friday Gene came early to get the kids, allowing me some extra free time for shopping. As I was cleaning up to go out, a thought occurred to me. I had been dreaming of buying a Pontiac Sunfire for probably five years now. Every time I saw the commercial for them, I just died for one.

Now I was still working on building my credit and the only credit card I had was Kaufman's which I used for the kids, but I paid the bill diligently. I bought the car I own now on a loan cosigned by my dad, but my payments were never late and I paid it off early.

I went straight to the Pontiac dealership. I walked in and said, "I want a Pontiac Sunfire." The only one they had was used and red, but it was clean, didn't have a mark on it, had low miles and they got it into my price range. I was over the top ecstatic when I signed that paper all on my own and drove off the lot with my dream car.

I got myself a bite to eat before going to volleyball. When I pulled in a lot of people were standing outside. I was beeping and honking like crazy. They all looked puzzled at first then came walking toward me. I got out and jumped up and down and said, "I got a new car, I got a new car!' They looked inside and out, saying how nice it was.

"What's the big deal?" Shawn said, laughing at me jumping around.

"This is the first car I bought without a cosigner," I said. "That's exciting for me,"

"Oh, well that's good," he said, not really seeming impressed, as everyone else was saying, "That's great Shelby! Good for you!"

I thought about this later that evening at home alone. *I thought I had fallen in love with Shawn. Perhaps what I was feeling was empathy. Maybe it was more codependency.*

These last few months have shown me that I could make it, despite all the hardships and everything we had gone through, I was able to not only survive but thrive, while taking care of my family.

As much as I would love a life partner, I really didn't need one, and that was a very powerful emotion. Now I needed to find a partner who could let me be strong and independent without being intimidated by it.

Was he out there anywhere? Could Shawn be what I needed?

Chapter 23

The Ghosts of Gettysburg

The North American Conferences for Separated & Divorced Catholics (NACSDC) were having their regional meetings in October. Since our region combined New Jersey and Pennsylvania, we needed to find a halfway driving point. The group we met at Notre Dame from New Jersey had been in contact with Randy and they had decided on Gettysburg for our meeting place.

Cindy called me one evening in September. "Are you going to be able to go? Sonny has been helping me as co-organizer of my group, so he will be coming as well. Randy has stayed active with the NACSDC after our leadership training in Notre Dame which is why he is putting this together with us."

"I don't really feel like I'm part of this group, but I'll go just for the fun of it," I said since they had so few people representing Pa. The folks from Erie could not come down nor could the group in Meadville make it.

There didn't seem to be a lot of folks committed to this program. Once again, the Catholic Church is marriage/family oriented and frowns on divorce, so those who are going through this tend to shy away from the church, feeling like they don't fit in. Or they are angry at the whole Annulment process. Or they just feel let down, embarrassed, or ashamed, and they walk away for whatever reasons they have, but it's a sore subject for any Catholic going through a separation or divorce.

"So, we thought Halloween weekend would be fun since we found a bed & breakfast called The Homestead, a big old house that was an orphanage during the war. It's supposed to be haunted."

     Shelby & Shawn   ©   2023

She explained.

"Oh, that will be fun! So, there's only four of us going from Pa?" I asked.

"Pam and Kathy are coming. Also, another guy named Frank from Pittsburgh is coming down. Randy's bringing his kids with him, and he told me he's just going to be spending time with them and doesn't want to be bothered otherwise except for the Regional Meetings."

"That's not a problem," I said, trying not to sound sarcastic. The trip to Notre Dame was a sore spot for me and Randy. "Do you know how many are coming from New Jersey?"

"No, I don't think we have a final number yet but probably the people we met at Notre Dame will all be there."

"Gosh, that seems so long ago, I don't think I even remember them," I said, trying to recall the names of all those people I'd met. "I remember the one guy I was dancing with; I think his name was Jeffrey or something." I laughed.

"Well, I'll give you the list before we go so, we can both familiarize ourselves with it and we won't be embarrassed." We both laughed at this.

We talked more about my vacation, her boyfriend, my new car and when we realized we'd been on the phone for two hours, we called it a night and hung up. I wrote Gettysburg on my calendar for October 27 – 29, I made some notes for my meeting on Thursday and went to bed.

Cindy and I would be riding down together and sharing a room, so I got a check out to her immediately for my share of the deposit. I thought about asking my kids if they wanted to go to

        Shelby & Shawn   ©   2023

Gettysburg with us, but I was unsure how I'd explain that Randy and his kids didn't want to be bothered by us. It was best to let them stay at Gene's that weekend.

As they were getting older, they didn't bother so much with Halloween anyway, so I had decided not to get a pumpkin this year either. If they wanted to trick or treat, they usually just threw on some old clothes and some fake blood and just went around the neighborhood. It was a big townhouse complex, so they always got a lot of candy without putting too much into it.

October was a busy work month. I had to travel to Pittsburgh a lot for staff meetings, I had to take some fairly long training CBT's on hiring and firing employees, and there were a couple of employee reviews that needed to be done by the end of the month.

The night before our trip I called Cindy to confirm plans for the next day. We both took Friday off so we could take our time driving down, stopping along the way if we wanted, and just enjoying the scenery. The leaves were in full color, and we would be traveling across the mountains. Gene would pick the kids up right after school on Friday.

"Hey, what time are we leavin?" I asked when she answered her phone.

"I'll pick you up around 10:00. We can check in any time after 2:00 so we should get there right around then if we stop and eat along the way," she said.

"Sounds good. I'll be ready," I said, and we hung up to continue packing.

I was going casual, jeans, t-shirts, sweaters, and boots. I brought warm and cool pajamas not knowing what the sleeping temp might be in the place. If we saw a ghost during the night, I didn't want to be running out not properly dressed, I thought and laughed to myself.

I got the kids off to school the next morning and Cindy arrived promptly at 10:00 am. She pulled up, not even getting out. I threw my bag in the back and jumped in. Putting my cup of coffee in the holder next to her cup of coffee to strap my seat belt on.

The drive was absolutely gorgeous. There were various colors like tapestries across the mountains like fall pictures seen painted by artists and hung in galleries for sale. It was hard to talk with the breathtaking view. I wanted to just absorb it and make it part of my soul.

We stopped at different markets and yard sales along the way, meandering along, in no hurry to get there. I found a couple of good books and some holiday decorations I liked. Cindy bought some books too; our love of reading was another thing we had in common. We stopped for lunch at a small diner with home- made food that was to die for. Cindy and I were comfortable and enjoyed each other's company, talking or not, but we always found things to talk about.

We arrived in Gettysburg at 3:30 and found The Homestead very quickly off the main drag of town. Others from New Jersey were arriving, and we were all reintroducing ourselves waiting to check-in. Seems nobody remembered anyone's name, so we didn't feel bad after all. Jeffrey and I remembered each other, "Hey, how are you?" hugging and chatting while we waited our turn.

An elderly woman named Joan Simmons had owned the place with her daughter, Kim, for many years. It had been passed down through her family, so she knew all the good stories to tell.

          Shelby & Shawn   ©   2023

Cindy and I got our room key and went to put our bags away. We were all to meet at 5:00 on the front porch to go to dinner as a group.

There were 15 altogether, so we needed to find a restaurant big enough to seat us all. At 5:00 we were all ready and waiting outside to find a place to eat. We ended up at a diner that was big and could put a lot of tables together to accommodate us.

Once we were seated and ordered our meals the group discussed some of the issues going on in the Church, with the separated/divorced ministry. I didn't know if this was supposed to be our official regional meeting or if the entire weekend was going to be a hit or miss kind of communication.

Whatever it was, I stayed out of it. I didn't really feel I was involved up to that point and wasn't going to insinuate myself into it now. When we turned to discussions the next day, it really seemed very casual and most of the group just wanted to go sightseeing, do the tours, and shop for souvenirs.

"I really want to do the tour of the battlefields on horseback," I said.

Randy's daughter, Leslie jumped at that. "OH, I want to do that too!"

But when we inquired about it, the reservations had to be made months in advance, which made sense, but we were disappointed anyway. So, after dinner, we all kind of walked around, exploring the different shops, some stopped at the pub for a drink, some turned in early and others just hung out talking or walked through the cemetery. Cindy and I were looking for a place where we could dance but there was none.

Exhausted from all the walking we turned in too. Of course,

everyone was on high alert for any supernatural events happening in the hotel. The story was the headmistress of the orphanage was very mean and abusive and some of the children died there. Their ghosts still roamed through the rooms at night. Joan didn't like to talk about that part of the house's history. She wanted people to know the history of the civil war and how her family and place played a part in that.

The next morning, when we all met downstairs for breakfast, we wanted to hear of any happenings, but no one had stories to tell aside from creaky floors and doors opening on their own. After breakfast, everyone went their separate ways, Cindy and I jumped into an SUV with a few of the guys, Frank from Pittsburgh and Jeff from New Jersey.

"You ladies okay with a tape and driving tour of the battle-fields, talking us through what was going on in the battle while we drove through the area it was happening." Frank asked.

"Sure!" We both agreed, not really knowing what other choice we had since he was driving.

"When we finished that we could go to the museums to check out the artifacts from the civil war era and videos of the famous battles." Jeff said, sounding really excited about it, so we agreed to that as well.

I was sorry I had not brought the kids with me, so I bought them a couple of souvenir shirts and hats with Gettysburg on them. We were all meeting back at the same diner for dinner at 5:00 because it was the largest in town to fit us all in. We got back to the Homestead at about 3:30 to freshen up before going over there.

Once again, the restaurant moved tables together to allow all of us to sit together. We had warned them the night before that we would be back tonight, so they were ready this time. I sat across from a couple from New Jersey who had just gotten married. I remembered them from Notre Dame, they had just gotten engaged then. He was very attentive and affectionate, and I was envious of her finding a man like that. They were few and far between.

She really didn't seem to appreciate him at all, and he knew it. In fact, he claimed she only married him for his money. She denied it of course, but I wondered. She was very attractive, and he was not so much. But he did spend a lot of money on her so in fact, maybe he used his money to get her. hmmm!

We all started talking about what everyone was doing for Halloween with costumes and decorating.

I said, "My kids are older and I'm just not into Halloween this year. They're giving me a hard time because I'm not even buying a pumpkin."

The others had various opinions about older kid's trick or treating but everyone agreed, magnanimously, "You HAVE to have a PUMPKIN!" I just laughed.

Later that evening we all gathered on the porch at the Homestead with Joan coaxing her to tell us about the civil war and her family's part in it. We listened attentively to her fascinating stories and enjoyed learning the history of the place well into the night. Finally, everyone grew weary and one by one we excuse ourselves for bed. It would be a long drive home the next day.

I had an interesting event occur the next morning in the shower I had to share with everyone at breakfast.

"When I was standing at one end of the shower, there was a shower mat at the other end hanging over a towel rack. The mat slowly slid off the towel rack down the tub to my feet. I don't know

        Shelby & Shawn   ©   2023

if it was a fluke, but it was weird that it moved so slowly."

We all laughed, fascinated by the only sign of a ghost in the house and how helpful it was that it didn't want me to fall. We lingered at breakfast not wanting to go but eventually, we had to pack up our bags, say our goodbyes, and go on our merry ways, vowing to meet again sometime but knowing we wouldn't.

Cindy and I left Gettysburg at about 11:00, only stopping for lunch, so I could get home before the kids got home.

As I watched the beautiful blankets of colors before us, even more now than two days ago, my mood became melancholy as I thought of Shawn. I hadn't heard from him since our hike and wondered if it didn't have something to do with my promotion. Cindy sensed the change in my mood and asked, "What are you thinking about?"

"Oh, not much." I replied, not wanting to confide in her yet about my feelings for Shawn, though she knew we were spending time together.

She dropped me off at my place at 3:30. I unpacked and settled in before the kids came in at 6:00. While I was waiting for them, I picked up the phone and dialed Shawn's number. His machine picked up and I left a message saying I was just thinking about him and wondered how he was. He didn't call back that night.

The next morning, as we all went out the door together, we tripped over a huge two-foot-high pumpkin sitting on our doorstep. The kids were ecstatic. I never found out who put it there.

     Shelby & Shawn   ©   2023

Chapter 24

Talk About Conflict

On the drive home from Gettysburg, Cindy mentioned she didn't know what she was going to do for her November meeting. She was running out of ideas for topics and asked if I could do a talk for her group. I was slowly overcoming my fear of talking in front of large groups and appreciated any practice I could get, since I would need that skill to grow stronger in my career now. I told her I would try to come up with something.

On Friday, at volleyball, it came to me. Conflict. Most relationships ended due to conflict not being resolved in a healthy way. Struggling to communicate was the prime reason. The situation with Roy was a perfect example. Our inability to resolve that conflict occurred because we did not communicate with each other in healthy ways, talking or listening.

While I was standing in the gym thinking about this, Shawn came walking over to me.

"I got your message Sunday night. Thanks for checking in on me. I went home for the weekend to see my mom and sister. I was feeling homesick, and I didn't get Kenny for Halloween, so I was upset about that."

"Oh, I'm sorry you didn't get to see Kenny in his costume. Did she at least take pictures for you?"

"No, probably not. She doesn't care if I'm a part of his life or not. She's seeing someone and they get to go have fun together and all I get is every other weekend."

I remember that feeling every time Gene came to pick up

the kids with Sherry in the car; it was the most painful emotion.

"I know that's hard for you right now. It gets better. When he gets older, he'll be able to say who he wants to spend time with. And the courts will listen to him." I hoped to help him feel better but there was no way to comfort someone going through that. The pain is too deep.

"Yeah, I know you're right. I just have to wait it out. I know when he gets older, he'll want to live with me. I'll be so happy then." His mood changed as he smiled, saying, "thank you." He winked at me. "We have to go out dancing some night soon," he said as he strode over to the guys while we took sides and started to play.

My heart was fluttering as I watched him walk away with his lanky shuffle of his. My desire for him was so strong, I wanted to be with him in that intimate way. I knew I had to control myself. I just got back into leading the new single's group; I had to live up to what it meant to be a leader in the church, living up to the standards of a good Christian life. I had to put it out of my head.

I didn't go out to eat after volleyball because I wanted to spend some time with the kids. When I got home, Robin had some girls over to watch a horror movie. I got out some snacks for everyone and plopped on the couch to watch Blair Witch Project with them. As the movie progressed, the girls were all laughing.

"Is this all there is to it?" Robin said and we were all laughing at the stupidity of it. Then I went to bed. Holy Crap!

Every time I closed my eyes that movie was in my head. I did not sleep a wink. Good thing I didn't have to work the next day. When I got up, the girls were sleeping all over the living room amid empty soda cans and snack bags. I wondered if the movie had bothered any of them.

Joel hadn't come home at all. I prayed he was somewhere safe. I took my shower, dried my hair, and came back down to the kitchen to cook breakfast. The girls had not stirred by 10:30, so I put the bacon and pancakes on the stove to stay warm for them, grabbed my purse, and went out to go shopping. When I came home an hour and a half later, they were up and had eaten all the breakfast food I had prepared and then got fruit from the frig.

I called for them to help me carry the groceries in. To my surprise, they all jumped up, grabbed some bags, and began unpacking them to put away.

"Did that movie keep any of you up last night?" I asked.

"No!" said one.

"Slept like a bear!" said the other.

"Not me!" Said another.

"Didn't even think about it!"

"I thought it was stupid!"

Apparently, I was the only one who got scared so I was keeping my mouth shut. "Well, that's good. Glad you all enjoyed it."

They were back in the living room watching something else, so I went upstairs to use the phone. In my room, I dialed Cindy's number.

"Hi," I said when she answered.

"Hey, how's it going?"

 Shelby & Shawn   ©   2023

"Well, my daughter's got a living room full of girlfriends that spent the night. We watched a horror movie, and it didn't bother any of them, but I didn't sleep all night."

She laughed. "Is anything going on tonight?"

"That's why I was calling you. Shawn asked about dancing last night. Is anyone from out there coming this way? Maybe we could get a group together and go down to Yesterday's."

"That sounds like a great idea. Let me see if I can round some people up. I'll call ya back."

Less than an hour later, she had a group of people who wanted to come in and dance. We would meet down at the club around 8:30. I called Shawn to let him know that we had a group going dancing tonight if he or anyone else wanted to join us. Could he pass the word along?

"Just so happens John and Bev are sitting here. 'You guys wanna go to Yesterday's tonight?' They said yeah so we'll all be there."

"Great! See ya there then!" I was so excited. I went downstairs to see if Robin could stay at Nickie's gram's tonight. The other girls had left already. Nickie and Robin ran over to ask Grace and came right back saying "sure. She can stay." Now if only I could figure out where Joel was.

I went upstairs to take a nap but had a hard time falling asleep. I must have dozed off at some point because I was woken from a sound sleep when Robin knocked saying they were going over to Nickie's gram's now. Her things were in the backpack she was holding. I looked at the clock. It was 6:30.

"Okay sweetie. I love you. Hey, any sign of Joel?"

"He's downstairs. He came in yelling about the mess in the living room so we're leaving."

Thank goodness. I wasn't going to be able to go out not knowing where he was. I went downstairs to check on him and he was on the phone. So, I messed around in the kitchen, making myself a sandwich, while I waited for him to get off the phone.

When he hung up, I asked "do you have plans for tonight?"

"Nope! I'm just hanging out here tonight. Look at the mess they left in here."

"I'll clean it up tomorrow. I'm going out so let me know if you need anything. I'll be leaving at about 8:30."

"I won't need anything. Have fun and be safe!"

I took a long, hot bubble bath feeling much better since I napped. The evening was warm for November calling for cooler clothes, especially when dancing. I wore my burgundy button down with sleeves that buttoned up at three quarter length and jeans with low heel boots. One quick look in the mirror ... *my hair came out great!*

I grabbed a light jacket going out the door and calling goodbye to Joel.

"Bye momma, love ya," he called back. He was back on the phone.

"Love you too sweetie! I won't be late."

When I arrived at Yesterday's, Cindy had two tables right

     Shelby & Shawn   ©   2023

inside the door to the right of the dance floor. She had quite a few people with her. Greg came, Joyce and Mary were there, Sonny and Al. Al did not have his girlfriend with him. I hung up my coat and grabbed a seat beside Greg across from Cindy. We barely had time to chat when Shawn came in with John and Bev.

Shawn sat beside me. "Did you just get here?" he asked.

"About 10 minutes ago."

"What do you want to drink?"

"Um, just get me a peach and ginger. Here let me give you some money."

"I got it." He and John went up to get drinks, so I moved over beside Bev to chat while they were gone. DJ Larry was setting up and would start to play so we wouldn't be able to hear well. I leaned over to Cindy and told her I had an idea for my talk at her meeting next week.

"What do you think of Conflict as a topic of discussion?" I asked her.

"That's a good topic! Something we all struggled with."

"Okay. I'll put it together and be at your meeting next Thursday."

The music started and everyone jumped up to dance. Shawn and John came back with our drinks and before I even had a chance to take a sip, he grabbed my hand and drug me laughing out onto the dance floor. We had a blast!

We danced all night, barely taking time to sit down. I was so happy to be with him. We both danced with others also but

          Shelby & Shawn   ©   2023

always came back to dancing with each other. As the hour got later the others dwindled out.

Soon it was after midnight and Shawn said he had to be up early tomorrow. John, Bev, and I walked out to our cars with him and said our good nights. I drove home on cloud nine. What a range of emotions I was feeling about him. It was exhausting and exhilarating at the same time.

Chapter 25

Cindy's Group

The next few days, as I was preparing my talk for Cindy's meeting, I found that Shawn was always on my mind. Even at work, I couldn't get him out of my head to concentrate on anything. He never called and I had to fight the urge to call him almost every day. I was becoming obsessed with it, which was very unhealthy.

After dinner on Thursday of the following week, I told the kids I had to leave right away.

"Why? Joel asked. "I thought we were going to see more of you now?"

"I have to give a talk to Cindy's Singles group tonight. She asked me to speak for her. It's a good opportunity for me to practice talking in front of groups. Would you two like to come? The talk is on Conflict. You might get something out of it and you'd get to see me give a presentation."

Neither one was interested in that.

"What time will you be home?" Robin asked.

"Not too late. Probably about 9 or so."

Now I feel bad leaving them. Something was obviously going on. *I'm going to have to find time to sit down with Joel for a heart-to-heart.* He seemed to be struggling with something. I was hesitating to leave but had to keep my commitment.

"If you're up to it when I get home, we can sit and talk for a while."

I pushed myself out the door and arrived a little late. To my surprise, she had twenty-two people come for this. *Good thing I didn't cancel on her.* She had tables set up and a blackboard up front for me. She and I chatted till everyone showed up and took their seats.

I took my place at the front and suddenly I began to have an anxiety attack. I still wasn't used to speaking in front of groups. My mouth became parched, my heart was racing, and my head was pounding, and I excused myself to go into the kitchen area to look for something to drink. There was nothing there. In a few minutes, I went back out and began.

"The biggest cause of conflict is lack of good communication …"

Once I got going, the anxiety let up and everything went smoothly. The talk lasted about 45 minutes. Some had questions that I answered the best that I could. We had coffee and cookies for everyone after.

"What happened?" Cindy asked after.

"Just a little anxiety. I'm so sorry. I know that was probably uncomfortable for you."

"Not at all. That was a very good talk." I knew she was just being nice.

"I thought it went very well once I got started. I got over it as I went along."

"The more you do it the easier it will get."

"Well, thanks for giving me the opportunity. I'm going to

need practice if I'm going to do these talks for work. If you don't mind, I'm going to get back to the kids. It was great to see everyone." I waved my goodbyes.

On the drive home, the temperature dropped, and it began to lightly flurry making the roads a little slick. I slowed down to accommodate the change in the weather and tried to concentrate on driving but once again my thoughts drifted off to Shawn. I desired him every single day, to talk to him, to be with him, to tell him how I felt.

I prayed for God to give me patience in this situation and that it will be that we are not together in the end, let me accept this now and move on.

When I got home, Joel was still awake in the living room watching tv. I got my coat hung up and things put away before I sat down with him.

"Hey, sweetie. You seemed a little agitated at dinner. Is there anything going on? Do you want to talk?" I suggested.

"I'm just hating school. I want to quit." He said and I realized we were going to have this conversation again.

"I know it's hard for you to be there. Are you struggling with your classes or grades? Is there anything I can do to help you with that?" I asked.

"No! I just … it's boring. I don't want to do it anymore. It just doesn't have any purpose."

"Well, the purpose is to get an education." I could feel myself getting upset and angry. "It's important for you. For your future. It's really not that much longer before you graduate." I was desperate to keep him going. It was so important to me.

"Fine." He said and shut down.

I did not know what to say or do to make him feel better or understand. I thought the parent was to tell the child they had to do this, and they just did it. Yes, Joel had to go to school because it's the law and I will go to jail if he doesn't.

But that's not what I wanted him to feel like. Obligated. That would make him hate it worse. I prayed he came to appreciate the opportunities an education would allow him, and he would come to understand how important it was.

But I knew when he turned 18, he would be making this choice for himself, and I would be heartbroken.

     Shelby & Shawn   ©   2023

Chapter 26

My First Presentation

The practice I had talking to Cindy's group couldn't have come at a better time. The next day at work, Dawn called me and asked if I could put together a presentation for the next manager's meeting.

"I'd like you to focus on motivating people and building teamwork in the office place. Do you think you can have it ready for next Thursday?"

"Yes, I can have it ready." I had a lot of material from previous training classes I'd attended. I just needed to dig them out and put them together into a format that made sense.

Let's see … where did I put all those CDs I'd gotten at that one training class I attended?

I found the CDs and started going through them, finding the ones that would apply to my talk. I spent some time listening while writing notes. I pulled out some of the books from the Steller Trainings I took and made a lot of notes from them. Soon my stomach was growling, and I realized it was afternoon. I had missed lunch.

I went to the lunchroom to get my pack out of the fridge. I brought a salad today with some nuts and cheese to snack on. Wendy and Amy were there making themselves coffee and chatting.

"You've been locked up in your office all day," Amy said.

"I have been asked to do a presentation at the next manager's meeting."

"That's exciting!" Said Wendy.

"I'm kind of excited, kind of nervous. I have always been scared about speaking in front of groups, but I've been practicing at some of my volunteer meetings, and I think I'm ready."

"I'm sure you'll do great." they said. It was nice to have support and encouragement.

"Thanks!" I went back to my office to eat and continued working till closing. I thought about taking all my notes home with me to keep working that night but decided not to. Home is for my kids.

I continued to work on the presentation during office hours and had it put together to my satisfaction by Wednesday. Thursday, as I drove to Pittsburgh for the meeting, I practiced in the car to have a lot of it memorized so I didn't trip up.

When I arrived, I checked in, got my name tag, then went for the coffee chatting with some of the other managers until it was time to sit down. I was glad to see I was the first speaker, so I didn't have to sit and bite my nails till my turn.

Once the announcements and introduction were over, I was introduced by Dawn.

"Shelby is our new Uniontown manager and she's going to talk today a little bit about Motivating People and Building Teamwork."

I stepped up to the front. "Thank you, Dawn. Hi everyone. I've been with the Auto Club for eight years and in that time, I've worked in three offices. It's been my experience that each office runs differently. Why is that? Because the staff is different?

Because the area is different? Because the customers are different? I'd say each one of these factors apply."

I went on to explain why I thought each of these areas played a very important part in how people interact, what makes them want to build camaraderie and teamwork, how important it is to build an atmosphere of trust and mutual support, each person working for the benefit of the other, whether it be coworkers or customers, we are all in this together for the best possible outcome. I wrapped it up in about twenty minutes and sat down. I was very pleased with myself. *I didn't say one stupid thing.*

During our lunch break, Dawn approached me, "that was a very good presentation. Can you put together more details in a report and send them to me via email."

"Sure. I'd be happy to." I said, feeling really excited now. The other speakers I thought were much better than me. *I must be doing something right!*

"I'd like a list of your resources too."

"Sure. When would you like that done?"

"No hurry. Maybe next week sometime."

"Okay. Thanks!" I said.

"Thank you!" She said and we walked back to our prospective seats to eat.

Monday, I arrived at work early to pull all my resources together for my final draft of the presentation for Dawn. I put reports together, made a list of the sources I used, and typed everything up into a more detailed report. This took me all day. *No lunch again.*

I spent Tuesday morning going over it again for a final review but still did not feel comfortable sending it. I kept thinking of more ideas to add and every time I reread it another thought came to me, or a different way of saying something.

By Wednesday I thought *I'm really obsessing now. That's as good as it's gonna get.* I attached the file to an email and hit send.

A reply came back a couple of hours later saying "Excellent job. Thank you."

I felt pretty good about it. Dawn was one of my favorite people in the company and I really didn't want to let her down. Although she was the kind of person who sees the quality in her employees and builds on their strengths, like I do, which is why I like her so much. She sees the best in others. That quality seems to be lacking in many executives these days, but she seems to hold onto that character in spite of what's happening around her.

I went out on the floor with my staff to chat and catch up since I had neglected them the last couple of weeks. They were all doing well. I felt an inner strength that was new to me.

Chapter 27

The Kidnapping of Shawn

We spent Thanksgiving Day with my mom and dad. My older sister, Debra's family was going to her in-laws for dinner but would stop by later to see us. The kids watched the parade with pap while mom and I put dinner on the table. She always cooked enough for an army and this time was no different. As we ate, we talked about my work, the kids' school, and what was on TV these days. We were a quiet bunch.

Just after we cleaned up, my mother's brother Gabe and his wife Mary stopped in for a visit. They came every holiday, bringing a bottle of wine and silver Virgin Mary medals she passed out to everyone. My mom always said, "put one in every window to keep evil out." And, true or not, we all did because who didn't want to keep evil away?

Debra arrived soon after them with Ben and her kids, Toni and Benny, who were the same age as my kids. They ran off to watch something on TV. We had finished eating but hadn't cleared the table yet. Mom was serving coffee and bringing out the pies. They had eaten earlier but grabbed plates and sat down to munch on cranberry sauce, stuffing and pies. Because no one made them like mom!

Debra's the talkative one, so the conversation got livelier when she came in. We caught up on what was going on in our lives, who did what, who said what, and got up to speed on all the news. Then the conversation rolled around to Christmas.

We always had Christmas Eve at mom's because she was the only one who knew how to make all that fish stuff. Being Italian Catholic, we celebrated the Feast of the Seven Fish. We had also been exchanging gifts between all of us on Christmas Eve since our kids were born and they loved this tradition. Mom made a point to have non-fish food, such as cheese pizza, butter spaghetti, and fried dough for the kids who didn't like the fish so much. That made them happy.

As it was getting later, Aunt Mary and Uncle Gabe had left. Everyone was tired, so Deb and I helped mom clean off the table, load the dishwasher and put food away, making sure we had filled containers of our favorite leftovers for home. We said our goodbyes and looked forward to Christmas Eve.

At home, Robin, Joel and I watched some TV before going to bed. The office would be closed on Friday, so I had a long weekend off. Gene was picking up the kids for his Thanksgiving celebration with them.

Volleyball had not been canceled. The group wanted to play and almost everyone showed up, giving us three teams. Shawn and I ended up on the same team, so we had some time together in between games.

During one intermission, we sat on the mats lining the wall together and talked.

"How was your Thanksgiving?" I asked him.

"I drove home to spend the day with mom. My sisters came and we had a nice day," he didn't sound convincing.

"Did you get Kenny?"

"No. I didn't get him for Thanksgiving. I don't see him at all this weekend. I got him for Christmas supposedly. I'm tired of thinking about it and worrying. I wish someone would just take me away from all this."

"Ah. Maybe some night I'll come and kidnap you to go dancing."

"I would love that!" He looked into my eyes and smiled.

Then we were called out on the court to play and broke the spell. *Darn.*

Saturday night I decided to act on it. I put on a clingy, yellow knit sweater with my tight jeans, and I drove over to his apartment. It was around 8:00 when I knocked on his door.

He called "come in." When I walked in, he was sitting in his recliner just finishing his sandwich. He cocked his head back and said "Hey! How ya doin?"

I sat down beside his chair and said "I'm kidnapping you."

"You are?" he said laughing. "Where are you taking me?"

"Yes. You'll see when we get there."

"Ok!" He sounded kind of unsure about this. "Let me get cleaned up."

He went into the bathroom, and I could hear him brushing his teeth. Then he went into the bedroom, coming out with a clean shirt on, and brushing his hair.

"How do I look?"

"Great!" I jumped up. "Are you ready to go?"

"Yep!" He turned off the TV, grabbed his wallet and keys, following me out to my car.

 Shelby & Shawn   ©   2023

I drove to the Sheradon Inn where a band was playing, which meant it was crowded. I paid for our cover and walked to the bar, Shawn following me. I ordered a tequila sunrise and Shawn a beer.

I waited for the drinks to come as he spotted a table and went to grab it. Just as I sat down with him, the band started to play, and it was too loud to talk. I downed my drink and told the waitress to bring me another one, then grabbed Shawn and took him out on the dance floor.

The Sheradon's dance floor was very small, always hosting a large crowd since it was the only place doing live bands anymore. Doing any kind of swing or cha-cha was impossible. Everyone just kind of stood in one place and bounced up and down.

We were laughing so hard we could barely stand up. Finally, they played a couple of slow songs, clearing the floor of those who had no partner. Shawn pulled me in close and held me tight as I nuzzled my face into his neck.

After two slow dances, the music got fast again, and the crowd was back. It had gotten very hot, so we decided to sit out a few songs. Back at the table, I was so thirsty, so I downed my drink and Shawn finished his off. I ordered another for each of us. Usually, I stuck to my two-drink limit, but I was enjoying the fun we were having so much, I didn't pay attention to how strong the drinks were.

We talked as best we could, but we were practically yelling and hearing was impossible still. We got up to dance some more and the effect of the tequila was starting to hit me. The last thing I remember was walking out into the fresh air, the cold hitting me in the face suddenly.

 Shelby & Shawn   ©   2023

I woke up on Shawn's sofa bed. I still had my under-garments on but I was wearing one of his long T-shirts. It took me a minute after opening my eyes to figure out where I was. I rolled over coming face to face with Shawn. He was laying on his back with his right arm over his head. He brought his left arm over to scoop me up and pulled me over to rest my head on his chest.

"How are you feeling?" He smiled at me.

"What happened?" I asked in a low raspy voice."

"You had a little too much to drink. I didn't want you driving home."

I looked up into his eyes and felt so much love, I couldn't resist; I leaned up to kiss him. He turned his head away. Feeling rejected, I rolled onto my back. He rolled over on his side to give me a peck on the mouth, but I didn't respond. The moment was gone. I got up to get my clothes, thanked him for being such a gentleman and taking such good care of me and I left.

I didn't know what to think or how to feel, I just knew I needed to get out of there. I was so embarrassed that I even let this happen. How was I going to face him again? What was he going to think of me now?

When I got home, I took a long shower and crawled into bed, crying until I fell asleep. I woke up around dinner time feeling melancholy and needing to eat. Once I got some food in me, I became less emotional and ready for the kids to come home.

He didn't take advantage of me. That's my hero!

Chapter 28

Dave's Party with Tequila

I didn't hear from Shawn over Christmas, and I didn't go to volleyball because of all the holiday stuff going on with the family. The Friday after Christmas, Gene took the kids for the week, so I was able to go play that night.

When I walked into the gym and saw Shawn, I blushed, giving him a little crooked-headed half-smile. He winked at me and smiled.

He must know how embarrassed I am.

No one there said anything about what happened. I felt a little relieved about that anyway.

We know how gossipy these groups are. And just what I needed was for Roy to get started again.

One of the regular guys named Dave Morgan was having a party at his house the next night and we were all invited. So, Saturday night, we all went to Dave's.

Everyone except Randy showed up. Bobbi came with one of her girlfriends, Amber, who was new to the group. They sat on the couch all evening just talking between the two of them but when Shawn came around, she got noticeably flirty with him.

Dave gave us a tour of his house. He had a nice-sized house with a lot of rooms and some neat artifacts, like a life-size suit of armor. *Money!* After the tour, some were all gathered in the game room, and some were in the kitchen talking.

Shawn was standing beside me leaning back against the kitchen counter when Tara said, "so we heard you like tequila, Shelby."

My face turned red. I didn't know what to say for a minute. I froze. My worst nightmare. I was feeling so insecure at that moment.

Then I backhanded Shawn's chest. "Did you tell them?"

"OUCH!" He said laughing as he pulled his arms up to protect his chest in case, I hit him again.

I walked past him into the game room as he followed. "Shelby!" Still laughing.

Roy was sitting on the floor holding a deck of cards. "You guys wanna play cards?" He said to us when we came in.

"Sure." We sat down on the floor and played blackjack for a while.

Soon someone noticed a blizzard had been going on and everything was covered. The guys jumped up to go out and scrape cars while the girls got on coats, boots, and hats to brave the cold.

As I was getting my hat and coat on, Shawn said "wait here. I'll scrap your car."

I laid down on the floor in the game room to wait with my head in my arms, closing my eyes, feeling very tired, a little insecure and very vulnerable.

He hadn't called me after that night. What was he thinking? How was he feeling about it?

I didn't want him to think less of me. And I knew he told his mother everything. What would she be thinking of me?

Soon Shawn came in, rousing me saying "Come on. Your car's ready."

I got up and walked outside with him. He put me in my car, *taking care of me again, warm fuzzies*, and said good night. The roads were horrible but thank God we all got home safely.

We never talked about it.

Chapter 29

Indoor Football?

Shawn called a few nights later to see how I was. "Did you have any trouble getting home the other night from Dave's?"

I was so relieved to hear from him. "No. My roads were cleared till I got home. When I woke up the next morning, it was bad though. I didn't have to go out in it at least."

"Me neither. So, let me ask you something." He changed the subject. "Have you ever heard of indoor football?"

"No, I can honestly say I never have."

"John is a big fan of this indoor football team that plays out of Johnstown, and he wants to know if we'll go to a game with him and Bev."

"Oh, that sounds like fun!" I said. "How much are the tickets?"

"I'll get the tickets."

"OK!" I checked my calendar for the Saturday in question and Robin would be with Gene. "Well, that weekend is good for me."

"Great! I'll give you the details when I get them."

"K. I'll talk to you later."

"Bye." We hung up and I wrote the date on my calendar.

When that Saturday came, I woke up feeling very sick to

 Shelby & Shawn   ©   2023

my stomach.

Should I cancel? But the money for the tickets. And I really want to go with Shawn.

We had decided I would drive to their apartment complex and meet them, so they didn't have to go out of the way to pick me up. When I arrived, they were waiting outside.

"I'm going to be honest with you," I said as I walked up to them. I have a bit of a stomachache, but I decided to muddle through. I don't want to miss this or waste the money for the ticket. But I wanted you to know if I seem a little off, that's why."

"I'm sorry you're not feeling well," Bev said.

"Are you sure you're okay to go?" Shawn asked.

"I think I'll be fine. Just don't ask me to jump up and down on the bleachers." I smiled.

"OK, let's go."

We jumped in Shawn's car to leave, and I began to regret it immediately. The roads were windy over the mountains which made my stomach churn even more. I tried to put the window down a crack to get some fresh air but it was so cold everyone yelled to put the window up.

What have I done? Sometimes, when things like this happen, like when things go wrong a lot, I feel like God is saying 'this isn't where I want you.'

I was glad when we arrived so I could get to the bathroom. Shawn had waited for me to come out, which was thoughtful of him, to walk me to our seats. John and Bev were already in their seats and the game had started.

"Can I get you anything?" Shawn asked when we were seated.

"Thank you so much. I think I'm okay right now."

"How bout some ice cream?"

"I don't think so. Maybe in a little bit I'll take a ginger ale."

He was very sweet, and I was grateful. I was a little embarrassed about having to run to the bathroom. So, we looked at our programs and John was explaining how this game worked. So, this was a gym with a 50-yard field set up and no sidelines. It was kind of fun to watch but when these guys went down, they went down on a hard concrete floor. Ouch.

At half-time the guys got us drinks.

"Feelin any better?" Bev asked.

"Not really but I think the ginger ale will help a lot. I feel bad that I can't have ice cream." We smiled at each other because ice cream was our favorite thing. "I hope I'm not ruining the evening for you all."

"Not at all. I'm having ice cream." she laughed.

"You should." I laughed back.

The game was just about over. John's team was winning. I asked Shawn if we could start walking out. I needed to get some air. We walked out toward the parking lot and stopped to wait for the others. We stood face to face, looking in each other's eyes as it started to snow, flurrying all around us. He leaned in to kiss me just as my stomach did a gurgling thing and I had to take a step back to pass it.

Ruined that moment ....

"I just have some kind of stomach bug and I don't want you to catch it." I said trying to cover up why I pulled away.

"I understand." He said. I wondered if he did. He seemed offended.

John and Bev came out happy that their team won. We got in the car to drive home just in time for the real snow to start falling. The roads in Johnstown got bad fast so we wanted to get down over the mountains quickly and safely.

Several times, because of my stomach, I had to roll the windows down and everyone yelled "It's cold!"

"I'm sorry." I couldn't wait to get to my car and drive home. I was so embarrassed.

He'll never ask you out again.

And he didn't.

Chapter 30

The Introduction of Joe

Now one person I didn't hear from often was Carol Tealing, or Carol Jenners now that she had married Peter. It was like she had disappeared off the face of the earth. Then one day, out of the blue, she called me.

"Hey! How are ya? How are the kids?" she asked very perkily.

"We are all doing fine. How are you and Peter?

"Well, that's the reason for my call. We are moving to Florida. I got a really good job offer and we're packing up. I was wondering if you could use our waterbed. We'll bring it over and set it up for you."

"Oh Wow! That's awesome. I think we could use it. Let me ask Joel when he gets home, and I'll let you know. Can I call you tomorrow?"

"That'd be fine. I'll talk to you then."

When Joel came in that evening, I asked him what he thought about it. I knew he'd like it and wanted it but I didn't want to presume.

"Heck yeah. I'll take it." he said without hesitation.

"I'll let her know to bring it over. We'll have to get down there and clean out your room so they can set it up for you."

"No problem. Just let me know when they're coming."

I called Carol back the next day and she said they'd come on Sunday with everything. That gave us till Saturday to clean up and make space for it. They were able to drive right up to the back door and carry it in. They worked very well putting it together and had it set up in no time.

"Are you sure I can't pay you anything for this?" I asked as they were leaving.

"No. Just glad someone could use it and we didn't have to throw it out."

"Well thank you so much! And good luck in your new job. Be safe traveling." I said all the right things and hugged.

"We'll still be here another couple of weeks to get the house ready to put on the market for selling. Want to have dinner one night before I leave?" Carol asked me.

"Of course. Let me know when and where."

A few days later, she called, "How bout the Sunset Cafe for dinner Tuesday?"

"I can make that. What time?

"About 6:00. And by the way, my friend Joe Barnes is coming too. He lives in Johnstown and wants to come say goodbye as well. Is that okay?"

"Oh sure. That'd be fine. I'll see ya then." I hung up smelling a set up. I never heard her talk about this Joe Barnes before. *This should be interesting.*

On Tuesday morning, I told the kids I'd be out for dinner. I made sure they had some stuff they could pull out and heat up for

          Shelby & Shawn   ©   2023

themselves. I left the office a little later so I could go straight to the restaurant when I got into town.

I hadn't eaten at the Sunset for a long time. It was a big house turned restaurant with many rooms, a closed-in deck with windows all around, and upstairs rooms, all wood and rustic looking. It used to be one of the best Italian Restaurants in town until it was bought out years ago. It went downhill after that, but now it's under new management. The smell was enticing when I walked in. Carol and Joe were there at the bar waiting for our table. They waved me over.

"Shelby, this is Joe Barnes. He's an old friend of mine and we used to work together. Joe, this is Shelby."

"It's nice to meet you," we said simultaneously, shaking hands and laughing.

Our table was ready, and we were led to one of the back rooms downstairs with a window view. The place was crowded and noisy.

"So, you're from Johnstown," I said to Joe as we looked at the menus.

"Yeah … My wife was from that area. She passed last year so now I'm looking for a place down this way. I'd like to be back in this area again, probably sell the house there, if I find a job here, that is." He kind of laughed.

"He has an interview with my boss tomorrow. He may be taking my position." Carol said.

"Oh, well good luck. I hope that works out for you." I said.

The waitress came, brought us drinks and took our order.

 Shelby & Shawn   ©   2023

"I've been thinking about that lasagna all day!" I said, mouthwatering from the smell of sauce and garlic.

"How's the waterbed working out? Peter and I gave our waterbed to her son, Joel. We didn't want to have to move that big thing to Florida."

"He loves it!"

"What kind of work do you do?" Joe asked me.

"I'm an office manager trainee for The Auto Club. My branch is Somerset. I just transferred from Pittsburgh as a promotion. I'm so much happier. The drive is easier, and I can be home with my kids more."

"How old are they?"

Our food came and we dug right in, eating as we talked. Carol ate quickly and left in a hurry.

Just as I thought ... a fix-up.

Joe was a nice enough man, very good-looking, well built, but he had this goofy laugh. We stayed and talked for a little while after we cleaned our plates. Then headed our separate ways.

"Would it be alright if I called you?" he asked while walking me to my car.

"Sure." I gave him my phone number, got in, and drove home thinking how nice it was to be with a man who seemed confident. But I know as well as anyone not to trust first impressions.

He called the next evening. "I got the job."

"Terrific, I think. Is it what you want?"

"Well, the money's not as much as I was making but it will be in a couple of years. Now to find a place to stay while I'm commuting until I sell the house in Johnstown and buy one here."

He was easy and comfortable to talk to. We spent a while on the phone and then he asked me to dinner the following Friday night to celebrate.

"I'd love to. My kids will be picked up by my ex on Friday night at 6:00. I can meet you any time after that."

"How bout the Sunset again? The food was good there and I'm not familiar with the area yet to venture out much further. Is 6:30 okay?

"I'll be there!" I said.

I was so shy and backward as a young girl. One of the reasons Gene so easily manipulated and controlled me. The flip side of divorce for a woman going through a bad breakup is gaining so much confidence and strength. Sometimes you don't see it till you look back on it. I am so confident with men now.

So, let's open this new chapter and see how it writes out. Joe began attending my monthly single's group meetings at the church. He came to a lot of the events we had going on. We began spending time together independent of the group also.

And he began to play volleyball regularly. I knew it was more than friendship on his part. He was respectful but attentive in a romantic way. Over time, he helped me around the house, got to know the kids, took me to his house in Johnstown, and we went on day trips to various places.

I let him stay at my house when the snowstorms were bad. I wasn't letting him drive over the mountain in bad weather. He slept on the couch and always had the coffee ready in the morning when I got up.

One weekend, he asked me to go to Lancaster with him.

"There's a play at the Sight and Sound Theater I'd like to see called Behold the Lamb. We'd have to get a hotel and stay overnight since it's a long drive."

This was a challenge. I knew he was expecting us to sleep together.

"Well did I mention I plan on staying abstinent until marriage?" I asked, thinking I had mentioned it before.

"You don't really mean that though, do you?" He said laughing.

"Ah. Yes, I do." I insisted. "So, two beds in the room and you'd have to stay on your own side."

"Okay," he said, still laughing that nervous laugh and I got the feeling he didn't believe me.

We did go and I made him sleep in his own bed which made the situation uncomfortable. Things went south after that.

In this time, we spent together, the talk involved 'relationship' conversation. We were trying each other on. Unfortunately, it didn't take me long to know he was not a fit for me.

Like trying to fit a round hole in a square peg. We couldn't force it.

He was a charmer though and it didn't take him long to meet some other women in the group he was able to dazzle. We continued to stay friends (*another male friend*) and spend time together. He seemed comfortable talking to me and I was okay with that, though some of what he told me made me nervous and even more convinced he was not the one for me.

I tried not to judge but I have to determine 'what's right for me,' to set a line where I won't allow behavior to cross. The key to happiness in any relationship is knowing *What do I really want?*... then don't settle for less.

And I still hadn't fully given up on Shawn.

Chapter 31

My Mother's Fall

One Friday night in March, after volleyball and Eat N Park, I came home at midnight to find a message on my answering machine from my father. His voice was frantic.

"We're at the hospital, your mother fell, I rode in the ambulance so I don't have my vehicle here, can you come and get us?"

I went immediately to the hospital, entered the emergency room, and asked for Sam and Toni Good. They took me back to the room they were in just as the doctor came in. Mom was moaning obviously in a lot of pain.

"There are three vertebrae ruptured right in the middle of her back. She will need emergency surgery. I'm going to set this up as soon as possible."

Mom had been having problems with her back for many years. She had surgery on her neck 20 years ago that was very successful, but the doctors refused to do the middle back for some reason. She had been taking pain pills ever since.

"If you'd done the surgery before, she wouldn't have fallen. She could have been seriously injured or killed." Dad was giving the doctor a hard time now.

"She's having it now dad," I said. "No sense in being angry about it. Thank God it wasn't a worse fall." I was always trying to be the peacemaker, but the truth is, I was angry too. Who knew how bad this was going to get? I walked over to mom. "What happened?"

 Shelby & Shawn © 2023

"I lost my balance and fell down the basement steps. Just the last 3 or 4." she said softly.

"Yeah, this is what it takes to get some help around here." Dad wasn't going to let it go, I knew that.

"Is there anything more we can do tonight?" I asked the doctor.

"No. We're going to strongly sedate her for the night. You should go home and get some sleep. Be back early in the morning. I'll call you if anything changes."

"Come on dad. I'll drive you home." Mom was on the verge of falling asleep from the sedative already. "We'll be back tomorrow mom." I gave her a kiss.

"I want to stay here," Dad said.

"We don't allow anyone to spend the night, sir. Get some rest tonight and she needs to rest too."

We convinced dad to go home so we waited till mom was sound asleep before we bid her good night and walked out. I drove him to his house and walked him in the door. He was kinda shaky himself and I didn't want another accident tonight.

"Call me if anything changes and let me know what's going on. I'll be back at the hospital as soon as I get up." I said as he went inside. "Did you call Deb?"

"No. I'll call her now." His voice caught in his throat, and I couldn't tell if he was crying.

I thought about staying but I had run out the door when I got the message without even showering or changing my clothes

 Shelby & Shawn   ©   2023

after volleyball. I gave him a hug before I left. When I got home, I took a shower, put my jamas on, and set the alarm for 7 am. I would jump out of bed and get up there right away to be with him unless someone called to say otherwise.

I couldn't sleep much. Tossing and turning, I thought about how old and fragile she was. She'd been on those pain pills for so long that she couldn't be without them now. *Why do these doctors prescribe pain pills instead of dealing with the issue to begin with?* I began to pray and soon fell asleep.

The alarm went off promptly at 7 am, waking me from a dead sleep. I got up slowly, dressed, made coffee, then headed to the hospital. No one had called me so I didn't expect dad to be sitting there when I walked in.

"They just took her down to surgery about 10 minutes ago. She had a rough night. The pain medication they gave her wasn't working or something."

"Oh no. I'm sorry to hear that. How long have you been here?"

"I got here at about 6. Debra said she'd come as soon as she got the kids off to school."

"Do you want some coffee?" I asked.

"I guess I could use some."

"I'll go get you a cup."

I had brought mine from home, but it was almost empty already. I had to go down to the cafeteria to get us fresh, not out of a machine. When I got back, he was snoring in the chair. I let him sleep, setting his cup down on the table for when he woke up. I

       Shelby & Shawn   ©   2023

wished there was another chair that I could have slept in. The bed looked inviting but that didn't seem appropriate, I laughed to myself.

I watched Good Morning America till dad woke up about 20 minutes later and wanted the news on. Deb got there about 8:30.

"Any word about what's going on?" she asked.

"No," dad said. "They took her down about 7, just before Shelby got here."

"Where's the coffee?" Deb asked.

"Well, if you want the machine, it's right around the corner there. The good stuff is down in the cafeteria." I told her.

"I'll go for the good stuff." She said.

"I'll go for a refill," I said and got up to go with her. "You ok dad? Are you ready for a refill too?"

"No. I'm good."

As Deb and I took the elevator down to the ground floor where the cafeteria was, she asked what happened.

"As far as I know, she fell down the basement steps, the last three or four she said."

"She could have been killed." She was just as upset as dad the night before.

"Yes, I know. Dad was telling off the doctors last night about that very thing. I didn't think I was going to get him out of here. After mom fell asleep, he was able to leave."

          Shelby & Shawn   ©   2023

"What are we going to do about them?"

"Well, let's see how the surgery goes." I understood her concerns and I had thought of that too. They couldn't stay in a house that had steps if she was going to be stubborn like she was. No one was going to tell her not to do something when she got it in her head to do it. "Dad's going to have to be firm and not let her do some things. He's going to have to do them himself."

We got our coffee with some Danishes and went back up to the room. Dad was snoring again, so I scrambled around to get some more chairs to sit on while we waited. We put on game shows to pass the time. Dad got up and walked the halls for a while, coming back to sit down again. He did this several times until about 12:30 when the doctor came in to tell us mom is in recovery.

"She did really well. We fixed 3 vertebrae. She's going to have to do some therapy, but she'll be home before you know it."

"Great news!" we all exclaimed.

"She'll be in recovery for a couple more hours before they bring her up." the doc said.

"Come on dad. Let's go down and get a bite to eat. You must be hungry." Deb said.

"I am!" I said.

"Ok." Dad said, sounding a lot better.

While we were eating, we made a plan to cover visits so dad could go home and get some rest.

Deb said, "I could visit in the afternoon so dad could go eat and take a break."

"I could come up in the evening," I said. "We could bring the kids for a visit to lift her spirits. We really need to play this by ear depending on how long she'll be in here."

We went back upstairs, chatting and laughing, feeling very optimistic about her quick recovery. At almost 3 pm they brought her into her room, adjusted her tubes, and hooked up her vitals. They said she would sleep through the night so there was no need to stay. Dad wouldn't leave but Deb and I went home to get some rest.

"I'll be back up around 5:00. What do you want me to bring you? Any food? Drinks?"

"No, I'll just get something here if I want anything."

"Ok." I leaned down and kissed his forehead. I went home and slept for a couple of hours. I woke at 5:30 and rushed to get out the door again not wanting dad to think I forgot him. When I got to the hospital dad was standing outside the door of mom's room with his hand up to his face.

"What happened?" I said as I approached him.

"I don't know," he said. "Suddenly she started convulsing. They kicked me out."

"It'll be okay, dad." I rubbed his shoulder to reassure him.

Soon the door opened, and the doctor came out. "She had an allergic reaction to morphine. Has she ever had that happen before?"

        Shelby & Shawn   ©   2023

"No." Dad and I both said at the same time.

"It wasn't in her charts either so I'm not sure what caused this. She has been on a lot of pain pills in the last few years. That might have played a factor. Well, we got this under control but she's going to have to get off those pills."

"Ok." Dad said. "Can I go back in now?"

"Yes."

I followed dad into the room and mom was awake.

"How are you feelin?" He asked her as he took her hand and sat on the bed beside her. I'd never seen my dad like this. Mom always took care of him. Wow! He must really be scared.

"I don't feel well," she said, soft and weak. "It hurts."

I stood beside dad, looking at mom, and said, "You're going to have to take it easy for a while, mom. You won't be able to do as much but it's ok. We'll all help."

We stayed a little longer until the nurse came in with a pain pill. "You'll have to leave now. She really needs to rest."

So, dad and I went home to rest. I called Deb and told her what happened with the medication.

She wasn't surprised. "Mom's been taking pain pills for so long it had to have some kind of effect on her sooner or later. It's another thing dad will have to keep control of. I'll be bringing the kids in tomorrow to visit her."

"See ya then." I hung up and called for Joel and Robin.

 Shelby & Shawn   ©   2023

Chapter 32

Final Family Time

When Gene answered the phone, I gave him some background on what was going on.

"My mom's been in the hospital for a couple of days. She had a bad fall and had to have surgery. I wonder if you could bring the kids home early to visit. She can really use the family around her now to boost her spirits."

"I'm sorry to hear that," Gene said. "Sure. I'll bring them home." He then said to Robin, "Here, it's your mom."

"Hi sweetie. I just wanted you to know your grandmas in the hospital." I said to her.

"Why? What happened"

"She fell and had to have surgery on her back. Then she was allergic to the medication. She's in a lot of pain now. Your dad is going to drop you off earlier so you can visit with her for a while. It might lift her spirits."

The receiver was muffled, and she got back on. "He said he'll bring us in around noon."

"Okay. Come to the house and we'll drive up together then." I hung up and went straight to bed, but still tossed and turned most of the night from bad dreams.

The kids and I arrived at the hospital on Sunday at about 1:00 pm. Deb, Ben and her kids were already there. They weren't happy that we had that many people in the room, so Ben took dad,

Joel, and Benny out for a walk around while Deb, Robin, Toni, and I stayed to visit for a short while.

Mom was really giddy from the meds, so she was slurring her words being silly and had everyone laughing. When she started looking tired, we went out and let the boys have a chance to visit. They were not in there long before she fell asleep. We all decided to take dad out for dinner to make sure he was getting away for a while and eating.

"She's been pretty good today," he told us at the restaurant. "She is sitting up, talking, and eating. Not complaining too much about the pain. Just when the meds are wearing off and it's time for another pill."

"That's a good sign." Ben said.

"Are you going to have any trouble monitoring her meds at home, dad?" Deb asked him. "Cause you know we can look into a day nurse for you if you want."

"I think I can manage but I'll keep that in mind." We all knew how stubborn mom could be.

"She was really giddy and laughing with us," Toni and Robin were telling him some of the silly stuff she was doing.

After dinner, we all went home, hoping to get a better night's sleep after the positive interaction we had with mom. I stayed up with Robin and Joel for a while till they went to bed then I followed.

At 3:15 am the call came. I woke Robin and Joel, and we went immediately to the hospital. Deb's family arrived shortly after us. They had moved her to intensive care. She'd had a stroke. They let us go in two at a time to see her, but she didn't know who we

 Shelby & Shawn   ©   2023

were. By 5:30 am she had passed.

We all sat in the hospital waiting area for a long time in shock, not knowing what to do, not wanting to leave, and just holding on to each other. Eventually, we knew we had to go home. The next day we met at dad's and began funeral arrangements.

I called work to let them know I would not be in for a few days. They sent flowers from the company to the funeral home. That meant a lot to me. It was a most difficult time for us all. The funeral was exhausting.

We were blessed to have so many friends offering support. Everyone from my office came to the viewing and brought food. My dear friend, Anne, was there with me all afternoon after the viewing. Most of my friends from volleyball and my singles group came to the evening viewing. Other relatives we hadn't seen in years showed up to support dad.

Shawn walked in that evening with Roy and John. When I saw him, I walked over and put my arms up to hug him. He grabbed my wrists and pushed me away. I was confused, but let it go. I turned to hug Roy and John who hugged me back easily.

Then I asked if anyone brought the volleyball. They just looked at me, stunned. I chuckled, "It was a joke. Almost everyone from volleyball has been here." *Just trying to ease a tense situation with a little humor.* I introduced them to my family, then they walked over to stand with the rest of the group.

The next morning was the church service. My mom and dad belonged to St. Bruno's in Greensburg. As we processed in behind the casket, I saw Randy, Greg, and Joe all standing in separate pews in the back. It was a comfort knowing they were there.

Randy and Joe came to the reception. They sat with me and the kids to eat. Father Blaine, who presided at the service, sat with us too. The conversation led to the single movement as I laughingly called it.

"The single, separated, and divorced in the church need support from our Christian community. This is a very difficult time for us. There needs to be a place for us here." I said to Father Blaine.

"You are right. We don't think about it like that. You're welcome to have the church hall for your meetings if you need to at any time."

"Thank you."

The guys both left at the same time. They made sure I got big hugs before leaving, letting me know "if there's anything you need."

We cleaned up and went home, feeling empty and sad.

Deb and I went to the house the following weekend and helped dad clean out her things. We split up what we wanted to remember her by, giving the rest to goodwill. I took her jewelry. Deb was more her size and build so she took most of her clothes. There wasn't much. Mom never believed in spending money on herself.

We cleaned the house thoroughly and made sure there was food. Dad didn't know how to take care of himself. At one point he exclaimed emotionally, "What about the bills? Who's going to pay the bills?"

"I'll come over and see that he gets that taken care of." Deb said. "I'll show you how to write out the checks to mail, dad."

When we left, we made sure dad would call us if he needed anything. The fact that I worked a full-time job and Deb didn't mean she would be picking up most of the care for him.

"I'll help when I can," I told her. "Just let me know what you need."

"I will." We hugged him and left knowing he'd have a hard time with it. They'd been married fifty-five years. How do you live without someone after that long? *Lots of Prayers.*

Anne stepped in and began calling me almost every day. We spent a lot of time together and I became another daughter to her. *And she is a second mother to me.*

     Shelby & Shawn   ©   2023

Chapter 33

Harrisburg on Business

The day after the funeral, I had to go on a business trip to Harrisburg for two days. This had been scheduled months ago and I didn't want to cancel out and lose money for the hotel and conference fees.

Gene had agreed to drop Robin off at Deb's Sunday night. Joel would have Tom and they could stay by themselves for a couple of days. I had so much food left over from the reception that I called some people to see if I could unload it. *No such luck.* What the boys didn't eat, I ended up throwing out.

On my way out of town, I stopped at Dollar General to get snacks for the drive. *Peanut M&M's, can't go without those!* I bought a big one-pound bag along with a bottle of water.

I took interstates to avoid toll roads and traffic on my way down. Spring had arrived, so the drive was full of natural wonders, farmlands, and such that I always love. The air had that pungent smell of fresh fertilizer you could only stand for so long before you had to roll up the windows and turn on the air conditioner.

Once I arrived in Harrisburg, I found my way to the hotel, checked in, and ran a hot bath, soaking for a long time feeling depressed and exhausted. *I just buried my mother. She didn't even get to see my house. What was going on with Shawn?* I felt weak and lonely. Crawling out of the tub, I dried off and got into bed.

When I woke, it was pitch black in the room. I fumbled for the light, turned it on, and looked at the clock. *10 pm. I slept all day. I'm starving.* I called room service and decided to treat myself to a steak with all the fixins, along with a glass of wine. It didn't take long to get to me, and I ate every bite while watching

 Shelby & Shawn   ©   2023

television. Oddly enough, when I finished, I fell right back to sleep, sleeping through the night.

Fortunately, I remembered to set the alarm for 7:00 am. I had to be at the conference by 8:15 to pick up my packets, badge and schedule. There was a long line when I got there but I recognized many employees from other area offices in Pa. Some others I talked to but never met in person, so it was nice to put a face to a name.

Once I got my packet, I went into the conference room, found a seat off to the side in the back, put my things down, and went for coffee. There were Danishes and cookies, but I was still full from the steak dinner the night before. I spotted Kelly Stone and Jenn O'reilly from Pittsburgh and went to talk with them while sipping at my coffee.

"What time did you guys get in last night?" I asked.

"It was late, like around 8:30 pm. We all went to the bar after checking in. When did you get here?"

"I was here earlier in the day."

"We're sorry to hear about your mom," Jenn said.

"Thank you." My emotions were raw, so I was glad they began to make announcements. We all went back to our seats.

There were many speakers lined up for the day, with a short break mid-morning and mid-afternoon. During the breaks, I always tried to chat with employees from other offices to get an idea of how things are done so differently. We got an hour's lunch, provided by the company, and the amount of food was incredible. They served soups, salads, sandwiches, and drinks with a couple of different desserts. It was hard to stay focused after eating like that.

          Shelby & Shawn   ©   2023

The speakers for these conferences tend to be very long- winded and boring.

We knocked off at about 4:15 and had some free time till dinner at 6:00. I brought my bathing suit to do laps in the hotel pool for about an hour so I would be tired tonight for better sleeping. When I got back to my room, I took a shower and dressed for dinner.

I got there in time for introductions and more announcements, then they started going up to the buffet by tables. I sat with Sonya, one of the directors of the conference who was on the support team for us. I talked to her on the phone every day but never met her. She looked nothing like I would have imagined. She was very thin, with mousy brown hair and a soft, gentle voice. I loved chatting with her; she was so delightfully friendly, everyone's go-to for questions and information.

"I remember when you were new," she said to me, "and working in New Kensington by yourself."

"I was learning everything on my own. You were such a huge help to me. I can't ever thank you enough." I said.

"And where are you now?" she asked. "Didn't you just get moved up?"

"Yes. I'm the manager in Uniontown now."

"Congratulations!" She said, "Look how far you've come. How many years did it take?"

"I've been with the Motor Club for 12 years now." I couldn't believe it myself.

Look how far I've come indeed. The withdrawn introvert

        Shelby & Shawn   ©   2023

coming out of her shell. That seems to be a thought coming to my mind a lot lately. Do I really want to be with a man who can't give me support and encouragement on my journey? Wasn't that part of the problem with Gene?

I snapped back to reality as Sonya was still talking and I missed part of what she was saying. Then I heard *mother* and realized she was offering her sympathies.

"Thank you." I said. "She had a stroke after having surgery from a fall. It was very sudden." I felt myself choking up. "Well, I think I'm going for more of that dessert." I said, excusing myself to compose my emotions.

At the dessert table, I ran into Joy Marshall. She had been moved up to supervisor when I left Pittsburgh and she was very excited. I was excited for her. She was one of my best girls and she surely deserved it.

"Congratulations!" I gave her a big hug.

I took my dessert back to the table and Sonya was mingling around the room with other people. The other girls at the table said a bunch of them were going to the bar afterward if I'd like to come.

"Oh. No thanks. I'm kinda worn out." I finished eating, excused myself, and went back to my room. My pajamas felt very comfortable, and the bed pillows were soft to sink into as I turned on the TV, found some old movie, and fell asleep watching it. However, I was up several times during the night for various reasons.

So, when the alarm went off promptly at 7:00 am. I struggled to get up. I had prepared the coffee machine the night before, so it was ready when I got out of the shower. I drank one cup as I dressed, disliking the taste of it and decided not to make

    Shelby & Shawn   ©   2023

more. I hurried down to the conference room where fresh coffee would be served along with the other breakfast items. Today I was hungry, so I filled my plate with pastries and cookies, taking them back to my seat.

The talks began on time but today would only be half a day. During our morning break, everyone ran back to their rooms to pack up and check out, getting back to the conference room in time for the speakers to begin again. They wrapped it up around lunchtime. Some of the ladies were going to eat before leaving, but I passed on that so I could get home to get Robin who was staying at her Aunt Deb's.

Driving the turnpike was faster so I made good time, stopping once at a rest stop to use the bathroom and grab a bite to eat at the fast-food place. Music always faded in and out on the mountains, so I had several CDs to play with my favorite songs. The weather was nice so the windows open and music blastin made the trip much livelier. I had a good time at the conference and learned a lot to bring back and share with my employees.

Once again, I thought about my life. *How blessed I've been to be thriving at establishing my career,* another goal I had set for myself when I divorced. *Funny! My goals were to finish my education, establish my career, build my credit and buy a house.* Not once had I thought about remarrying, although I had been dating a lot, had a couple of serious relationships, and was engaged once *but deep down I knew I wasn't going to marry them.*

Perhaps the meaning of life is not to find a man to love but to find a life to love.

Chapter 34

A Visit from Cindy

When I picked up Robin from Deb's, I swung by and got Joel and Tom. I took them all out for dinner. We had a nice time chatting about their cousins, Toni and Benny.

"Aunt Deb let Toni and Benny stay home from school today. We went to the mall, then for some lunch." Robin told us.

"Wow! So you're getting to eat out today twice!`` We laughed. The boys didn't think it was funny.

"We've been eating leftover lunch meat and food from gram's funeral for two days." They crumbled but they really weren't mad about it.

We finished eating, went home, found a movie to watch, and before we knew it we were all tired and went to bed. The next morning, I let them sleep in, leaving a list of chores on the table for them to work on that day. They will get back to school tomorrow.

When I arrived at work, I immediately began going through my notes, putting together a spreadsheet for my boss on what was gone over at the conferences.

One of the girls came knocking on my office door at about 11:30 am saying someone was here to see me.

"Oh." *Who is it?* I wondered. "I'll be out in a minute."

I finished up what I was typing, making sure I saved it, and went out to greet the person waiting for me. It turned out to be Cindy.

 Shelby & Shawn   ©   2023

"Hey!" I said, surprised to see her down here. "What are you doing here?"

She came up and hugged me. "I'm sorry I didn't make it to the funeral. I was out of town at my daughter's. I'm just getting back now and since I was going this way, I wondered if I could take you for lunch."

"You're so sweet. I'd love to. Let me get my things." She followed me into the office where I got my purse and a rain jacket, just in case.

"Wow! Look at you!" She said when she saw the office.

"Oh, it's nothing." I said. I did not want her to make a big deal out of it.

"You have really come a long way." She said.

"Thank you!"

She took me to the Smokehouse Restaurant in the historic district for lunch. It was very nice, and the food was delicious. I told her about what happened to my mom. She talked about her trip to her daughter's. We had a nice visit to catch up.

"Are you still dating that guy?" I asked since she had not mentioned it.

"Yeah. I still see him. He drinks a lot so I'm not looking for this to be a long-term relationship, but he's fun to hang out with and someone to date."

"Oh. Okay. As long as you're aware." I said feeling concerned about her again. I wondered if she wasn't settling because she didn't think she could do better. Cindy wasn't beautiful but she was cute.

I knew she could find a great guy if she wanted. But then again, like so many after the divorce, perhaps she just didn't want to be hurt or disappointed.

If we don't expect anything, we don't get let down. I know that feeling.

"You know you can do better, right," I said.

She just kind of shrugged and said, "Thanks for caring."

We hugged as we left the restaurant and she drove me back to work. It *was* raining.

 Shelby & Shawn © 2023

Chapter 35

Getaway With the Girls

It wasn't going to be much of an Easter this year. No one felt like celebrating, even the kids. Deb said we could come to her house for dinner, but she always went to her in-laws, and I didn't want to take that from her. She would need that from now on.

Gene took the kids for the weekend, and they were able to celebrate with his girlfriend and her kids. I stayed home alone and slept.

The following week, I got a call from a casual friend who I talked to occasionally. She was a member of my new group and came to the monthly meetings but didn't come to any of the events.

"Hi Shelby. This is Theresa Gerome. How are you?"

"Oh, hi Theresa. I'm fine, how are you?" I tried to keep the surprise out of my voice.

"I'm good. You're probably wondering why I called," she said rather shyly. *Yes, I was.* "Well, I wanted to say how sorry I am about your mother."

"Well thank you. That's so kind. And it's always nice to hear from my group members. I'm always interested in your opinions, ideas, and suggestions for group activities. Is there something you were wanting to do?"

"Well, a friend of mine, Mary Noble, and I want to go to Gettysburg to tour the battlefields on horseback. We heard you talk about it once and we would both love to do that. Maybe we could go for a weekend."

"Okay. Well, let me pull up some information and see what I can do. Is there any time that's better for you to go?" I pulled out my calendar to look at my schedule.

"No. Any weekend is good. Of course, we would want nice weather but who can predict that." She laughed.

"Yes, but you're right. The closer to spring and summer the better the chances of getting a nice day. Let me work on this and see what I can put together. I'll announce it at the next monthly meeting."

As soon as I had a chance, I got on the computer and checked out the prices for the horseback tour as well as the dates available. They were booking about six weeks in advance right now and required payment up front. I put in a date and let them know that my group would be calling to make their own individual reservations and payment.

The Auto Club didn't have any Marriott's in Gettysburg, so I searched for the lowest price with the best quality and found a room to sleep five with a patio entrance. I booked it with a free cancellation just in case.

I also found a ghost tour that I wanted and reservations in advance were also required. I typed all of this information into my newsletter to be passed out at the meeting.
At the meeting, I spotted Theresa coming in.

"Hey. I was able to put that all together. I have the information in the newsletter. I'll let everyone know when I make the announcement to see if anyone else is interested."

"That's great! Thank you." She sat down as I went to the podium and began with the announcements.

"There's information about a trip to Gettysburg in the newsletter with all the details. Thanks to Theresa for the idea. I have phone numbers for the tour of the battlefields on horseback. You must make your reservation and pay in advance. Please let me know as soon as you are locked in so I can adjust the hotel if necessary. Right now, I have a room for five booked. There's also a ghost tour that needs a reservation in advance but not payment so that's a little more flexible."

I made a few more announcements and we ate. The meeting that night was casual, but we were still getting large turnouts with new people who were coming back. Everyone was just enjoying the food and fellowship.

The following week I got a call from Theresa. "Sorry, it took so long. I had to leave a message and wait for a callback. Mary and I are locked in for the horseback tour and the ghost tour. We are so excited. This should be fun."

"That's great. So far, the only other person I've heard from is Joy Shannon. She doesn't want to do horseback riding but she's up for a weekend getaway. So there will be four of us."

That weekend came quickly. We all met at my place that Saturday morning and piled into my car. We packed snacks and had our coffee for the three-hour drive down, stopping only for bathroom breaks.

The last time I drove down this way was fall and the leaves were a blanket of color. This time, in the spring, the buds were coming out on everything, and the smell of fresh manure was strong everywhere. When we arrived in Gettysburg, we checked into the hotel, unpacked our things, and walked around to find a restaurant for lunch.

After lunch, Theresa, Mary, and I headed off to find the

stables. Joy went back to the hotel to chill. When we arrived at the battlefield, we checked in and then had to wait for the guides to get organized. We were given a short lesson on how to handle the horses and what to do in certain situations.

They let us pick the horse we wanted to ride and helped us mount. We were put in a single line, with probably 30 horses, a guide was in front, one in the rear, and one guide was positioned somewhere in the middle but occasionally got out of line to check that everyone else was staying in line.

Once everyone got moved into position, we were given headsets with cassette players that had cassettes in them. We proceeded forward and they told us when to turn on the cassettes, which transported us to the Civil War era and we were transformed into battle. Each step of the way, the speaker gave us details of all that was going on around us as though we were there in the middle of it.

It was extremely hard for me to not transcend the boundaries of the line we were told to stay in, to give the horse a swift kick in the side and run at full gallop across the fields. The two-hour tour embraced every nook of the imagination, and we were all sorry to see it be over.

That was fabulous!

We sat atop our horses waiting for our turn to dismount and our horses lead away to water and brush down by the stable help. We drove back to the hotel, where we all needed showers before going to dinner. Joy was still sleeping, so while Mary went first, Theresa and I sat on the deck and talked.

"Thank you so much for suggesting this trip, Theresa. I didn't realize how much I needed a getaway." I said. "This was a perfect choice."

"Well thanks for making all the arrangements for us." She said, "I think so too. That tour was incredible."

"Didn't you just want to take off in a full gallop across the field?" I laughed.

"Yeah! I kinda did. But some of those stories were so sad," she said.

"Yes. It's a part of our history that we don't want to think about. All the women who lost husbands and the children who were left orphaned."

Just then Mary poked her head out to let us know the bathroom was free. Theresa was going next, and Joy had come to life.

"What time is it?" Joy asked as we all walked back into the room.

"It's about 6:00 and I'm famished. Is the Irish Pub good for dinner?" I asked.

"That's good for me." Everyone agreed.

Theresa didn't take long, and I was next. We were all dressed, after checking each other's hair and make-up, and ready to go in no time. The pub was across the street and down a block, so we walked. The evening was cool and overcast with rain expected later. We brought jackets but no umbrellas so we may be running back to the hotel.

The restaurant was packed but we managed to find a tall table with stools. Across the room in the corner was a man playing the guitar, but no one could hear him for all the noise. The service was fast though, and the waitress had our drinks and our orders in right away.

"Shelby, I was sorry to hear about your mom passing. Was she sick for a long time?" Mary asked.

"No. She had a fall that required surgery. That all went smoothly but before she even left the hospital, she had a stroke caused by a blood clot. It was hard for us but at least she didn't suffer much." I started feeling emotion. "I don't want to bring the group down. Let's drink," we clicked our glasses together "To friendship."

"How was the horseback riding tour?" Joy asked.

"Oh my gosh! That was the most fabulous activity I think I've ever done." I said.

We told her all about the horses, the headsets, and taped stories as we quickly ate. We managed to finish, get out of the restaurant, and arrived in time for the ghost tour. That involved an hour and a half walking around Gettysburg, listening to stories about the war, the soldiers, and the ghost sightings reported by people over the years. We were all on high alert but disappointingly, nobody saw any ghosts that night.

It was a long walk back to our hotel in the rain that had managed to hold off until then, just as we expected. We all poured into the room, stripped off our wet clothes, put on warm, comfy pajamas, and crawled under thick, soft comforters. Someone turned a movie on, but I don't know what it was as my lights were out as soon as my head hit the pillow.

We were up early, packed, and checked out by 9 am. No one was quite hungry yet, so I went to the gas station and got some coffee to get us going. There was a miniature horse farm a few miles west of Gettysburg, right on the way home, that the girls wanted to stop at. When we got there, it was closed and didn't open for a couple more hours. No one wanted to wait so back on the road.

A little past Chambersburg, we found a small, quaint family-owned diner to stop at for brunch.

"I love finding these off-the-wall places. The food is delicious!" I said, as everyone agreed this would be a great place for brunch.

The rest of the drive home was long and quiet. When we got back at my place, we piled out, said our goodbyes, and each went our own way. I threw my overnight bag into the laundry room, flopped down on the couch, and crashed.

What a fabulous weekend! I was thinking about Shawn less and less.

When the kids came in from Gene's at 6:00, I told them all about my weekend and the fun we had.

"When are we going to do something fun? What are we doing this summer for vacation?" Joel asked.

"Do you have anything in mind you might want to do? I asked them.

"No. I hadn't really thought about it until now." Joel said.

"I'd like to go to Disney," Robin said. "That would be nice if we could go there."

"When I get to work tomorrow, I'll check out some prices on things and see what we can afford."

If it weren't for this job, I know I couldn't afford to do anything with the kids. My dream in high school was to be a teacher. That dream was never realized but I am grateful to have these opportunities now that I might not have had otherwise.

Turned out we were able to do a couple of things that summer, Disney being one of them.

Chapter 36

Summer Picnic Again

Cindy called one night at the beginning of May. "The traditional Memorial Day picnic hosted by Catholic Charities is coming up. Sharon is not participating much but has given me some instructions for what to get. I need you to pass the word along to your group members, so we know how many are coming. We're ordering food and some people are bringing items to pitch in."

"I can pass out some invites. I'll let you know a number when I have it."

I really didn't take part in the planning like I had the year before since I was not part of the original group anymore. I was glad to be under the umbrella of Our Lady's church now. I felt safer and more valued there.

Not too many from my group were interested in coming. They were all moving on from the typical separated and divorced functions, spending more time in the single life now.

"One woman who brings her seven foster kids every year insisted on bringing a whole sheet cake." Cindy said.

"That's very generous of her."

"And the guys have graciously offered to auction off themselves for a home repair of some sort. We thought this would be a riot. The proceeds will go back to Catholic Charities."

"That will be fun!"

"Bring your cash."

"Okay! Is there anything else you need?" I was anxious to get off the phone. I just didn't feel like I was a part of it so I didn't want to act like I was.

I announced it at my May meeting and got all the names of anyone interested from my group to her by the end of that week. They got their invitations a few days later and were calling me, excited about the auction. A couple of ladies I had lunch with one day were talking about finding the love of their life this way.

"That's a little far-fetched," I tried to tell her, but she would not hear it.

"You never know," she said. I could see trouble brewing here.

On the day of the picnic, I went to the pavilion with my contribution of macaroni salad. I walked around mingling then sat with the people from my group to talk while I ate.

Before long a big red truck came down the road and pulled into the pavilion parking lot. Randy has brought his entire clan, including cousins, as well as his new girlfriend. Kathy was a member of his old singles group, someone he had shown interest in then, but she had not reciprocated.

Apparently, she has changed her mind.

Randy hadn't been to volleyball in a while, so I didn't know he was dating her. I was happy to see it. Of all the women I had in mind to fix him up with, she was top of the list. I thought she'd be perfect for him. And I was glad to see them trying each other on for size.

I went over and gave them both a big hug.

"I'm so happy to see you both. How have you been" I sat with Kathy to catch up on how things were going, what she was up to, and all that. It was a good feeling to know they had found each other again. But as we talked, I got a gut feeling she still had reservations about it.

I also sensed some discomfort from Cindy and Randy, that this might be uncomfortable for me. And Cindy loved her drama anyway, so she was always making things out to be more than they were.

Again, that inability to be a friend without expectation. Just ignore it.

We got the auction started and it was a lot of fun. The men had been very generous in donating their time. The bids were things like a two-hour carpentry job, three hours of yard work, one drywall repair, and so forth. The women went crazy forking over a lot of money for this.

When this event wrapped up, I packed up my things to leave after hugs and goodbyes to those I was close to from my group. It was a fun day but I was tired and didn't want to deal with any more drama.

A couple of months later, I attended a Women's Day of Recollection at St. Joseph Center through the Dioceses of Greensburg. Kathy attended as well and it seemed she and Randy didn't work out after all. They had gotten engaged and then called it off. I was disappointed but understood why.

Randy's tough to be with.

I admired her ability to stay calm and reflective, keeping her composure, and not saying anything against him as some women might. Although she was taking all the responsibility on herself.

"Don't do that Kathy. I know Randy well and he's very difficult to be with." I told her, not wanting to see her beating herself up over him.

It seems like time goes on, the more failed relationships we have the more we look for blame. There must be something wrong with him or me. Otherwise, it would have worked out. I would be finding someone by now if I weren't so screwed up.

It took me a while to learn how inaccurate and immature that way of thinking is for, I have thought that way myself. It's no one's fault. It just doesn't work. People are different and don't always click together. It's just life.

A few days later I sent him an email telling him I had seen Kathy at the retreat. "I heard about the breakup. I'll be praying for you. I know this must be hurting you a lot. If you want to get together to talk, I'm here." I knew he'd drink his way through it.

He responded thank you and withdrew for a while, licking his wounds as we all do.

After a while, he came back to volleyball but didn't talk much to anyone.

 Shelby & Shawn   ©   2023

Chapter 37

Disney AND Philly

So, at work, I started working on our summer vacation plans. I called our travel reps for Florida. "Do we have any perks for Disney?" I asked them.

"As an employee, yes you do get Disney and Universal tickets. One of each is free. You would have to buy any more you may need after that."

Because my cousin, Tom, his wife Tammy, and their family, lived in Kissimmee and offered to let us stay with them, I drove my kids to Florida that summer. Now the drive to SeaWorld in Ohio last summer was the first time I'd ever driven out of state on my own.

This was a bigger challenge yet. And I'll be honest. I had a panic attack the day before I left. What am I doing driving across the country with a couple of kids?

But guess what. Not only did I drive down and back, I also drove all over the Orlando area. I took us everywhere. We spent a whole day at Universal Studios and that was a blast.

Now since Joel and Robin were teens and Joel had already been to Disney with a friend a few years ago, I wasn't sure how they felt about Disney. It was the 25th Anniversary and tickets were hard to get. But I would try if they wanted to go," I asked them.

"What do you want to do about Disney? Would you want to do Busch Gardens in Tampa instead?" I asked them.

"Tampa," Joel said right away.

 Shelby & Shawn   ©   2023

"I'll go to Tampa with you all. My kids love it there." My cousin suggested it.

Robin agreed to Tampa without too much arguing, though I knew she wanted to do Disney and was disappointed that we didn't. But we drove to Busch Gardens and spent a whole day with my cousin and her three kids who were 5, 4, and 2 years old and they really had a good time.

The rest of the time we spent on our own going out to eat and checking out the sites around the area, like Lego Land and Downtown Disney. Robin enjoyed picking out souvenirs and eating at the Hard Rock Cafe. It was a good time.

On the way home, we stopped to check out the Kennedy Space Center. This trip was an incredible milestone for me. By the time we got home, I felt like I could do anything. I prayed that I was being a good example to my kids.

No matter how much hardship we went through, we could overcome it and thrive.

Our second trip that summer was to Philadelphia. A representative from the visitor's bureau in that area came to the office and offered everyone a packet.

"This consists of a free hotel stay and a VIP pass to the city's attractions and trolley systems." He said handing us a manila envelope full of brochures and coupons from the Philadelphia area. "Just give me a call when you want to come, and I'll make all the arrangements for you."

When I got home, I told the kids about it. "Is this something you'd like to do? Do you want to go? I asked.

"Sure." Said Joel.

"Sounds like fun." Robin said.

"Fantastic! I'll make the arrangements for next weekend when you'll be home."

We got up early Saturday morning since it was a four-hour drive, stopping for lunch along the way. At about 11:00, we arrived and checked into the hotel.

There wasn't much time, so we took off right away to see the sights of the city. We went to the science center and the Ben Franklin Museum, kind of rushing through those to try and get as much in as possible.

We grabbed the trolley up the hill to the Museum of Art. They had a cafeteria there, so I got the kids a sandwich quickly. There was so much to see that we missed the trolley's last run back down to the city.

"What are we gonna do now?" Joel started to get a little upset.

"It's okay. We'll figure something out. We may have to walk down."

"We can't walk down. Look how far it is."

Fortunately, there were others coming out who missed the trolley as well. A nice security officer came out and, realizing what happened, got hold of the main dispatch to have them send another trolley up to get us.

"See. Everything's fine. We just must wait a little while longer for the ride down." I said to Joel as he calmed down.

I was a little nervous being on my own and responsible for two kids, but we were really getting the hang of this traveling thing. It was getting easier every time.

Once we got back down in the city, we found a nice restaurant to eat dinner just around the corner from the hotel. It was close enough to be safe walking back at night. A classy place, very crowded but the food was excellent.

Back at the hotel, we changed into our jamas and had ourselves a good old-fashioned pillow fight. That put us over the brink of fatigue, and we were ready for sleep. The next morning, we checked out and went to the Liberty Bell for the presentation and pictures.

On the way home, I drove through the Amish Country of Lancaster for lunch to give the kids a glimpse of what it was like to live there, the horse-drawn carriages and workers in the fields.

We ate at the Good N Plenty Home Style Restaurant for lunch, a unique experience for them. It was a good educational trip. I was so happy I could give them this experience and have this memory.

This would be the last summer I had my kids home with me.

Chapter 38

A Bon Jovi Kind of Summer

The summer was going by quickly as time always was these days. I enjoyed my work, my kids, my friends, and my alone time. It all seemed balanced now.

At my single's group meeting in July, Greg approached me.

"I heard somewhere you are crazy about Bon Jovi," he said.

I smiled. "I sure am. He's one of my favorites."

"He is going to be at Star Lake on August 24th. Would you like to schedule this as a group event? Do you think anyone would be interested?"

"Well, I'll tell you what. I'll announce it as an interest and see who bites. If no one is interested, we'll plan to go ourselves. Would that be okay?" I asked.

"That'd be great."

As everyone was eating, I got up to the podium and called for everyone's attention.

"I've been asked to see if there is any interest in going to a Bon Jovi concert at Star Lake in Pittsburgh on August 24th. The tickets are on sale now, so we must be swift to purchase them before they sell out. Anyone who's interested, please let Greg know by the end of this evening. Thank you."

Later, as the group was breaking up and everyone was leaving, I went over to ask Greg if anyone had approached him about it.

"Not one person," He laughed. "Either too much money or too far to go, I think."

And I agreed that was probably true. "Well, I am. Go ahead and buy the tickets. I'll pay you back when I see you next."

"That sounds like a plan. In the meantime, I'm putting together another peddle/paddle at Ohiopyle for the end of July. And what do you think about a baseball game?"

"That all sounds great. Call me with the details and I'll put them in the newsletter."

He called me the next night. The peddle/paddle was scheduled for the end of July, the baseball game at the beginning of August and he got the Bon Jovi tickets ordered. My head was spinning.

I got the newsletter updated and mailed out immediately, so everyone had time to sign up for the events they wanted to attend. I put my name in for the peddle/paddle and made my reservation. So did Joe Barnes with his son and another guy named Troy from Cindy's group was bringing his five daughters.

I asked Joel and Robin if they wanted to go but Joel had other plans and Robin feared being on the water in a boat. She would go to Gene's that weekend.

The day was beautiful. The peddling was easy. The paddle not so much. I ended up with Troy's 16-year-old daughter in my canoe with me. He took his 8-year-old with him and got a rubber ducky for the other three girls, two 12-year-old twins and a 14-year-old, to float down on. All the girls were full of energy and had a blast.

I was concerned about the safety of the girls. Troy wasn't. They were jumping out of the boat and splashing around as we were still moving down the river. When we got to the rapids, they were hanging over the sides screaming. Even the young lady sitting up front with me wanted to be daring and was always heading for the rocks.

Joe was with his son sharing a canoe and Greg had his own. They stayed as close to us as they could to jump into action if needed. I was at least grateful for that.

When we found a clearing and pulled over for lunch, I asked Troy if he was okay with them being so wild like that.

"Yeah! Their having fun!" was all he said.

"But aren't you afraid they're going to get hurt or worse," I said, still fretting over it.

"They'll be alright. They can handle themselves."

Well. They're his kids.

I had to admire him for teaching his girls to be strong and self-sufficient.

A few days after our adventure, I got an email from Troy with only an attachment. No explanation. Turns out the Outfitter at Ohiopyle, who randomly took pictures and sold them to the participants, had captured my concern for safety on film. The picture was of me and Troy's daughter in our canoe, in the middle of rapids, aiming for a very large rock, me behind her with my mouth wide open and a look of shock on my face trying to avoid said rock.

It was priceless. I replied, "Thank you! I'll treasure this forever."

Then of course he posted it on the internet for everyone to see. *I'm gonna kill him!*

Greg and I ended up going to the baseball game with John and Bev. I drove us all down in my car. The evening went without a hitch, and we had a really good time.

But the Bon Jovi Concert was the bomb!

 Shelby & Shawn   ©   2023

The man kept the crowd on their feet for three hours. He did all his best songs, number one hits, and had two ovations. For my favorite song 'I'll Be There for You' Greg and I danced right there in the field. We didn't even mind that we had to sit in the traffic of the parking lot for almost two hours to get out.

"That was the best concert I have ever attended." Greg said.

"Oh, man. I agree. He played all my favorite songs."

Greg's divorce was finally over, and his wife had moved out. He seemed much calmer now without all the paranoia. And they hadn't killed each other. *Like War of the Roses,* I chuckled to myself.

But he was ready to get out and date now. He called me more often and wanted to make plans to do things together independently of the group. One night he called to ask me for a last-minute date to Kennywood.

"My company is having their work picnic and I haven't been there since my kids were young. Do you wanna go? It's this weekend. I know it's short notice." He said.

"I don't have any plans at all for Sunday. I would just like to be home by 6:00 when my kids get home from their dads." I replied.

"That's not a problem. I'll pick you up around 10 am if that's okay."

"Sure, I'll be ready." I felt like a kid.

Wow. I haven't been to Kennywood for a long time either.

     Shelby & Shawn   ©   2023

We rode every roller coaster. His company had a nice spread of food for them, so we ate and rode some more. It was the most fun.

Greg and I got along well and he was very easy to talk to. But when I hung out with the guys in my group, I didn't consider it dating. *Another best friend* was always in the back of my mind.

Because the man I wanted to be with wasn't calling to ask me out. And the only time I saw him was at volleyball ...

when he came....

     Shelby & Shawn   ©   2023

Chapter 39

The Camping Trip

A few weeks before Labor Day weekend, Joe called to ask if I'd like to put together a camping trip for that weekend.

"Well, it's kind of the last minute. I can go 'cause the kids are with their dad but I'm not sure we're going to get anyone else interested." I said.

"I have another female friend, Althena, who wants to come on Saturday. Her son and grandkids will come on Sunday just for the day. Prince Gallitzin State Park is a nice area. I'd like to go up on Friday and set up to stay till Monday."

"Okay. Well, let me put the word out and see who bites. Go ahead and make the reservation. I'll definitely go. I'll see if my kids want to go but don't count on them. They hate camping, especially in tents." I laughed.

"Let me know when you know. They only allow two tents on one campsite so if we need more than that I'll have to reserve two sites."

"Okay." I called Cindy first.

"Hey, do you think anyone in your group would be interested in going camping over Labor Day weekend? I have a member putting together the trip. I know it's last minute, but I told him I'd put the word out."

"I doubt it. Not on this short notice. I'll check and let you know but don't count on it." She said.

"Okay. Thanks!" Next, I called Joy. I knew she liked these

last-minute getaway weekends so I thought she'd be interested if she could get off work.

Sure enough, she was. "Let me check my schedule and I'll get back to you but probably count me in."

Joy was much younger than most of us but seemed to like hanging out with the older crowds. And we all got along with her so it was a pleasure to have her along. She called me back a few days later and said she'd be coming. No one else responded.

I took Friday off and Gene picked up the kids early so I could get on the road. I had the tent, sleeping bag, and all the camping gear I had packed up to leave right away. I headed to pick up Joy, squeezing her gear in the trunk and back seat. My Sunfire wasn't very big for these adventures, leaving me at a disadvantage now.

It was a three-hour drive to camp. Joe was already there and had his stuff unpacked and set up. He had brought his canoe which he took down to the shore to sit for anyone who wanted to use it. A big blazing fire was going strong for roasting hot dogs, with a pot of beans set to the side.

We quickly unpacked and set up our tent before dark. The fire was inviting as the evening got cool and we were very hungry. Of course, we had to go into the woods to find our sticks for roasting hot dogs and marshmallows. They had to be long, thin but sturdy enough to hold the weight, meaning thicker down toward the holding end. It took great skill to find just the right one to last the entire weekend.

"I got mine," I said, coming back and handing it to Joe who had the knife for scaling the end to put the hot dog on.

"This is a good one." He said.

        Shelby & Shawn   ©   2023

"I've had a lot of experience finding sticks. I can get you some good kindling for the fire as well." I bragged a little, feeling like a child. "My dad always sent us off to find the kindling to make a good fire when I was a kid. It had to be thin and dry, no wet stuff. And bark was always a good fire starter."

"Your dad just told you to get you out of the way while they were making the fire." Joe said laughing. "He just wanted you out from underfoot."

"That's not true!" I said I was very offended. "He always used what we brought back, and I've always made fires easily with this tactic."

He just continued to laugh, not saying anything else. Joy came back with her stick, and we made hot dogs for dinner with the beans that had started to burn in the pot. We sat around the fire chatting about nothing much till the mountain air made us tired. One last trip to the bathroom before crawling into our sleeping bags for the night.

I woke to the sound of Althena arriving. Joe was already up to greet her. Joy was still sleeping so I crawled out of my sleeping bag quietly to not disturb her. Joe introduced me to his friend who was apparently someone he'd dated.

"We're old friends." She was very bold about telling me. "We dated a long time ago but now we still see each other as friends."

Joe just stood there laughing that nervous laugh, not knowing what to say.

"Well, I think that's great." I said and I truly meant it. She was sweet and really attached to him. It was easy to tell she still

 Shelby & Shawn   ©   2023

had feelings for him and wasn't giving up hope for a relationship there. I had to admire her for hanging in with him.

She hadn't brought very much in the way of gear. Seemed she was going to sleep on the ground by the fire. She was short, chubby, and blonde and I was unsure of how comfortable she would be sleeping on the ground, but Joe said he would sleep out there with her. They must have done this before.

"We're going out in the canoe for a while. What are the plans for later?" he asked me.

"I understand the Cambridge County Fair is going on. How would you all feel about going there?"

Joy stuck her head outside the tent saying, "that sounds like fun."

"Well good morning sunshine," Joe said to her. "Glad you could join us. This is Althena."

"Hi." They both said.

"Well, that sounds like a good plan. Let's eat there too so we don't have to get food. I have mountain pies for later when we get back."

"Oo that's a treat." Joy said. "But what's for breakfast?"

"I'm about to make some bacon and eggs." I said and started retrieving the items from the cooler, igniting the gas stove, and greasing the cast iron pans.

Joe and Althena headed for the lake to take the canoe out. Joy headed for the bathrooms to shower and dress. I had breakfast ready with plenty extra for anyone returning at any time who was

 Shelby & Shawn   ©   2023

hungry.

After eating my breakfast, I went for a run around the trails available in the campground. It was a beautiful day, sunny and warm with just a hint of color in some of the trees. *Fall is my favorite time!*
And I loved being in the mountains by a lake. Maybe one day I'll buy a lake house.

I dreamed of what that might look like someday as I ran a couple of miles through the camp. The smell of bacon cooking was everywhere. Some people were riding their bikes, and others just walked but everyone had a sense of peace and contentment about them.

When I got back to camp the others were sitting at the picnic table eating the leftovers and having coffee.

"How was your run?" Joy asked.

"Fabulous! I'm dreaming of buying a lake house."

"You do that. I'll come to stay with you." Joy laughed.

"You would be more than welcome. I'm headed to the showers."

I got my things to go take a shower and dress for the day. The water was cold by that time, so my shower was quick. I took time to dry my hair, I didn't go anywhere without my blow dryer, but refrained from putting on any makeup. I didn't feel the need for it.

Back at camp, everyone was getting ready to leave for the fairgrounds, which were about 30 miles away. Joe would drive in his truck that had a back seat for us so we fit comfortably.

"I want to go see the animals," Joy said when we arrived. So that was the first thing we did.

Althena wanted to see the craft tables and we walked all over the grounds looking at handmade crafts and the 4K projects. Joy and I rode some rides until we got on one that went backward, making us sick. After that, we had to eat something to settle our stomachs down. More walking around to look at crafts and it was getting dark. Time to head back to camp.

"I want to light the fire," Althena said to Joe when we were riding back to camp.

"Althena's making the fire when we get back." Joe said to us.

"Okay." We said, not understanding what the big deal was.

So back at camp Althena lit the fire and Joe made us mountain cakes. It was apparent she was in love with him and may have been a little jealous of me or threatened by me. I had no interest in him, so I didn't know where this was coming from, but I also didn't know what he was telling her. Maybe he was using me to make her jealous. *Oh, the games we play.*

We sat around telling jokes and stories till it got late and cold. I was the first to turn in.

"If you don't mind, I'm getting up early to take the canoe out." I said to Joe.

"That'd be okay," he said.

Joy came in a short time after me. We both fell asleep quickly, exhausted from the day. I woke up at dawn. There was

 Shelby & Shawn   ©   2023

still fog on the water. I paddled around the perimeter of the lake staying close to the shore, so I didn't get lost. When I got around the other side, the fog had lifted, and the motorboats were coming out.

To my surprise, I was pushed out to the middle of the lake. I had a difficult time getting back to shore. Every motorboat that went by swung me around to go the wrong way. I would no sooner get turned around and aimed back at the dock again than another motorboat went by and swung me around again. This went on for a good hour. Some people on shore fishing were watching and getting concerned.

"Do you want us to send you some help?" They called.

"I think I'll be okay. Thank you." I called back but I was exhausted, and my arms were hurting.

I finally got well enough into the peninsula that the motorboats were not coming around. They were out in the deeper water. I paddled past the dock to the shore where Joe had tied the boat, putting it back where it was supposed to be. I walked up to the camp area where Althena and Joe were sitting at the picnic table having coffee. I made myself a cup and sat down, telling them my canoe story. Joe was upset but I was laughing.

"Don't worry about it. Who knew all those motorboats would be out there practically running me over. I'm fine. I made it back. It's no big deal."

Joy was still sleeping, and no one had made an effort to cook breakfast, so I got up and started pulling everything out. Just then Althena's family arrived. Her son, his wife, and their three-year-old son who was just as cute as a button.

I made a huge breakfast for everyone, consisting of bacon,

sausage, eggs, and pancakes. They brought donuts and we had a lot of food. Joy got up in time to join us.

After eating, Joy and I got our bathing suits on and took little Jeremy to the beach for swimming and sandcastle building. We taught him how to dig tunnels with our hands all the way through the castle. He loved it. Joe was sitting in a lounge chair on the grass watching us.

"Where's Althena?" Joy asked.

"She wanted to spend some time with her son." He said. I remember Joe telling me once he didn't get along with her son and that was why they stopped dating. Soon her son came down and got Jeremy to go home. Althena got packed up and left as well.

Joe, Joy, and I lay on the beach for a long while till the sun started to set and the air got cool. We all showered and dressed for a cold evening. Back at camp, we packed up as much as we could to be ready for leaving in the morning. I helped Joe get the canoe in his truck.

In the morning we got up early, made coffee, and had the leftover donuts from the day before, since the pot and pans were already packed. Joe stayed for a while but soon left. Joy and I took our time with the tent and packing everything up. We were tired on the drive home, so it was quiet.

I dropped her off and couldn't wait to get home for a long hot shower.

It was a good tired.

Chapter 40

Football and Rock Hall

When I arrived at the gym the following Friday night, everyone was standing outside waiting for the person who had the key and ball. John and Bev were leaning against their car talking to Joe and Sam when I walked up to join them.

"Hey," they turned to me when Joe and Sam walked away. "Shawn couldn't make it tonight, but we wanted to ask you about something."

"What's up?" I asked.

"We want to go to the Football Hall of Fame and the Rock N Roll Hall of Fame some weekend. Would you want to go?" John asked.

"Oh yeah! That sounds like fun. Have Shawn give me a call to set it up. I'll see what kind of discounts I can get at work. I'm sure I can get a hotel room at least."

"That'd be great! We'll all pitch in," said Bev. "There are discounts online for the Rock Hall if we join their club or something."

"Ok! Count me in!"

I was feeling very excited. Another weekend getaway with Shawn. Of course, the more time we spent together, the more we'd get to know each other to determine if we were fit. The attraction was definitely strong, but avoiding that temptation was difficult. This time we would be sharing a room with John and Bev so there would be no temptation to worry about.

Weeks went by waiting for Shawn to call me. He didn't show up Friday nights either. I wasn't sure what to think. Finally, I asked John and Bev one Friday night what was going on.

"I'm not sure," John said. "We still want to go."

"Shawn seems to be dragging his feet. I asked him why but he didn't really say." said Bev. "We thought something was wrong between you two that he didn't want to tell us about."

"I don't know what it could be." I said, but I had a hunch. I believed he was intimidated by my success. *He is so insecure. I didn't think he could handle it.* "I'll talk to him." I felt like we were good enough friends for this to be a non-issue.

I waited a few days and then gave him a call. "Hi Shawn," I said when he picked up the phone.

"Hi Shelby." He sounded friendly enough.

"So I hear you and I are going to be travel partners again."

He laughed. "Sounds like trouble."

I laughed too. "Only for you." I said.

"Oh. So, what's that mean? You're all going to gang up on me."

"Sounds like a plan." I said. More laughing "So when is this happening? I'm available any weekend."

"Let me look at my schedule and talk to them. We'll get back to you."

"Ok. Take care." I hung up before he said goodbye. I was

 Shelby & Shawn   ©   2023

beginning to have a bad feeling about it. Something felt off in my gut. I felt like I was begging him to do this.

A couple of days later, Bev called me. "Hi. How are ya?

"I'm good. How's everything with you?"

"Good. Shawn said any weekend would be ok with you, so we picked the 20th & 21st. That's the weekend before Labor Day. Is that ok?"

"Yeah, that'd be great. I'll get right on booking a hotel room for Saturday night in Cleveland. We're all staying in one room, right?"

"Well John and I would like to be alone, but it'd be ok to share and save money."

"Ok cause I can only get one room at my discount. And I can get tickets to the Football Hall of Fame. They're free."

"Oh, thank you so much. Then John and I will get the Rock and Roll Hall of Fame ticket discount off their website. I'd really like to go to the zoo and I think those tickets are really cheap."

"Well before you buy the Rock Hall tickets, let me see if I can get a discount?"

"Okay."

"Sounds like everything. That was easy."

"Cause the women did it." she said as we laughed. I really liked Bev. I think we would be friends without John and Shawn.

"I'll touch base with you when I have everything finalized

and let you know."

"Ok. Talk soon." We hung up and I got right onto the website to see what Marriott's were available in Cleveland. With my auto club discount, I got a very nice room very cheap, so I booked a double queen with an indoor pool in case anyone felt like going for a swim after dinner.

Thank God I got a queen. Some of those beds are so small for two people to fit and Bev's a little chubby.

The next day at work, I called my contacts at the visitor's bureau in Ohio and asked about getting some tickets to events in their neck of the woods. She offered me the Football Hall of Fame tickets, as I knew she would, but just as I thought, could not come up with any Rock Hall tickets. She did offer tickets to the Science Center in Cleveland, which I took not knowing if they'd want to do that, but no harm to having them. I thanked her and the tickets arrived in a couple of days.

I called Bev that night. "I got the Hall of Fame tickets, the hotel booked and as an extra bonus, she threw in Science Center tickets in Cleveland," I told her.

"That sounds great. If we leave at 6:00 am Saturday morning, we should arrive at the Hall of Fame just as it opens. We'll have the morning there before heading to Cleveland. We can spend the afternoon at the Zoo and then check in to the hotel before dinner."

She had it all planned out. *Now there's someone I can travel with.* I loved knowing we had a plan and wouldn't miss anything. *Without a plan, it's always chaos.*

"Sounds like you've thought of everything. Who's driving?"

          Shelby & Shawn   ©   2023

"Shawn said he'd drive. We'll pick you up around 6:00 am Saturday."

"See ya then!" I hung up feeling a little better about this trip.

On Friday night, Gene picked up Robin and I finished packing, then set my coffee pot on auto for 5 am and went to bed. I woke up needing that cup of coffee to get going. They pulled up out front and waited for me to come out. Shawn jumped out to throw my overnight bag in the trunk. I jumped in front saying hi to John and Bev in the back.

"Good morning," they both mumbled barely audibly.

I got comfortable enough to lean against the window and doze off. Shawn knew the way and didn't bother us for directions. Ninety minutes into the trip we were up and ready for a bathroom break that included fresh coffee.

On the road again we were right on schedule and arrived at the Football Hall of Fame as they were opening. Just as we were going in I got a call from the office. I was going to turn off my cell phone for the weekend, but I knew the office did not have a manager available. I walked off to answer it, knowing it would be a problem to solve. Fortunately, it was a simple one and I joined the group at the door to go in.

"Work?" Shawn asked as I walked over to him.

"Yeah. Nothing important."

"I get calls from work too." he said and walked on ahead of me.

OK! What was that about?

We walked through, talking about our favorite players, wanting pictures with the busts, reading all the plaques and watching all the videos. We were all huge football fans so it made sense we would all know a lot about the game, but it seemed to bother Shawn that I knew as much as he did.

Am *I being too arrogant about it? I was just excited.*

We came to an arcade room where there was a game of throwing a football through a hole in the backboard. They all tried once and missed. John and Bev walked away but Shawn watched me. I threw it right in. I turned to hand the ball back to him, but he walked over to them and I heard them mumble "She get it in?"

"Yep." Everyone walked on leaving me behind.

"I can't help it I'm good at throwin a football," I tried to redeem myself, but no one was listening.

I really felt uncomfortable after that. I tried to make a joke of it but I felt like I was being shunned. Shawn walked with John and Bev and I was just keeping up. Every time I got excited about something we saw, they all walked away from me.

After a couple of hours, we headed to Cleveland. We could not find the hotel exit, so I looked for the map.

"The map's back here," Bev said and pulled it out.

I tried to tell her what we were looking for, but she didn't get it.

"Here," I said impatiently, annoyed that we had missed the exit. Taking the map, as Shawn pulled over to the side of the road, I spread it out across the dash. We looked at it together and figured

     Shelby & Shawn   ©   2023

out where we needed to go. Once Shawn knew what roads to look for he was fine and got us there with no problem.

"Good job," I said to him as we pulled into the parking lot.

"I'm pretty good with maps and directions," he said.

"I can tell," I had redeemed myself this time. *Does being a woman really mean catering to a man's insecurities all the time? Is that what love is?*

When we got into the hotel, we realized the rooms were very small with only double beds. I knew Bev wanted to be alone with John, so I suggested we get separate rooms. John and Bev were agreeable. Shawn seemed annoyed but went along with it.

We checked in and were off again to the Cleveland Zoo. It was a cool day, so we had to wear jackets to walk around outside. Bev was enjoying herself with John, but Shawn was avoiding me, keeping on the other side of John all day. I walked beside Bev.

This is not the Shawn I spent New Year's Eve with, I thought.

As it grew darker, we left to find a place to eat. I had some information about an Improv Club and Restaurant open, but no act was playing, just live music. We got there and ordered food, then Shawn started teasing me about getting up to dance.

"There's no dance floor, Shelby."

"We could dance right out there in the middle of the floor." I said.

He laughed. "Want to?"

     Shelby & Shawn   ©   2023

"I don't know. They might kick us out." We both laughed.

Ok, there's the Shawn I was falling in love with.

We got our food and ate quickly, exhausted from the early start that morning. Back at the hotel, Shawn and I took turns in the bathroom, changing into our versions of jamas, which turned out to be mostly sweats, then crawling into bed. Something got put on TV. Shawn didn't seem interested in talking, which was alright with me. I was out when my head hit the pillow.

I was the first one up in the morning, so I grabbed a quick shower to have time for blow-drying my hair.

The first thing Shawn said when I walked out of the bathroom was "Are you going to take an hour?"

"Yes! That's why I got in there first." I set myself up on the floor where there was a plug out of everyone's way.

"I'm goin for coffee then," said Shawn.

Roy had come in. "Bev's in the shower. I'm coming with you for coffee too,"

They came back with coffee for everyone. I was done with my hair and Bev was out of the shower, so we had our coffee while we packed up and the guys showered and dressed. We checked out and headed for the Rock N Roll Hall of Fame.

Shoot! I forgot to tell them I couldn't get tickets to the Rock Hall. We had to pay full price to get in. Another reason for Shawn to be mad.

"I wouldn't have come if I knew I had to pay full price. This isn't what I enjoy doing."

"Sorry," I said flatly and didn't even try to redeem myself.

The place was huge, and we spent most of the day there. I was especially impressed with the new display of John Lennon's work on the top floor of the museum. There was one wall of nothing but pages from a song he wrote that depicted the process from beginning to end, from his rough draft to the final product, and all the pages in between where he crossed out and wrote in the margins. This was well before computers and word processors.

"I find his creativity amazing," I said to Shawn who was coming through behind me.

"You hero worship a drug addict?" He said sarcastically.

"Actually No! I would use him as an example of how a genuinely intelligent, creative man can be destroyed by using drugs and alcohol." I said, feeling a little defensive. "Look at how much potential he had and yet his life was cut short by the lifestyle he lived."

Shawn didn't respond. He walked on by me and went on by himself. I was about over this roller coaster ride. I didn't know what was happening with him or why he was acting this way, so I just wanted to go home. I went and found the others to see if they were ready too.

Turned out the Science Center was right across the street from the Rock Hall, so we walked through there quickly. Roy and Bev looked like they wanted to play around but I could tell Shawn wanted to leave as much as I did.

By that time, it was getting dark, and we had a three-hour drive ahead of us. We got most of it under our belt before stopping for dinner at a Cracker Barrell. We were all very tired and cranky

     Shelby & Shawn   ©   2023

from lack of sleep, so dinner wasn't very pleasant as we were all edgy with each other. I didn't even feel like I could ask for a dinner roll without being treated like a leper.

The energy is not flowing smoothly in this group right now.

When they dropped me off at my house, I got out of the car. Shawn had popped the trunk from inside and I had to get my own bag out before they pulled away. I hadn't even gotten to the porch yet.

The light wasn't on, so I struggled to get my keys, unlock the door and step inside. Dropping everything on the floor, I went to my bedroom, changed into PJs, dropped into bed and burst into tears, crying myself to sleep.

Chapter 41

Penn State Football

A lot of the time, when people perceive you as strong, they don't understand they can hurt you and they don't care. Your perceived strength makes them feel weak. Treating you badly makes them feel strong.

I didn't see them much after that. John moved in with Bev and they all stopped coming to volleyball. When Shawn did come, he hung out with Roy and the other guys or talked with Bobbi. We had some new people. Things were changing again.

One afternoon I was shopping at Giant Eagle when an old boyfriend of mine came walking up to me.

"Hey, Shelby! How are ya?" Sam Walkins was one of the lusts of my life for a short time about 10 years ago. My kids hated him. His kids hated me. It was doomed from the start. But we had stayed friends, getting together once or twice a year for lunch or dinner or just to go for a walk, to catch up on what's up with each other.

Over the years, I came to realize how wrong we were together. One time during lunch, he said to me "you have really grown." When we dated, I had a serious inferiority complex. He and his friends were very upper class. I was just coming out of my days of poverty and getting on my feet. He saw me as very insecure. *I was very insecure!*

I laughed about his comment later, realizing I had outgrown him. Our conversations now, from my point of view, left him looking shallow and lacking integrity.

The sex was great but all else failed the commitment test,

which is why my policy now is 'friends first.' But he owned Penn State season tickets, the only thing I loved doing with him more than having sex.

"I'm great! How are you?" I replied, stopping to talk.

"Good. Hey, I can't make the next home game *(no explanation necessary, knew exactly what he was talking about)* on October 6th. They're playing Michigan. Should be a good game. Do you want the tickets?" He asked.

"Oh my gosh, I'd love them. I haven't been to a Penn State game in forever." I said so excitedly and knew the first person I was going to ask to go along.

"I'll drop them by your place next week."

"Awesome. Thanks. Wanna come for dinner?"

"That's nice of you to ask. Sure," he said.

"We can catch up!" We both said at the same time, laughing.

Tuesday, I made roast and potatoes with a vegetable casserole. The kids found other places to go eat. *Of course! They really hated him.*

Sam arrived at about 7:00. *He was always a late eater.*

"Come on in and sit down. Dinner is ready."

"Smells delicious. You were always a great cook. So, what's going on with you?" He asked me.

"I got a promotion at work. I'm a manager trainee in the

 Shelby & Shawn   ©   2023

Uniontown office now."

"Wow! That's great!" He was genuinely proud of me.

"I'm leading a singles group at the church. You should come to a meeting sometime. We do a lot of fun, crazy stuff, like the peddle/paddle at Ohiopyle."

"Not my thing but sounds like fun. I just bought a house, and it takes up a lot of my time with repairs and remodeling and such. I'm seeing Jennifer Pyle. You remember her. You met her and her husband when we were dating." *He always had a new girlfriend.*

"Were they the ones with the big piano that took up a whole room?" We both laughed.

"That's them. Well, they got divorced and now I'm dating her." He said boastfully.

"Well, she was nice. I hope it works out. I'll be looking for a house soon too. I really don't want to rent anymore."

"It's the best decision I've made since divorcing Diana." he laughed. I just shook my head, wondering how long this new girl would last.

He really is such a misogynist. *Breaking up with you was one of the best decisions I made.*

He didn't stay long after eating. I was just as glad. I cleaned up, washed dishes, went into the living room, picked up the phone and called Shawn.

When he picked up the phone and said hello, I said "I've got some exciting news."

"What's that?" He asked.

"Well, if you're not busy on Saturday, Oct 6th, how would you like to go to a Penn State football game in State College?"

Silence.

"I ran into an old friend of mine who has season tickets." I continued. "He can't go to the game on the 6th and said I could have them." Still silence. "What do you think?" I was feeling awkward and regretting that I called him.

"Ahhh … No. I can't go." he said, sounding like he was in anguish.

"Oh. Okay. Well, I'll have to find someone else." I said feeling very disappointed. This was a chance for us to really have some fun together. We both loved football so much.

"Good luck." he said and hung up quickly.

Wow! He said no to a live Penn State football game. Something's really wrong.

Not knowing any women who loved football more than me or even as much, I thought of asking Roy. But did not want to give him or any guy the 'this is romantic' impression, I called Randy.

"Sure! I'll go." He said without hesitation.

"Great!" We talked about the plans for that day, what time to leave, what to do for lunch, and so forth. "See ya then!" I said when we confirmed everything and hung up.

Gene picked up the kids that weekend, so I had no worries

about what time to come home. Randy and I made a day of it. He picked me up early and we took our time driving. The leaves were beautiful along the route, changing to yellows and oranges early in the season.

When we reached Beaver Stadium, we parked, found our seats first, then went for food and drinks.

"I'll buy lunch if you want since you got the tickets," he said as we were standing in line.

"You really don't have to." I said, but he insisted, so I let him.

The day was beautiful, sunny and warm. The seats were good, and the game was exciting. My throat was raw from cheering. We pulled out a win in the 4th quarter. As we pulled out of the stadium, Randy suggested we find some interesting things to do in that area and north, since we're up here.

"That sounds like fun!" I was always game for an adventure.

We left Beaver Stadium parking lot and drove north for a while. At a gas station, we found fliers for things to do. Penn's Cave was a good option but was closed that day. A little farther, we found an old church with some very interesting artifacts, monuments, and displays of the area's history. We walked through, reading some of the plaques about history.

One plaque I was reading was about the Indian girl the church was named after, Kateri Tekakwitha. When we got in the truck, Randy asked what I was reading. I told him the story of Kateri, also known as Lily of the Mohawks. Her entire family died of smallpox, but she survived with severe scars on her face. She became Catholic, never married, and was named a saint after her

     Shelby & Shawn   ©   2023

death in 1680.

"Wow. You even remembered her name." He said sarcastically.

What was that supposed to mean? I always felt like I was being looked down on by him.

We spent some time looking for other places to stop but found none, so we headed back home. We decided to stop at the Home D Pizzeria in Bellefonte, where Robin Hood Brewing Company sells their beer out of State College. We had some food and of course, Randy had beer, a lot of it.

"I heard Shawn is seeing someone. A neighbor?" He said while we were eating.

K. Where'd that come from?

"Ah, he said something to me about going for walks with one of his neighbors. I don't really know much more than that." I answered, wondering what this was about.

I had no intention of discussing any of the private conversations I had with Shawn. Nor should Randy be telling me something Shawn should be telling me. Randy didn't say anything else about it.

My comfort level with Randy was strained after dating and breaking up, just as I thought it would be. We were best of friends, comfortable in any situation before we decided to 'give it a try ... see where this will go.' *Therein lies the trouble.*

Now, there was an uncomfortable atmosphere between us, as though he was thinking that more was being anticipated from me. The worst part is, I never fell 'in love' with Randy. I never even told him I loved him. So, there was never an expectation of more in the first place.

And yet for the same reason I didn't feel comfortable with Roy as a friend now because I knew he wanted more in the past. But how do I know his feelings haven't changed as well?

We don't know and therefore it can never be the same. You can't go back. Men and women cannot be friends, date, and then go back to being friends without that expectation. Is it really a true friendship if you have to constantly say 'we're just friends.'

I also knew if I was with Shawn now, I'd be having a lot more fun on this adventure. At least the Shawn I fell in love with. But THAT Shawn hasn't been showing himself much lately.

Randy did not have a playful side like Shawn had. In fact, Randy thought having fun was considered 'folly' which is to be avoided, as it says in the bible.

My mother believed in the suffering Christian, following the suffering Christ on the Cross. But the bible also says to fill your hearts with joy for the Lord.

I hoped that Randy didn't fill himself with too much joy in the form of beer here so that I didn't have to master driving his big truck home. Not that it mattered since he hid alcohol in his glove box, under his seat, and in that little flax in his coat pocket as well.

We got home safely, well after dark and I thanked him for accompanying me and being a gentleman. He said goodbye and drove off, not even getting out of the truck, but reaching for his glove box as I saw him pull away. *God protects him and anyone in his path while driving home.*

The following Friday, when I walked into the gym for

volleyball, Shawn and Roy were waiting to approach me. They walked right over to me with a purpose.

"So did you go to the Penn State game last Saturday?" Shawn asked me.

"Yes, I did. It was a beautiful day and an exciting game."

"I know. I watched it on TV." Shawn said, sounding like he regretted not coming with me. "So, who'd you end up going with?

"Randy."

Shawn looked at Roy. "He tells us to say no to her..."

"What!?" I said. They both walked away from me. I thought about this for a moment.

Awww! A lot of things were making some sense now. I laughed to myself, knowing how much Roy and Shawn both loved Penn State.

Fools! Why are you listening to Randy?

I wondered if Shawn was really dating the neighbor girl he'd met and why he wouldn't have told me. That might have been the reason he was weird on our trip. And why he's been distant lately. I would have been hurt and disappointed, but I would have understood. I want only the best for all of these guys. I would hope they would want the best for me as well.

Knowing how I feel about him, he should have been the one to tell me.

We're all just trying to find the right partner, the one that comfortably fits, to spend our lives with. How could I call myself a

     Shelby & Shawn   ©   2023

Christian, or say I have love in my heart, if I didn't wish joy and happiness to my friends?

Because we're all broken, that's how.

Maybe I have been chasing Shawn too aggressively. Maybe? More like I've been throwing myself at him. I'll have to take responsibility for that.

I've seen he is not calling me anymore. The first clue was when my mom died. He was so cold toward me for no reason. But I didn't let go. My brain did not connect to my heart just yet. It will now.

I wonder if this was love at all or more like codependency. I thought when I first studied codependency for self-improvement, I would be able to recognize it right away. Maybe not. I guess it fooled me again.

And part of me knew there were times I self-destructed with Shawn, sensing it wasn't going to work out, to avoid the heartache. Maybe I unconsciously pushed him away.

I still have so much more growing to do. This process may take a lifetime!

        Shelby & Shawn   ©   2023

Chapter 42

Thanksgiving Without Mom

Debra called me just before Thanksgiving to ask if we'd come to spend the day with them. It was going to be a difficult time getting through the holidays without mom. Dad would come too.

"Thanks for thinking of us," I said. "The kids are going to be at Gene's for the long weekend, so I'll be by myself. I'd love to come. What can I bring?"

"Well, I'm making turkey, stuffing, mashed taters, and gravy. What do you think?"

"Okay. I'll bring some cranberry salad and a corn muffin casserole. How's that sound?" I said off the top of my head. "How about pies?"

"I have ordered pies from the church, pumpkin, apple, and cherry. It won't be the feast mom used to make but we'll have plenty of food. That all sounds great!"

On Thanksgiving morning, I got up and made the kids a big breakfast. Gene was picking them up at noon, so I had time to spend with them. I wanted to make it special. Pancakes, eggs, bacon, and hash browns, with plenty of syrup and chocolate milk. We lingered a long time at the table even after we finished eating, just wanting to be together. We were all feeling the loss.

After Gene picked them up, I sat on the patio for a while alone, just breathing in the fresh air while enjoying the view of the stream and the fall leaves. It was a warm day for November, the leaves were late falling so the tapestries were in full color. The stream was flowing heavily from the rain and the ducks were

 Shelby & Shawn   ©   2023

enjoying splashing around in it. *They remind me of me.*

Mom and dad taught me to enjoy the outdoors, camping, fishing, boating, and anything to be outside. We were always going on picnics with the aunts, uncles and cousins. Or we were at each other's houses, all the cousins playing hide and seek after dark and scaring the bejeebers out of each other.

I was the youngest and Debra was always made to look after me. The others would scare me and run away, screaming. Deb would always come running back and get me.

Campfires were the best, roasting the fish dad caught, toasting marshmallows, listening to the men tell their stories, and enjoying each other's company. The memories were flooding over me, and I began to cry, just letting all the raw emotion come pouring out.

I wanted so much to give that life to my own kids. This is where I have to stop. I can't keep beating myself up for the life I didn't have. Who knows where God is taking us?

I wiped my tears and got up to make cranberry sauce and cornbread. Then I showered and left for Deb's.

When I arrived, I hugged everyone, and we had a wonderful day together. After dinner, dad went for a nap on the couch. Deb and I sat on the patio to watch Ben, Benny, and Toni shoot hoops in their driveway.

"I broke down in tears earlier remembering mom, all the outdoor fun we had camping and such," I told her. "I remembered being so little, waking up needing to go to the bathroom. She would get up in the middle of the night to take us to those dreadful outhouses. Remember?" We laughed.

"I had a meltdown in the shower this morning too. I can't believe she's gone." And now here we are both crying and hugging. "It was too soon to lose her. She should have lived another 10 years."

"Maybe dad was right about the doctors and the medications being detrimental to her. Maybe that is what killed her."

"Doesn't matter now. Won't bring her back." She said and she was right. What good would suing the doctors do?

It finally started to cool off outside. Dad woke up and wanted to go home. We said our goodbyes to him then pulled out some board games to play, going back for seconds and thirds on the food. It got late and it was time for me to leave. Deb packed up a care package full of goodies to take home with me so I could have leftovers tomorrow.

Hugs and kisses brought more tears as we said goodbye. When I got home there was a message waiting for me from Cindy. I hadn't heard from her much, so I called her right away.

"Hey, how's everything?" I asked. "I haven't seen you in ages. I'm surprised you're home on Thanksgiving."

"My daughter couldn't make it home for the holiday cause she had to work, so my dad and I went out for dinner earlier. I hung out at his house for a while till he conked out." She said laughing. "I was wondering if there was any place open tonight but the few other calls I made said no, everything's closed. So how bout tomorrow night? Do you have anything planned?"

"No. They even canceled volleyball this year. No one is around for the holiday weekend. What'd you have in mind?"

 Shelby & Shawn   ©   2023

"Yesterday's!" We both said in unison, laughing. "Sure! I'll meet you down there, probably about 9ish."

"Okay. See you then."

I hung up and started pulling out my Christmas decorations. I thought it might cheer me up and put me in the mood for the holidays.

I had never shopped on black Friday because I hated the crowds but this year, I got up early and went out to grab a couple of things I'd seen on sale in the paper.

I continued cleaning and decorating all morning, playing Christmas music, and it did help. My mood improved considerably. By the afternoon I had finished the whole place and it looked pretty good, especially the window clings on the sliding glass doors. I was the window cling queen. I loved them and put them on every window.

I was pretty pooped out, so I decided to lay down for a rest since I was going out tonight. Turned out I was really pooped out because I woke up three hours later and it was dark outside. On top of that, I hadn't eaten all day. *Leftovers!* I pulled out my care package from Deb to warm everything up and chowed down while watching the news. It tasted even better today. *Doesn't it always!*

A long hot bath was in order, with bubbles. As I lay in the bath I wondered if I should let anyone know about tonight. Most of my group weren't of the club and dancing types. Cindy's group was more about that. The only person I thought of was Shawn and I knew I couldn't call him anymore.

Our time is over ... Now I'm sad again.

I pushed back against that heartache and got myself up and

dressed. I put on a long, below-the-knee skirt with boots and a sweater. I felt pretty good.

When I got to Yesterday's, Cindy had arrived early to get us tables. Just as I'd thought, most of her group was there taking up three of them. We did a lot of dancing and laughing.

"Hey, thanks for setting this up and letting me know. I really needed this. This is the first holiday without my mom." I said to Cindy when I had a chance to move into a seat beside her.

"I really needed some fun too. I was getting tired of sitting around the house all the time with Chad drinking. It's a drag. He never wants to go out."

"Well, we'll go out with you," I said. She laughed and we toasted to that. Then a good song came on and we were back on the dance floor.

It was a good time.

 Shelby & Shawn   ©   2023

Chapter 43

Mom's Christmas Dinner

The weeks went by as we celebrated, having parties at work, out with friends, and with our single groups. It was a busy time, and I didn't have any energy to waste on sadness. I was happy to have the kids with me to celebrate Christmas too.

Deb and I decided while talking one evening, "Let's go to dads on Christmas Eve to keep the tradition going."

Mom always had the Feast of the Seven Fish, though dad was the only one who liked fish, there were some dishes we wanted to keep going in mom's memory.

"I've never made any of that stuff. How about you?" I said.

"We'll figure it out." She laughed.

We met at dad's house in the afternoon of Christmas Eve, the house where we grew up, to spend the whole day cooking while dad, Ben, and the kids watched football.

Deb made her favorite tuna spaghetti. Ben liked the anchovy spaghetti as did dad. I liked the shrimp cooked in various ways and the kids just liked fish sticks. But mom's specialties, and dad's favorites, were smelt, squid, octopus, and crab. We did the best we could to make these, though neither one of us had ever had before.

"I can't believe we pulled this off," I said while we were eating. Everyone was diving in and really seemed to enjoy it.

"Everything's delicious," Dad said, trying to hold back the tears in his eyes.

 Shelby & Shawn   ©   2023

"The crab salad we were able to buy from the famous local Italian store called Delallo's." I said. "That one was easy." Everyone laughed.

Anything Italian could be found at Delallo's and would be 'to die for.' People came from all around to shop. They sold items you couldn't get anywhere else, and it was all fresh.

So, we had our Feast of the Seven Fish for mom. It all turned out well. Dad ate some of everything that night and leftovers the next day.

The kids were happy. We also had buttered spaghetti, which was Robin's favorite, cheese pizza and fried dough dipped in sugar, a favorite of all the kids.

There was so much food. And we were so exhausted after cooking and cleaning up we barely had the energy to exchange gifts. But we weren't going to get out of that. It's what the kids waited all day for.

The basement in our family home had a big game room with a pot-belly fireplace. One wall was covered with shelves holding fish aquariums from dad's 'breeding fish' days. They were empty now since he had moved on to his next hobby, gardening. He put up a greenhouse in the backyard and grew vegetables all year round.

Dad had a fire going when we got down there. There were big piles of gifts everywhere. Suddenly it was complete chaos as everyone was handing out gifts at one time. Then wrapping paper flew everywhere! Then it was over.

The snow began to fall out the big picture window. Ben, Benny, and Joel had made hot chocolate for everyone to drink. We

          Shelby & Shawn   ©   2023

sat back to enjoy sharing with each other what we got as gifts.

Dad was quiet. There was contentment in us all. We had kept her memory alive, at least for a while.

Chapter 44

Joel's Done

In January, Joel turned 18 and quit school. I was heartbroken.

We sat down and talked about this many times so I sorta knew it was coming. One night after work, we were having dinner and I asked him what he wanted to do for his birthday. I stopped having parties for them at 16 so generally, I made them a dinner of their choice, homemade or restaurant, whichever they preferred.

"I want to quit school," he said.

"Joel, you have six months left. Can't you just get through six months?"

"I haven't been going anyway, mom. I've missed them so much they're going to make me repeat this year. I'm not doin that."

"What will you do then?"

"I'll take my GED then get a job."

"Can we go in and talk to your guidance counselor before we make a final decision? Please."

"Fine. But this is my decision and I'm not changing my mind."

I called the school the next morning and scheduled the meeting for that day. Arriving a little early for our appointment, we were asked to have a seat and Mr. Saxonburg would be right with us. During our wait, the bell was about to ring.

Joel said, "Watch mom. It'll be like a herd of cattle."

The bell rang and sure enough, the halls were packed with students, wall to wall, with barely any room to move to their next class.

"See," he said. "That's why I hate it here."

I attended this school district all of my life. This was the school I graduated from. Wow! So many memories rushing back to me.

"I don't remember it ever being that crowded when I came here." I said to Joel.

"Mr. Saxonburg will see you now. You can go ahead down to his office," the secretary said.

We walked down the hall to Mr. Saxonburg's office, entered and sat down.

"So how are you, Joel?" he asked, directing his attention immediately to my son.'

"I'm fine." Joel said in a very dry apathetic voice.

"He wants to quit school. I'm hoping we can do something to change his mind. He's not going to get into a good college. He won't be able to find a good job." I started pouring my heart out.

"Why do you want to quit school, Joel?" asked Mr. Saxonburg.

"I hate it. I'm bored. I don't want to learn any of this stuff. I don't want to be here."

"Well, how old are you?" he swiveled in his chair to open a file on his desk, then turned back to me, "He's 18. He can make this decision for himself. There's nothing we can do to stop him. If we try to force him, it won't do any good. He won't get anything out of it."

It's church all over again.

"Mom, I'm going to get my GED, and then I'll get a job. I promise."

"What kind of job are you going to get without even a high school diploma? What about getting into a good college later?"

"I'll figure it all out."

And he did. Within a month of quitting school, he had passed his GED. He got a job at a Sheetz in Greensburg that paid decent wages. He moved into a house with some friends about a block away from the store, so he was able to walk there since he didn't have a car. He was on his own and he'd figured it out just like he said he would.

I had held him off as long as I could and had a hard time adjusting to this change. I missed him a lot, but I still had Robin at home to cushion the blow. *The nest is not empty yet.* She did not mind at all that he was gone. Now the place was all hers. I think there were times when she missed him as well, though she'd never admit it.

Joe Barnes helped us move him. Joe called me one evening a few weeks later to see how things were going.

"I miss him terribly," I said. "I still have Robin here but it's just a matter of time before she goes too.

 Shelby & Shawn   ©   2023

"You're an empty nester," he said.

"Oh my gosh. I don't want to think about it. I mean he still comes around to visit and do laundry."

"I always take my laundry home to mom," he laughed. "It's a guy thing."

"And I love it." I laughed too. "His laundry will always be welcome here."

"So, how's house hunting going?" He asked.

"My lease on the townhouse is about to be up in February. I got a notice they would be raising the rent a significant amount. I guess I should get on the ball. I'm sure they'd let me stay an additional month, if necessary, but I don't want to have to. I think they know about the cat, and they are not happy about it. So I know I'm not going to see the security deposit back. And Robin's about to turn 16 so I have that party to plan."

"Well let me know if you need any help," he said.

"Thanks! I appreciate that." I was truly grateful to have these good guys in my life. The ones who genuinely cared enough to help when needed. That was a gift.

Chapter 45

Sweet Sixteen

"What would you like for your sixteenth birthday party?" I asked her one evening during dinner.

"I want a red devil's food cake like grandma used to make for me." she said. Mom made her cake every year since it was her favorite.

"Okay. I'll try to find the recipe." I had no idea where mom would have that recipe. I don't remember seeing it when we cleaned the stuff out. "I will have to go to the house and see if grandpop kept her recipe box. *Or maybe Deb has it.* Okay. What else?"

"Umm, maybe a sleepover with my friends on Friday and then my party with family on Sunday."

"Okay. That sounds like fun. We can pick out some invitations at the store tomorrow and we'll get them sent out." I said.

"I can just make some homemade invitations for my friends."

"Good idea." We worked on making some invitations that night while we watched TV and she was able to hand them out to her friends the next day. While we were at it, we just made two more to send to dad and Deb for the Sunday party. I put Deb's in the mail the next day. I would just have them over for dinner.

On my way home from work I stopped in at dads to see if he had the recipe box of moms to get the one for red devil's food cake. The box was under the cupboard and sure enough the recipe was in it. *Thank goodness we didn't lose this treasure!* I brought the whole box home with me.

While I was there, I gave dad his invitation and sat down to visit for a while. "You can come over early and spend the day with us if you want." I told him when he opened it.

"Oh, I don't know. I'll probably just come after my nap in the afternoon. What time is it?"

"I'll have dinner after church at about 1ish. Just going to be us and Deb's clan. She's having a separate party for her friends."

"I'll be there for dinner."

"How are your finances looking? Have you balanced your checkbook and paid your bills this month yet?"

"Deb was here the other day and went over all that."

"Good. Ya know, I'm starting to look for houses. I want to buy a house soon. Maybe you could go around looking with me. I could use some advice on what's good and what's not." I said, thinking maybe it'd be a good idea to get him out of the house some. He spent so much time alone.

"I guess," he said, not sounding too enthusiastic.

"Ya know, furnace, water heaters, stuff like that. I don't know anything about that stuff. How'm I supposed to know if a water heater is any good? Well, I'll let you know if I find anything. You can go check it out with me."

When he just kind of grunted, I got up to leave, kissing his forehead before walking out. I'm sure he fell fast asleep as soon as I was out the door. It struck me again that dad isn't going to be

 Shelby & Shawn   ©   2023

with us much longer either.

"I found it!" I declared when I walked in the door at home.

"What'd you find?" Robin asked from the living room.

"I found grandma's recipe for red devil's food cake. In fact, I grabbed her whole recipe box for safekeeping. I didn't want pap throwing it away."

"Good thinking." She said, "You'll have to let Aunt Deb know you have it. I'm sure she'll want some of them."

"Hey, ya know. That's a good idea. I should buy her a recipe box and copy all mom's recipes in it. I'll give it to her as a birthday gift in May. I won't even let her know I have it so it will be a surprise."

"Make one for me too for when I move out." She said.

"Don't even talk about that." I said. *God! Not her too!*

She just laughed.

A few weeks went by and Friday night the girls all showed up. Nickie, of course, and four others. I made the cake, bought her all the snacks and drinks she'd asked for, ordered the pizza and we were havin a party.

I welcomed all the girl's parents as they dropped them off to let them know I'd be there all night. Once they were settled in with sleeping bags all over the living room, movies and games, I got out of the way and went upstairs to my room.

I reviewed some projects for work and then read my medication book until I fell asleep. At some point, I was roused by noise outside my window. There was a lot of loud talking and laughing from both male and female voices. *Is a neighbor having a party?*

I threw on some sweats, glancing at the clock saying 1:30, and went downstairs to check on the girls. To my surprise the living room was empty; there was not a girl to be found. The party outside was mine.

I walked out the door and called for Robin. She was on the other side of the parking lot leaning against the back of a car with a boy beside her, a little too close beside her. The others were scattered around, sitting on the grass or standing in the parking lot somewhere.

"Robin, it's time to come in," I yelled to her.

She walked over to me. "What's wrong? We're just having some boys over. We're having fun."

"Well, the original plan didn't include boys when you asked for a party, or I would have planned it differently. It's late and we need all the boys to go home so the girls can come in and be safe."

"You're such a drag!" she yelled at me.

"I probably am." I said. "Let's go girls. You boys need to leave now." I called the others.

They got up groaning and got in their cars to leave. The girls filed in as I counted them to make sure no one snuck away in one of the cars. When they were all in their sleeping bags and settled in again, I asked them "please don't leave the house again."

"We won't!" they all said together.

 Shelby & Shawn   ©   2023

I went back up to bed and thought *it begins!*

After a night of tossing and turning, I woke up to hear them giggling downstairs. I went down to make breakfast.

"What would you girls like to eat?" I asked.

"CAKE!" In unison.

"In that case, help yourself to the cake. There's milk in the fridge."

"Mrs. Good," One of the girls named Ashley asked, "Are you going to tell our moms about boys being here last night?"

"Do you think I should?" I asked her.

"No. Please don't. I would get in soo much trouble. I'm not allowed to date yet."

"How old are you?"

"Fifteen. But I'll be 16 in August and that's a whole summer."

"Oh well, I don't blame your parents for making you wait until you're a little older. My parents didn't allow me to date till I was 16 too."

Yeah? What's the big deal between 15 and 16? It's just a year."

"You'll be surprised how much you'll grow in a year, especially over summer. It doesn't seem like much, but it really is. I'll tell you what. I won't say anything, but I'll leave it up to you to tell them if you think it's the right thing to do. Okay?"

"Um, Okay." She said walking into the living room with her cake.

I chuckled knowing she'd never tell her parents there were boys here last night. I knew it was going to be a long summer for them.

I intended to have a long talk with Robin about it. Yes. She is sixteen now and will be allowed to date but we still have to have boundaries and guidelines. It was going to be a long summer for all of us.

Joel arrived Saturday night to sleep on the couch so he could be here for Robin's birthday dinner on Sunday.

"How have you been?" I hugged him so tight when he walked in the door. He looked so much older. It was almost like he was a guest instead of someone who lived here all those years.

He and I sat at the dinner table for a long time while he talked about what was going on at his job, in his home, and in his personal life. Robin had bailed out on us to run with Nickie.

"They're probably out meeting some boys." I told him what happened the night before with her party friends here.

"Ot oh. She's gonna be outta control now." he said laughing.

"I'm not going to get much sleep this year." I laughed with him.

On Sunday, Deb and her family arrived at 1:30. They stopped and picked up dad. Joel had just woken up and was taking the blankets off the couch down to the laundry. *Humm I'm*

     Shelby & Shawn   ©   2023

impressed.

"We just got out of Mass and came straight here. Sorry if we're late." They said coming in the door. "Happy birthday Robin!" Hugs all around.

"No, you're fine. Right on time. I'll have dinner ready in a minute." Everything was ready. I just had to put it all out on the table. I made spaghetti with meatballs, Robin's favorite dinner, and another red devil's cake for dessert with ice cream after dinner.

Robin opened her gifts after the cake and we all just sat around talking for a while. It was very low-key.

"I hear you're looking for a house." Deb asked. "Dad told us you want him to help."

"Yes, I could really use his help with checking it out, ya know, furnace and stuff I know nothing about."

"That's a great idea!" Ben said. "Make him go looking with you. He'd be good at that." I could tell everyone was thinking the same thing. *Get him out. Make him feel useful.* It was definitely what he needed. But I wasn't sure it was going to help. He seemed to have given up.

     Shelby & Shawn   ©   2023

Chapter 46

I Bought A House

So I decided to start the process. The first step was to apply. When I got pre-approved for a small loan, I was ecstatic. I couldn't believe it!

I did it. This was the last goal I set for myself after my divorce.

I then began looking for houses in that price range. There weren't many available. One morning, when Robin and I were sitting at the table eating breakfast, I told her my plans.

"Since our lease is up soon, I'm looking to buy us a house. We would be able to have a yard, a garden, more pets, and the freedom to do what we want without asking anyone if we're allowed. What do you think about that?"

"Fine," she said not very enthusiastically.

"Wouldn't you like that?"

"I'm tired of school! I don't want to go there anymore. Joel quit school. Now I'm going to have to change schools. What about Nickie? I won't get to see her anymore either."

"Alright. That's a fair argument. And you're right. That's a lot of changes. First, I promise you will get to see Nickie. I will take you there or she can come here to our house anytime. Is that ok?"

"Yeah. What about school?"

"Well, I've been thinking about that too and if we move out

of the school district we are in now, I can pull you out and you can home-school for the rest of this year. Then next year we'll talk more and make some decisions that will be best for you. How does that sound?"

"Sounds ok," she said, sounding a little better.

"Ok. I brought some magazines home, and we can look through them, hopefully, find something in our price range that we like."

We looked through the magazine and checked out a couple of places but didn't find anything I liked in my price range. One day, as I was driving my regular route home from work I spotted a cute little yellow ranch-style house with a for sale sign in the yard.

I called the Realtor to ask about it. It was a two-bedroom, with a finished basement that could be a game room or bedroom, a small yard, an enclosed back porch, and a one car garage in a very good neighborhood.

"When can I come to see it? I asked.

"How about Saturday?" I made an appointment to view the home that Saturday. I called dad and told him I'd pick him up to go along. He was agreeable.

When we got there, the first thing dad looked at was the basement, having a difficult time going down the steps. He checked out the furnace and water tank. He looked at the bathroom toilets and said everything looked okay.

The kitchen cabinets and closet space in the bedrooms were my area of concern. There had to be enough space to put all our stuff. I was pleased and dad was pleased.

         Shelby & Shawn   ©   2023

"Let's do it!" I told the Realtor.

The process of purchasing was very stressful with all the paperwork that needed to be done. Joe helped me with some cash up front to set up an escrow account while I was waiting for my income tax check to come, and I was able to pay him back.

I took Randy up on his offer to do the inspection for me and except for a few minor repairs needing done, it passed. We did find a termite infestation, but the seller took care of the extermination before we closed on the house.

"I'm so grateful for your help." I said to Randy when he brought me the final report. "Here's a check for your service."

"I don't want paid for this. I was doing you a favor."

"No! I insist you take payment. This was a lot of your time, and you deserve it. It's still less than a professional would have charged me. I can't thank you enough for this."

He finally gave in and took the payment. He also came to help Robin and I painted the weekend before moving in. We painted the entire house to cover the crazy colors that the previous owners had put on like pink and purple.

"I want to paint my room white with black splatters on the walls and ceiling." Robin said. She loved painting and decorating in school and was very good at it.

I got her the paint she needed, and she did a great job. It was late and I had fallen asleep on the floor in the living room. Randy helped her get it done before they woke me.

"It looks awesome." I said when I saw it finished.

The following weekend, Debra, Ben, and the kids came to help me move in along with Randy Brown and Joe Barnes. With all the trucks and help it only took a couple of trips. I ordered pizzas for us and we sat out on the patio for a while resting after the last load was unpacked. I looked around and thought, I am so blessed to have family and friends who believe in me and support me. It's an incredible feeling.

Lowes came and delivered the washer, dryer, stove, and refrigerator so the guys were able to make sure everything was hooked up well for me. Since I bought an electric dryer and the house had a gas hook-up, Joe ran a 220 electrical line that was required.

After everyone left, I sat in my living room with boxes all around me, feeling so full in my heart. *I can't believe I own a house. After working my way out of poverty since my divorce.* I was overwhelmed with joy.

Then I thought of Shawn. I had not seen or heard from him. He never offered any help. He never said congratulations. In fact, the one time at volleyball when I was telling everyone about buying a house, he said *I'll never buy a house. I hate mowing grass and having all that responsibility.*

Here I was growing and changing my life, getting stronger, feeling so good about myself and I got nothing from him in the way of support or encouragement. I was right to let it go.

I wasn't going to let him rob me of my joy. I got up and started unpacking.

Chapter 47

Settling In

I didn't go to play volleyball on Fridays for a couple of weeks so Robin and I could get the house turned into a home. I also didn't want to leave her alone in the evenings until she got used to the house and the neighborhood. So I took a week off work, taking this time to bond with Robin and our house.

"I want a black bedspread and drapes for my room," she said. "That'll go well with my white and black walls."

"Ok, let's see if we can find something like that."

We went to several stores and finally found what she wanted. We also went to some second-hand stores and found chairs for the porch, metal shelves for the basement and plant stands. We put everything together ourselves and I helped her arrange her room the way she wanted. I bought a new caddy for the kitchen, to give us extra shelf space because the kitchen was rather small.

Of course, I needed a mower for the lawn. The yard was not big, about a quarter acre with a slight hill in the back. It wasn't that hard to mow if I started at the top and went side to side all the way down. I enjoyed doing it. Afterward, I would sit on the back porch looking out at it, the smell of freshly mowed grass, with the most accomplished feeling.

There were flower gardens around the side and front to tend to with weeding and pruning. I planted a vegetable garden in the back with cucumbers, peppers, and tomatoes. I got a pretty good yield, passing a lot out to neighbors.

I can't believe I own a house.

 Shelby & Shawn © 2023

I home-schooled Robin for the rest of her tenth-grade year. I only had to transfer her into the new school district, then send in the papers and itinerary for the work we would be doing. I found the books we needed that the school didn't give us in a stack of my old college boxes. She worked well independently with math and science but needed some help with English and history.

"What book would you like to read for Literature?" I asked her when we planned her program.

"Anne of Green Gables," she said, so I bought her that one.

"How about another book called The Secret Garden? You can take your time reading them and that will get us through till the end of the year."

For home economics, I had her research foods, and nutrition to create menus for us. I also made up a fake bank account and checks to help her learn to manage money, something she was very weak with. She still resisted the whole learning process. "I hate school!" was her mantra and I had to push, shove and fight to get anything out of her.

When she began to struggle with Algebra, I asked Randy if his son Liam could tutor her since he was good in that subject and wanted to be a teacher. At first, he said yes, then later for some reason changed his mind, saying he did not have time to come. A rumor came out that he didn't want Liam to be alone with Robin because she was emotionally immature and might accuse him of something. I paid no mind as I know how people talk and rumors tend to be untrue, so I gave Randy the benefit of the doubt. *But I will never forget it.*

We ended up seeing a lot of Joel after we moved. He came for dinner often and brought laundry with him. I loved his visits,

     Shelby & Shawn   ©   2023

sharing conversations about his life, and watching him interact in a very different way with his sister. He gave her hugs and helped her with her homework.

I think he actually misses us!

On the weekends when Robin went to her dad's, I was alone for the first time in my life. I went from mom and dad to Gene and the kids. *I have never lived alone!* I thought and again that overwhelming feeling of accomplishment came over me, filling me up with peace and joy. It is so hard sometimes to not look back on the past.

How did I make it through all that pain, those years of poverty, going to school, working, shuffling my kids from the day-cares to babysitters, leaving them with people I shouldn't have trusted?

Somehow, I had … but my kids still had a long road ahead of them to recovery. My job wasn't done yet. There would still be consequences for some of the bad choices I made. I wasn't finished feeling the pain. And they were just starting their journey.

But God will be there to carry us through to healing...because, as you can see, the greatest lesson I learned is this:

In his way, in his time, he will bring us love in many different ways.

 Shelby & Shawn   ©   2023

Chapter 48

Icicles on the Falls

At work one day, I walked up to the reception counter to chat with the girls while we were slow.

"Whatcha guys doing?" I asked.

"Check out these pictures of the falls with icicles hanging on them," they said, handing me a travel book.

I picked up the brochures they were looking at about travel and the ad caught my eye. A package to Niagara Falls, and a beautiful picture of the falls with icicles hanging from it. I was hooked. I suddenly felt the urge to see that beautiful sight in person.

At my next Christian Singles meeting I made the announcement.

"I'm putting together a trip to Niagara Falls if anyone is interested in going. I have the details for the trip on the table with the news and information. The package consists of an all- inclusive price for a two-night hotel, two breakfasts and one dinner. See me with any questions."

Of course, Joy was interested. She was becoming one of my regular travel companions. And Greg wanted to go. I put the word out to Cindy, and she had a fellow in her group who wanted to come.

"That works out great." I told her when she called with his information. "Greg will need a partner to get the double occupancy rate on the hotel."

"He also has a female friend he wants to bring along." She said.

"Okay. Even better. That gives Joy and me the triple occupancy rate." It always bothered me that hotels charge more for solo travelers. *Almost double!*

Once I talked to Sam Jones from Cindy's group, we set a date that everyone agreed on. I called and booked the hotel, two connecting rooms with two occupants in one and three in the other. We had to put the men's room in Greg's name, so he called and gave them his credit card to hold the reservation.

I then put together an itinerary of our trip, so we didn't miss out on anything we wanted to see. Everyone had different tastes and it was easy on this trip to accommodate them all. Greg and I just wanted to see the falls.

"I just want to go shopping!" Joy said when I called her to confirm our plans for leaving.

"Okay, I'll work that in. There's a quaint little town called Niagara on the Lake that is just right for shopping. I'm picking up Greg Friday afternoon and then we'll pick you up."

"I'll be ready. I can't wait!" She was always so excited to go with us.

Joy, Greg, and I drove up on Friday and arrived early to check-in.

"Let's put our things in our rooms and then go walk around down by the falls. We can find a nice little place for dinner."

"That sounds great," Greg said.

 Shelby & Shawn   ©   2023

We threw our things into the room and headed off to explore the falls. It was indeed beautiful! Although it was cold, we didn't linger long there before finding a restaurant.

We found a nice Italian place that was not crowded. The food was excellent. We were all tired from the drive, so we didn't talk much.

When we got back to the hotel, Sam had arrived with his friend. Joy and I walked into our room and there she was, unpacking her clothes.

"Hi! I'm Jenny." She said.

"Hello. I'm Shelby."

"Joy!"

There was a knock on the door that was attached to the men's adjoining hotel room. I went to open it and was blasted with squirt guns. I screamed and quickly closed the door. Instant confusion ensued when there was a knock at the hallway door.

"If that's them?" Joy exclaimed as she opened the door and was promptly blasted with squirt guns. More screaming and laughter until the guys realized we weren't going to continue to fall for this.

Sam and Jenny decided they were going exploring while Joy, Greg, and I said our good nights and got ready for bed.

The next morning, everyone went to breakfast at the hotel's restaurant because it was included in the package. After eating, we left for Niagara on the Lake to go shopping. It was indeed a quaint little town of gift shops and little coffee shops, just as the brochure

 Shelby & Shawn   ©   2023

had said. It was an hour's drive over so we spent the afternoon walking around, buying souvenirs and snacks.

On the way back to the falls, we stopped at Riverview Estate and Winery for a tasting and purchasing if you were so inclined. We all got a bottle of something or other.

"My favorite wines are the fruity ones, grape, and blackberry mostly or strawberry," I said. "But strawberry is a little too sweet." So, I purchased a bottle of blackberry.

Greg bought a couple of bottles of Zinfandel and a red Merlot. Joy was not a wine drinker, so she just hung out. Sam and Jenny went off doing their own thing.

Back at the falls, we went to our hotel to freshen up for dinner at the Fallsview Restaurant that came with the package. When we arrived, they sat us by the fireplace, which was very warm and comfortable since it was very cold out that night. The place was elegant, and the view of the falls was beautiful from anywhere in the dining room.

Sam wanted to visit the casino, so after dinner, we did a walk-through, plugging in a couple of slots, but not staying long, moving on to the next thing.

But at night we found this club called The Island. The dance floor was an island with a moat of water around it, wooden railings, and bridges we had to cross to get on and off from the main area of tables. The DJ was great, and the music was good for dancing. We had drinks and danced until it was late and we were tired.

It was within walking distance from our hotel, and we walked along the waterway so we could see the falls again at night. That was a spectacular sight. The icicles were more beautiful in

 Shelby & Shawn   ©   2023

real life as in the picture with the lights shining on them. It was too cold to stand out there long with the mist from the water rising up to soak us before long, so we moved by quickly.

I'll never forget that view.

This was a good group of people and a lot of fun to travel with. Sunday morning, Sam and Jenny took off early. Greg, Joy, and I took our time to have breakfast and check out.

It was the last trip I took with my group, and it was a blast. Greg and I began to spend a lot of time together, talking on the phone every day and seeing each other often.

I spent time at his house and met his family. I considered him a friend but did not see a future with him. After a couple of years, when he did not see a romantic relationship developing, he moved on to marry someone else.

This time I really missed the relationship we had. Though we were only friends, there was a bond, a closeness that I hadn't felt in a long time. I loved that we talked every day. We traveled well together and were very compatible. But there was no attraction for me physically and that was important to me too.

I just can't seem to find the one that fits ...

 Shelby & Shawn   ©   2023

Chapter 49

Moving On

In 2004, I once again stepped down from leading the Christian Single's at Our Lady's church to go back to school and finish my degree in Psychology. It has always been my dream to work with kids. At this stage in my life, I didn't know what I would do with this degree, it just felt important to finish it.

A young woman named Stephanie Page, who was new to the group, took over with the help of Joe Barnes and some other women. She and Joe became a couple. They were just right for each other and stayed together until she passed many years later. After she passed, he went back and married Althena. I stayed in touch with them for a while but soon our lives took different paths.

The volleyball group dwindled down to just a few people showing up every week. We had to give up the gym for lack of players to make a full team or funds to pay for the rental. Randy continued to come till the end. He and I stayed friends until he got married, then I became friendly with his wife. She was a perfect fit for him. Soon they got caught up in their own lives and I stopped seeing or hearing from them.

Cindy's group also dwindled down to no one coming so she quit. I didn't hear from her about going dancing or anything after that. I guessed eventually she gave in to her codependent relationship and stayed home with her boyfriend. I hoped and prayed she found love and happiness.

As time went on, I ran into people here and there I knew from the groups. Most had gotten married, some had not, and some had married and divorced again for a second or third time. Some had lost partners due to passing.

I did learn that Shawn had gotten married. I never knew who she was, but I prayed he found love and I was very happy for him. Once, years later, I ran into him at a grocery store. We exchanged 'how are ya's' and moved on. The spark was gone and there was nothing much to be said. But those old feelings still grabbed my heart strings.

I remember those times as leader of the Starting Over Single group fondly with an appreciation for the relationships I had and lost, with all the lessons I learned from them.

After several dead-end jobs, Joel did go to college and build a career. Robin got married and gave me beautiful grandkids. They struggled as they grew but eventually found their way and began to thrive with their jobs, relationships, and kids of their own.

As they grew older, they realized what all we had gone through together was hard on all of us and we did the best we could. Down the road, I would be pleasantly surprised to rekindle an estranged relationship but that is for another story.

I finished my degree and then focused on my career until retirement. I continued to enjoy my volunteer work. I loved traveling and found different places to go every year, sometimes dragging the family with me.

My best friend, Anne, and I shared a bond that's unbreakable, talking every day and doing everything together. When she passed it was as great a loss as losing my mother. I miss her every day.

I enjoy being single. My real commitment is focusing on nurturing my inner peace. I spend time with my family. My heart is full and indeed love has found me.

Mary Ann has been enjoying retirement while pursuing her dream of writing books. This is her second book in a series called Starting Over Single about Shelby Good, a woman who finds herself a divorced, single mom. She has created this character depicting some of her own life experiences, making her books relatable and inspirational.

During her free time, Mary Ann volunteers for the Westmoreland County Food Bank and various hospitals in the area. She participates in church and community projects such as the Christmas Angel Tree and Toys for Tots.

She is a long-time member of a women's group in Westmoreland Co. She has also been an avid hiker all her life, recently leaving a more advanced group of Pittsburgh hikers to co-lead a less strenuous hiking group, who are active in Allegheny and Westmoreland Counties.

Mary Ann plans on enjoying kayaking and other adventures with her grandkids, family members, and friends at various lakes and rivers in Pa. Currently, an extensive trip as a solo traveler to explore the National Parks around the country is in the planning stage.

 Shelby & Shawn   ©   2023